ESCAPE
FROM
THE TEMPLE

BROOKE FIELDHOUSE

Matador
Unit E2 Airfield Business Park
Harrison Road, Market Harborough,
Leicestershire LE16 7UL
Tel: 0116 279 2299
Email: books@troubador.co.uk
Web: www.troubador.co.uk/matador
Twitter: @matadorbooks

ISBN 978 180514 023 8

British Library Cataloguing in Publication Data.
A catalogue record for this book is available from the British Library.

Printed and bound by CPI Group (UK) Ltd, Croydon, CR0 4YY
Typeset in 12pt Adobe Garamond Pro by Troubador Publishing Ltd, Leicester, UK

Matador is an imprint of Troubador Publishing Ltd

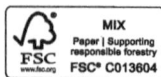

Janusz

Illustrations inside end covers:

Front: hand drawn maps by the author showing i) The fictitious location as it might have looked in 2000BCE, and ii) showing the Chateau de Galets farm as it might have appeared in 1939 with the fictitious German additions of 1942 marked up in green.

Back: Top: German artillery casemate in the Boulogne area, photo taken by the author in 1975.

Bottom: Dolmen de Plouezoch, Brittany,photo taken by author in 1969.

EPIGRAPH

... Long before human beings mapped their world scientifically, they developed what has been called a "sacred geography". Certain places – mountains, groves, or rivers – have seemed to speak of "something else".

The devotion to a "holy place" was one of the earliest and most universal expressions of the religious impulse, and is so common that it must tell us something about the way men and women have experienced their physical world as a place of wonder and mystery. Even today we have not secularized the world entirely: many of us have special places to which we like to repair in a moment of crisis, or for renewal...

Karen Armstrong, Introduction to
Iris Murdoch's *Nuns & Soldiers*, 2001

PART ONE

Secrets Hidden

PROLOGUE

We are made of stone. We stand on a rock high above the sea. A resting place for dead souls, we were built by those who worshipped the sun and who made tools from iron and bronze.

The bodies of the upright ones – male and female – were buried within our walls, often generations apart. They were laid to rest with treasure that told of the skills of an age when folk made weapons and ornaments by smelting bronze from copper ore.

Over years, our mound became part of the land on which it had been set; overgrown with grass, thistle, groundsel, and rosebay willowherb. Later we were given names – "the knap", "the tump", or "tumulus", as if we were a tumour growing on body earth. They (the upright ones) knew about the treasure, and some of them came to take it so that they might exchange it for treasure of another kind.

Later still, our mound became a source of study for those who call themselves historians. They gave it a human name – Le Vieux Vicente – as if we were a single entity, not for the many.

These so-called historians – not content with trudging over the turf and knowing that their ancestors were lying comfortably beneath their feet – embarked on a search for evidence. 'Four thousand years,' they boasted. But that's only a hundred generations; it's nothing! This is a particular trait of the upright ones. Nothing is proven except within the tiny sphere of the upright ones.

Our mound was intended to be a place of peace and liberty, but over time, it bore witness to conflict. Those who sought to subdue their fellow being made it a place of war. Our stone was cut into, strengthened with concrete. It was made into a fortress for young, upright ones wearing uniform and became a place of a different kind of death.

Many believe that stones are dead just because we do not grow, like trees or ideas. But do we not absorb and reflect light? So, do not scorn our powers, for we possess energy, made from the same stuff as the stars which make light when hydrogen fuses with helium. Stars which the upright ones see fit to spend hours gazing at, use as guides, worship, and even attempt to travel to.

We stones run through space and time, and the stories hidden within our many layers are legion. But *we* cannot tell our tale. Only the upright ones can do that. They are our ciphers. *They* are the narrators.

Two upright ones are approaching, riding upon a strange metal machine which swings to and fro beneath their bodies. They are being pulled along by four-legged creatures.

The dense bracken is broken by great swathes of fireweed. It is the time when the seeds of the plant become airborne, and the gentle breeze pulls them free of their cerise pagodas to drift in their tens of thousands, seeking a hold everywhere. The clothes of the upright ones – and the manes of the horses – are full of them.

We stones of the burial mound try to be still, but the earth and those upon it move constantly like the seeds seeking places to take root. The upright ones are also desperate to plant their seed, to fertilise, to grow. Even the smallest particles are always moving – molecules, atoms, protons – never resting, always moving.

CHAPTER 1

HIDDEN SECRETS

The north-west coast of France,
early September 1939

Jean had been moving all morning and he needed to rest.

The bluest part of the sea is generally where it meets the sky, he thought, as he gazed down into space. It wasn't really a question, but if it had been, then it was one to which he knew the answer. That it all depends on the finer details of the weather and that there *are* memorable days when time seems to stand still, and earth, sea, and air appear to be limitless.

He could see no movement in the water, hear no seagull sounds, and the harsh grating cry coming from behind him was that of a corncrake.

From somewhere far below came the *pa-pa-pa-pa-pa* of a Kelvin petrol motor engine, accompanied by the soft murmur of men's voices, and a small boat appeared as noiselessly and timelessly as one of those tiny black dots which Jean sometimes saw floating in the fluid of his eye. He raised his arm and the two figures in the boat waved back. He could hear their voices, yet he remained silent, knowing full well that the vastness of cliff and sea would make his own talk seem as if it were intruding upon nature.

He could feel the afternoon sun on his left cheek. Hot as it was, he was wearing what he nearly always wore: his knitted wool Guernsey pullover. He clenched his teeth down against the stalk of a short clay pipe – the kind purchased for a few francs at the local tobacconist. Cigarettes for necessity and pipe for pleasure was Jean's maxim, and this was indeed pleasure.

He turned, walked a few paces, clumsily scrambled up a stone wall, and found a different vantage point. This time it was the clover-clad roof of the old burial mound known by locals as Le Vieux Vicente. They say that every person has a special place they can retreat to and be themselves. This was Jean's place. Not only could he see as far as the marine horizon, but by turning his back on the sea, he could glimpse the light playing against the old stone circle on the hill opposite and was able to detect a knob of vegetation in the distance, under which it was rumoured were buried ancient chieftains.

Jean turned again to face the sea. Standing upright and facing it as only he could, with feet fixed firmly onto the roof of the tumulus. Jean had the biggest feet imaginable. He knew it, and he just had to accept it when his siblings sometimes mocked them.

The surface of the tomb on which the mighty-footed Jean stood had been there for four thousand years – difficult for anybody to believe and a source of great fascination to the young man. He fancied that he could feel *the power* rising, entering his body, giving him strength – that's what he liked to believe anyway.

From his sublime position, he could take in the whole geometry of the mound. He had even once paced it out, so he knew that it was exactly seventy metres long, fourteen metres wide at its southern point, and tapering away to a slim seven metres at its opposite end. It was about the height of a man at its northern extremity and rose to half as much again at its wider southern end.

Standing on its roof, Jean felt as if he was on the deck of a ship, but it was a strange vessel. From where he stood, it resembled a giant stag beetle with two horns. The horns were berms of stone and earth, which stretched either side of what his father used to call the "false portal".

'Why should it be false?' Jean had asked. Surely an entrance was an entrance? Why did "the ancients" put so much time and trouble into building something which was a fake? His father had told him it was to fool would-be grave robbers and prevent them from stealing the "riches and treasure" hidden within. The thought of someone stealing from a grave, and all that effort going into deceit, had filled Jean with dismay.

The mound stood at the neck of a bluff of land above the sea. It virtually sealed off a quarter hectare which Jean had nicknamed the Champ de Mars because it was – like the tumulus itself – special to him, and he imagined that all sorts of ceremonies had taken place there, thousands of years ago. All that connected the Champ de Mars with the mainland were two narrow strips of land running either side of the tumulus: one six metres wide, the other measuring a mere three.

From inland, the tumulus was easily approachable through the wheat fields which stretched out from each of its extremities. But along its length, the ground fell away steeply and was overgrown with rosebay willowherb, bracken, and gorse. Jean knew it was selfish of him, but he felt as if it was *his* special place, belonging to nobody else. He wondered what the lives of the people who were buried below him had been like and whether the world in which they had lived had been as humdrum as his seemed to be.

Pipe in mouth, Jean felt as if he was suspended in time and space. The fragrance of the tobacco mingled with the cool bitter marine air as it was drawn up the face of the cliff and into his nostrils. He had never ventured inside the tumulus, and nobody could get in there now.

He recalled the time when he and his elder bother Joseph helped their father Arnaud block up the entrances. Arnaud had told them that it was to "stop folk getting up to no good in there", but Jean had always felt that there was another reason. He had enjoyed helping their father mix the concrete, but how Joseph seemed to have hated it! He remembered Joseph being sick and Arnaud having to send him home.

That was twenty years ago when he was six, and Joseph was eight, but he so wished that he had gone inside, and he often pictured himself doing so, stooping with difficulty and looking rather like an injured crab as he tried to scuttle forwards within the confined space.

Jean enjoyed his far-off imaginings; they didn't frighten him at all. In his mind's eye, he would try to avoid touching the stones inside the mound; they were so cold. Most of all, he remembered their smell. He knew that such a memory was impossible because he had never been in there, but the feeling was sometimes so intense…

In one particular fantasy, he could hear scraping sounds as another man shuffled along behind him… scratching, stretching, searching, scaring, scarring… and the beating of his own heart. Who *was* that other man…?

Again, came the grating of the corncrake but this time followed by a *click click click, whirrr* and the comforting sound of a horse exhaling.

'Come on, wake up, my little brother! We haven't got all day. *You* need to get back to work.' Jean felt his heart sink. As he turned, he could see Joseph sitting on the steel seat of a harvesting machine, a whirring contraption being pulled by a team of two horses.

'I see what you're looking at. Thibout and Amaury have gone out lobstering; they didn't tell me. We're two men short, so buck up, will you! I know you'd stand here all day if you could, but we need to get this lot cut and stooked – by tonight. Have I got to do everything round here myself?'

No doubt Jean's face had a look of disappointment, even misery. This is what his elder brother was always doing: wrenching Jean away from his world of dreams into Joseph's own dark and imperfect sphere of discipline.

Joseph was a bundle of activity. His jaw was so square it looked as if it had been produced by machine. His eyes so brown and liquid, they resembled dark, bottomless pools. He was constantly pushing his long, dingy, copper hair back from his forehead. He was never still.

Any horizontal surface which happened to be near would be turned into an improvised lectern, upon which he would thump to emphasise a point. If no such deck was available, then he would stamp on the ground to produce the same effect. Jean amused himself with the thought that if the right equipment existed, the family could wire him up and he would produce enough energy to run the farm for years to come.

Joseph grinned a lot, but his eyes never smiled. Jean had a secret name for him: The Dark Night. It was silly really, but the phrase had always stuck in his mind. It had come from a story their mother, Constance, read to him as a child, and the words "the dark night" had frightened him. That very moment he had looked up and seen his elder brother grinning at him with his mirthless grin, and he had got it into his head that *he* was The Dark Night.

It was strange that whenever Jean was near the tumulus, he felt calm, relaxed, at ease with himself and the world, enjoying his fantasies, whereas when Joseph had to go near it, he seemed even more agitated than he normally was. Jean liked to tease him about it, but you had to watch your step with Joseph.

'Come on, come on, I've four more rows to go then I need the other team,' bellowed the one-piece, blue-denim-clad man.

The two brothers had always worked with five horses, whether it was ploughing, sowing, or harvesting, as today. Two pulling, two waiting in the paddock below, with one resting – Bertrand was the oldest, so it was usually him. He didn't seem to mind.

One pair worked the morning, the other the afternoon, and it was now Jean's job to make his way down to the paddock to collect the second duo. He needed to be back in the field as Joseph finished cutting the last row.

Off lumbered Jean at his usual leisurely pace. It was tempting to take the most direct route to the farm, but it was the steepest, and although when they were children, he and his siblings used to hurl themselves down the bracken-clad slope, he *had* to accept that now he was in the adult world of work.

He crossed the ford over the stream, planting his feet on one flat stone after the other, so wanting to stop and delight in its sound and vision, but every minute counted. It was nature, it couldn't stop, and this was work, so neither could he. They were both part of an endless process.

He entered the paddock, dragged the harnesses and bridles from where they were hanging on the wall of the barn, and led the docile animals up the hill to where Joseph was waiting.

'Come on, come on! You're just in time.' His brother was yelling. Joseph had completed the final row, unharnessed the team, and was standing waiting for Jean, while nervously glancing across at the tumulus. Already, the outgoing horses were being watered.

Jean helped his brother push the harvester to where he had stationed the new horses. Pipe back in his pocket, he grasped the shafts, his nostrils full of the tang of oiled leather, cropped wheat, and dung. He hooked the loops to the harnesses and attached the holdbacks to the breeching body. Jean could feel the hooks of the tugs going taut as he pulled to prevent them from slapping the horse's legs as they moved, and the fresh beasts were ready to work.

Jean gathered the old team and returned them to the paddock. This time, on his way back up to the wheat field, he dared to allow himself the luxury of a few moments to stand and gaze at the stream and watch its frantic progress. All those molecules of energy bouncing along! The water winking at him as it surged over the stones seemed like life itself, racing along from one mysterious source – to finish up Heaven knew where? – while he and Joseph were standing by, prisoners of their own self-appointed tasks and never really taking part in life's grand scheme.

Back in the field, Jean contemplated the job ahead of him. Had Thibout and Amaury been here, they would have stood on the rear platform of the harvester, taken hold of the ears of wheat as the machine cut them; would have formed them into bundles and sent them rolling down the canvas webbing, back onto the field ready for stooking. But they weren't there; they were out lobstering, so Jean and his brother would have to do the stooking themselves, and it was going to take all evening.

Neither man spoke as he worked. That gave Jean more time to think. He knew he was impulsive and idealistic – what was wrong with that? For pity's sake, look at him! He glanced across to where his brother was a flurry of limbs, pulling, stretching, lashing, and looking as if he was trying to work out a fit of temper. *Joseph's body may well be lithe, but his mind is rigid*, thought Jean, *like a sheet of corrugated metal that will only bend one way.* Thibout and Amaury had annoyed him alright, and it was their younger brother Robert's eighteenth birthday party in two days' time – maybe he was jealous about the trouble sister Helene was going to?

Anyway, Jean had been halfway through a fascinating vision concerning the tumulus. Where was he before The Dark Night so cruelly interrupted him? He was in the prehistoric world, still inside the tumulus, watching as his unknown dark, copper-haired companion felt inside his cloak, withdrew an object, and placed it next to his own hunting bow. It was a dagger, triangular in shape, its edges bevelled, and the length of one and a half adult male hands. Three dome-headed rivets held in place its handle: a flattened tube, dull, and dark. The blade seemed to emit its own light, rich with unearthly colours, and as he placed it on the stone, it gave out two distinct sounds. The handle delivered the hollow click of bone, while the blade produced a pure note, its resonance forming images in Jean's mind which he was unable to comprehend: an ethereal ringing. It seemed to signal the beginning of a ritual...

* * *

At last, the work was done, and Jean could see the sun about to vanish below the horizon. He could feel the air – only moments ago warm – rapidly begin to cool.

'I want one more pipe break, Joe, before we take the horses back.'

'That's right, keep your sister waiting, won't you.' It was true; Helene would have the supper waiting for them. It was selfish of him to want to get that final view of the sun as it disappeared and watch the blue sea turn to grey and then to silver.

Instead of climbing onto the roof of the burial chamber, Jean walked the three additional metres to the edge of the cliff. Here he stood, his big feet on a flat stone which seemed to form a threshold between land and sea. He could feel the sun's last rays upon his neck, see its shadows at his feet. In the corner of his right eye he could see the movement of a man – Joseph, his head turning and bobbing as he gathered up the water containers and loaded them onto the harvester – some fifty metres away.

Jean shifted his gaze out over the sea at the towering pillars of cloud, hanging over the water. To him, the scene looked like a shadowy village built for giants, and as he stared, he had the awful feeling that the giants were somehow doomed and that all was about to sink beneath the ocean.

He didn't hear anything at first, just watched as a long, irregular shadow fell across the stone on which he was standing. It had to be Joseph standing right behind him – there was nobody else around, but this time there was no "Come on, come on!". Jean could almost see him there in his mind's eye, posing like some statue. But he could still see Joseph adjusting the harnesses. He couldn't be in two places at once.

Jean fought with a terrible urge to turn around, his eyes travelling between the hanging cloud, the small black dot of a boat which had reappeared in the bay, and the motionless obscuration at his feet.

Suddenly, the shadow elongated itself, and Jean felt both his shoulders being gripped. He recoiled from the pain in his upper arms as unseen digits clawed into the soft front muscles of his shoulders. He was helpless; the pressure on his upper body increased; and he felt himself being pushed forwards out into space. It must be Joseph! But why the hell was he behaving like this?

In a strange moment of calm, it came to him. He's going to kill me, because that's what he's always wanted, because I was the outsider – the odd-looking one with the curly blond hair and the big feet . I'd been smuggled into the family as a baby. Father loved me and didn't love him…

Everything was happening so quickly Jean hadn't had time to absorb the shock, but he didn't care – why struggle? If this is what he wants, so be it.

He glanced down at the yellow-and-black skewbald pattern on the rocks thirty metres below him. How queer it looked – like the skin of a dead animal. What would it feel like to hit the rocks at sixty kilometres an hour? What noise would his body make, and would bone make the most noise, or would it be skin?

His thoughts seemed to act like a generator, and the powerful, unseen hands pulled back from his shoulders and transferred to his stomach, wrenching him away from the brink.

'Saved you!' roared Joseph's voice from just behind him. It was a shout of triumph. 'Christ, you scared me. I thought you were going to fall forwards. Thank God you're alright.' He was bellowing like a stag on the point of rushing an opponent. It was all show, staged for Jean's benefit – what the hell was going on? Jean swung round and looked into Joseph's eyes, but the pools of dark brown liquid were impenetrable. Where were Thibout and Amaury? Only metres below them on the water, but they might as well be in a different galaxy. Nobody had seen Jean and his brother on the cliff.

Jean could feel his body shaking. When he had been pinioned in space and within a moment of possible death, he had been in a perfect state of calm, like a melancholic in a crisis. Now the danger was removed, he was close to collapse.

Joseph had tried to kill him. It must have been him. All that puffing and panting, pretending he had seen Jean about to fall and come running over was nonsense. He had crept up while Jean was immersed in his daydream. He laughed inside himself at the irony – I mean why wait till now to do it, when he'd had the whole of Jean's life? What was different about today?

He badly wanted to yell at Joseph: 'What the hell did you do that for?' But Joseph had got there first; Jean had been standing too close to the edge – he lost his balance, could have fallen; it was plausible. Jean would never know, and all he found himself saying was, 'My bloody pipe's gone over!'

CHAPTER 2

THE FOURNIERS

The two men rode back to the farm. Jean shakily grasping the reins, his long body folded over the steel seat, while Joseph perched heroically on the platform behind him.

Without even turning around, Jean knew very well that his brother would be pushing back his hair while scrutinising the back of Jean's blond head and thinking: *Goodness knows where he got that mop from!*

Constance, their mother, Arnaud, sister Helene, and their youngest brother, Robert, all had dark, copper hair, but Jean had to be different, didn't he? "A strange cuckoo", Joseph would call him. 'Don't worry,' he'd say, 'only joking.' But it was hurtful all the same. Joseph had never cracked a joke in his life; he might go around grinning at people, but everything he did was deadly serious. What had just taken place on the cliff edge had churned up all those thoughts in Jean's mind about how Joseph went around telling everybody that Jean had been adopted.

'You'll be able to tell your mother I saved you,' came the voice from behind Jean, a comment double-edged and preceded by that little click just audible on the roof of Joseph's mouth.

'And if I don't, what will *you* tell her?'

'Nothing! I don't need to go around boasting about what I do.'

But what *had* Joseph done? Jean wasn't sure.

The machine careered back down the track towards the farm. Every few metres, Jean caught sight of a rabbit, bewildered by the upheavals of the day and making a dash for safer ground. *It isn't fair on them*, he thought. This was their natural home; they'd been here for thousands of years – like the tumulus – while modern farming men, Jean and Joseph, *they* were the interlopers.

For a few seconds, Jean felt himself relax again. His brother's presence on the platform behind him seemed no longer important as Jean slipped away into another of his fantasies, imagining that his ancient self had a family who came from what he called "Shadoward" and that his mother had died when he was two summers old. The smell of burning fireweed. The darkness, out of which emerged men who whispered in unison. He could almost feel someone's hands tugging him awake, tapping, and patting him, wrapping him in smelly wool cloth. Then he was running, being pulled faster and faster. But it was no good – he couldn't keep up. He was hauled up onto someone's back, and there he stayed, his head nodding with the thumps and bumps of his host's body, as he fell into sleep.

It would serve Joseph right if Jean *were* descended from those prehistoric chieftains who were buried in Le Vieux Vicente! As the two brothers garaged the harvesting machine, stabled the horses, and walked towards the farmhouse, Joseph began to air his thoughts – views which in Jean's mind had reached a pitch of tedium so intense as to drive him back into his world of burial mounds, wool cloaks, and bronze daggers.

'Crop sharing, bloody useless! Subletting to tenants who pay us back with a proportion of what they produce or don't produce because they've buggered off lobstering.'

'All right, calm down, Big Brother; you're away from the tumulus now – you can relax.'

'Bollocks to you as well!' muttered Joseph.

'Look, Joe,' Jean could feel himself straining every nerve to sound as convincing as he could, 'I know the crop sharing isn't going to make us a fortune, but you've got to look at it from this point of view: you let go a perfectly good milk herd because they weren't producing fast enough for you. That leaves us with only arable... nothing wrong with that, but we've got to move with the times. Sharing's a fair system.'

'So, it's my fault we're losing money, is it? Why don't you just go and give the crop to the whole bloody village for free!'

'I'm just saying, let's stick with the crop sharing for now. We owe it to Father – all that research he did on meadow grass...'

'You leave Dad out of it. I'm in charge now.'

'I just thought I'd mention it because Mum's had a letter. Her widow's pension's been cut. She's frightened. It's 'cause of what happened to Dad during and after the war. She thinks that you and I will go the same way in this next war.'

'All the more reason to pack in the crop sharing and start the building business. We can't compete with the larger farms inland.'

'For Christ's sake, Joe, everybody in their right mind knows there's a war about to happen. The question is, what part are we all going to play in it? Even if it doesn't happen, the Fournier family need something to work on together because, at the moment, we're going nowhere.'

Emotional talk – it felt good for Jean. It was helping him cope with the incident on the cliff edge, but there was an underlying feeling of sickness. How could they work together as a family on something none of them could agree about? How many times had they had this conversation? It was as if the two of them were working to a pattern – taking it in turns to say the same thing, as if each were mechanically reciting lines of a script.

While the two men had been standing talking outside the farmhouse, the sunlight had been replaced by another kind of light. The sky was still bright, but the land looked grubby. The buildings had the appearance of something artificial and reminded Jean of the model farmyard his younger sister had played with only a few years previously.

'Look at these buildings.' Joseph raised both his arms and turned full circle. 'We could transform them into a *gîte*. The building work we do here will spark other projects.'

'Such as?'

'Ohhh, Joe, here we go again! You just haven't thought it through, have you?'

'God, Jean! I'd hate to live in your world – spending all your free time sitting in bars with Raymond. You spout politics, but you never have any aims in life. You're good at following someone else's instructions, but when it comes to actually making something work...'

Jean was used to Joseph's argumentative gambits. They usually involved promoting his own ideas by undermining the character of the person he was trying to convince. He did it with everybody: family, suppliers, or the hands he hired to help run the farm. Jean could feel himself blushing with embarrassment at his own innocence which had been exploited by his elder brother.

How he had smarted – aged ten – when he, his sister Helene, and several village children had been having a class with their teacher! Jean was sitting with the others outside the farmhouse. The teacher had left the group alone for a few minutes, but Joseph was around somewhere, doing farm duties.

Jean felt a shadow fall across the pages of the French dictionary into which he was gazing. He turned and saw Joseph grinning that humourless grin.

'Father is furious with you.' That pang of fear at hearing of his father's fury, his trepidation at what was to come, but worse was the feeling of embarrassment as the other children all looked up. Jean ignored Joseph, hoping that he would just go away.

'You've made a right mess of those garden tools. Do you know what he's done?' he announced theatrically – all the children were interested now. 'Those tools were red when they were delivered – brand new – last week. Well, "somebody" has turned them green.' Everybody was laughing – even Helene. Jean had turned as red as the tools had been before he'd found the pot of green paint and thought they'd look nicer that colour. Most of the farm machinery was red; it would provide an elegant contrast.

Joseph wouldn't let it rest and forced him, crimson, to his feet to explain to the others in the class exactly why he'd done it. Dumbstruck, Jean longed for the teacher to return.

'Farms are not art galleries; they're places for grown-up adults. You've wasted time and materials!'

Nobody else ever knew, but when the class was over and Joseph dragged Jean off to show Arnaud what he'd done, all he said was, 'The lad's made quite a good job of it.'

Now better equipped to deal with his elder brother, Jean still knew that all who were in Joseph's company had to be constantly on their guard.

'Joseph, you donkey, you have to look at it from the point of view of the people, and round here there aren't many of them. They've all gone off to Calais, Boulogne, or Cambrai, so who are you going to build for, Big Boy?'

Still the answer didn't come, and Jean knew he was right. For a start, where would they get the extra money to convert the farm into a *gîte*, and who would come and stay *here*?

Jean suddenly felt chilled. The men had spent too long hovering outside the farmhouse, and by now the glow emanating from its squat windows looked more than inviting. His right thumb and forefinger felt instinctively for the wrought iron latch. He pushed the door gently with his left hand, and the brothers stepped into the interior warmth.

In the kerosene-lit room, Jean lowered his head, so as not to get a clout from one of the oak ceiling beams. They perched by the door on the wood settle to remove their boots. The air was warm; there was no longer any need to hurry.

Throughout his life, Jean had known no one other than suppliers, tax inspectors, midwives, and funeral directors visit the house. The kitchen where he now sat was the space where the whole Fournier family gathered every morning and each evening. It was where their meals were prepared and consumed and where they shared the experiences of the day. Most of all, every important decision the family needed to make was made here.

The slab-like scrub-top table in the centre of the room was set for five, but there was no sign of any other person yet. Save for the winking of the lamplight as a figure passed to and fro at the end of the kitchen, in front of the coke-burning stove.

'That smells good, Amber,' boomed Joseph, as the figure made circular motions with its arm over a maslin pan. Yes, Amber. When they were very little, Jean thought that the amber pendant – which his mother sometimes wore – looked just like his sister's eyes. So, Helene – as she was christened

– became Amber, and like a piece of the gemstone itself, she gave out warmth that their mother, Constance, did not.

'Apple puree in here...' came the voice '...and Daddy Girard's been on one of his poaching sprees, so it's pheasant!'

Jean never failed to be amazed at how the family could live so well when the farm earned so little money. Supper was usually roast chicken – well, more of the elderly broiler sort but still eminently edible. When Arnaud was alive, they even had beef when one of the dairy cows reached the end of its life. It wasn't the best, because the cattle were bred for milk, not meat, but it was acceptable.

Thibout and Amaury may have let them down with the harvesting, but when their fishing expeditions were successful, the family could expect bass, cod, and lobster, and something that folk referred to as "woof". It was catfish, delicate of flavour, but far too ugly to be called by its proper name.

As long as Jean could remember – well, since his father's death – he and Joseph had been responsible for bringing in the food and making repairs to the estate. Younger brother Robert was old enough to be taking an interest in the farm, but Robert was a strange one, for the Fourniers that was. He actually read books. Not farming manuals; it was novels, history, and goodness knows what else.

Jean was in awe; although he could talk with Raymond and his other friends for hours about Marxism and Dialectical Materialism, he knew very well that he hadn't read a "damn thing", and here was Robert, off to university within a matter of weeks.

The Fournier house was one where nothing was wasted, and time only seemed to exist to be filled with tasks. Robert was breaking the family mould. For goodness' sake, until their Dutch Aunt Icie came to look after them after Arnaud's death, even the rare recreational events had been somehow turned into duties.

Jean looked across at the window, just in time to meet the eyes of Balzac as he raised a head above the parapet of his basket. In the light of the wall lamps, the dog's eyes looked like two globes of black glass, bulging forth from golden sockets. Jean enjoyed watching this privileged creature. The collie's mother and sister were banned from entering the house, though neither seemed to ever want to. As he peered, Balzac's dark snout seemed to split open, revealing an enormous pink tongue which quivered violently with the effort of a yawn, then disappeared from sight.

Balzac was special. Not only was he Helene's dog, but she and Balzac were companions for life. When Jean made one of his good-humoured references to his sister as a "white witch", he would announce theatrically, 'The Lady Amber… and her *familiar* Balzac.'

Joseph went off to wash, leaving Jean to enjoy the simple activities of sitting upon the settle, feeling the warmth of the room, and watching his sister work. He would go and wash in a minute. It was a relief to be away from Joseph.

He could see Helene moving backwards and forwards and placing the hot tureens on the table. She was the soul of the family, tall, big-boned, and with a genuine smile. It was a smile which always seemed to be there, even when her mouth was still. Her eyes were always smiling.

A second female figure drifted into view. 1890, the date of Constance's birth, seemed a world away to Jean. She was a slim build – the big bones of the family had come from Arnaud. Constance had the same triangular-shaped face as Helene but had not been blessed with her daughter's spontaneous smile. As Jean's eye travelled to where the family photographs stood, it seemed to him that even the more informal images, showing her in the act of bouncing the newly born Joseph on her knee, revealed a shy and nervous young woman, uncomfortable with life. All her attempts at gaiety seemed to fall flat; even the flowered print dress, which moved elegantly enough on her – as she carried the bowls of butter to the table – would have looked more comfortable on a woman with her daughter's personality.

The two women of the house never strayed beyond their roles, as preparers of food, cleaners, accountants, and nurses. Helene was a natural with herbs and remedies, while Constance took charge of the bookkeeping.

Yet this business with Robert had really got Jean thinking. He knew Joseph was ambitious, but who wanted to be a building manager? Jean wanted more out of life. He just wasn't sure what at the moment.

'How's Jean-Paul Sartre?' asked Jean as Robert came into the room.

'I'm… I mean *he's* good.' He was pushing back an even thicker and darker thatch of copper hair and grinning.

Unlike their older brother, the grin was genuine. Robert had the warmth of his sister about him. Talk about chalk and cheese; if you had to put the family in teams based upon temperament, then it would be Helene and Robert versus Joseph and Constance. Exactly where Jean fitted in, he'd never been quite sure.

'Been keeping our eldest brother calm, have you?' asked Robert, with a smirk. 'I mean, you haven't been giving him an attack of tumulusitis, have you?'

Helene gave a loud cough and dropped the last tureen onto the scrub-top with a bang as Joseph returned from his wash.

The family took their seats, except for Joseph, who remained standing by the door looking at nobody in particular. The lid of every tureen was removed, sending a pillar of steam rising to the ceiling, each with its own specific aroma. Jean still hadn't washed. He'd been so enjoying those moments without Joseph shadowing him.

He left the others and went into the lean-to wash house. As he pulled off his shirt, he could feel the presence of the ancient, prehistoric Jean stepping out of the cold and damp late air into a humid interior, where the atmosphere was a choking mix of smoke from fires and steam which billowed from a number of sticky earth-fired cooking pots.

In this Bronze Age refuge, clay-fired vessels swung from timber frames. Each urn tended by a woman in the act of decanting the shadowy ooze of its contents into smaller containers which might be fit for human hands. Jean's prehistoric alter ego could see figures waiting in the gloom, some already in the process of shovelling the grey sludge into their mouths and slurping a diluted version of the golden liquid with which he and his strange copper-haired, dagger-wielding companion had grimly toasted one another at their sunset meeting. In his fantasy, Jean stood in silence. There was no talk; eating and drinking was no more than the act of fortifying one's body against the discomforts of the day...

As Jean arrived back into the kitchen, Joseph was still standing by the door, as if he had been on guard while his younger brother went about his ablutions.

'Do you realise?' proclaimed Joseph, following Jean to the scrub-top table. He seemed to be addressing no one in particular as he strode across the room. 'Our tenants have all the advantages. Whilst we as landlords have all the responsibilities of estate management and administration.'

It was like a speech. 'Quite right!' seconded Jean in mock committee style. 'We're supposed to have had a bloody revolution, and here we are, living as fat cat landlords!'

'Don't you swear in front of Robert!' whispered Constance.

'Oh, there'll be plenty of that kind of talk at the Sorbonne. You have to look at it from the point of view of the student, you know,' said Jean.

Constance's face looked hopeful for a moment, but anxiety was never far behind.

'That's if he actually gets there and doesn't end up in the German army.'

'The war may not happen, Mum. Anyway, this time the Germans might not be such a bad thing. This area could be repopulated and start to thrive.' Joseph's face had an artificial look of optimism about it. 'We could all be millionaires!'

'I told you that you've got to have political upheaval for society to develop.' Jean knew the phrase wasn't his own, it was something he'd heard Raymond say, but it sounded good. 'But it's got to be the right politics, and the Nazis have got it wrong – can't you see?'

There was a pounding on the kitchen door and Jean felt a sudden chill. The companionship of Helene and Robert had warmed him; now he remembered what had happened on the clifftop little more than an hour ago.

'Can you see who it is, Robert?' said Constance.

'Did you think we were all asleep or something?' bellowed Joseph as long-boned Eugene stood awkwardly at the far side of the room, looking as if he was trying to hide under his cap. Robert had disappeared – probably to say hello to Eugene's two Labradors and Spaniel.

Eugene always looked uncomfortable, and the group sitting round the table staring at him was making it worse. He balanced, first on one leg, then the other. He pursed his lips as if to speak.

'Come on, spit it out!' goaded Joseph.

Don't be so bloody unkind, thought Jean.

'Your tomb…'

'Yes?' barked Joseph, his voice rising two octaves higher than usual, the grin wider than ever, but eyes deadpan.

'Your tomb…'

'For Christ's sake, what *about* "the tomb"?'

'Your tomb – he open!'

CHAPTER 3

THE RELIQUARY

Poor Eugene! Helene had always felt sorry for him, and hoped she'd made him feel useful when he brought her comfrey flowers, mugwort, meadow clary, St John's wort – he knew just where to find them.

After being verbally prodded by all present, the young man – still wearing his cap – blundered through a description about a hole – "for human men to wriggle through" – which had mysteriously appeared in one of the blocked-up entrances to the tumulus.

Why did he refer to it as a "tomb"? The biblical reference was clearly upsetting Jean, and poor old Joe was looking downright uncomfortable. The two of them would be up at the crack of dawn tomorrow mixing fresh concrete. All right for Jean, but Joe was practically throwing up every time he had to go near the place.

'That damn thing, waste of fertile ground. It's taking up the space of two hundred loaves, but the Government's made it a "protected historical monument". I'll just have to keep ploughing round the wretched thing.'

'Ooooh that will keep the *deildergheists* happy,' mocked

Jean in theatrical "ghost" voice. He seemed to be perking up a bit.

'They're *never* happy,' cried Helene. 'The poor things live in perpetual misery.'

'Do you actually *know* anybody who's ever seen – or who even knows of anybody who has seen – a *deildergheist*?' snapped Joseph, his right finger poking at Jean, while his left hand grasped a pewter serving spoon and was heaping parsnips and carrots onto his own plate. 'It's myth… to frighten people into doing things… like religion…'

'There are lots of stories of the demons,' said Constance in that don't-go-too-near-the-edge voice.

'Daemons,' interrupted Jean. He looked self-satisfied with his correction and perhaps also with the fact that he had just neatly – but rather shakily – cut two braces of roast pheasant into halves. One half each plus seconds for him as wants. Talk about fat cats!

'There are good and bad ones, you know – daemons that is – and the ones up there are just doing their job trying to get back the stones which were stolen from their borders. The poor buggers aren't just working at it from nine to five like office workers in Boulogne, you know – they're at it all day and all night for eternity!'

'Well, I wouldn't go up there at *night*,' said Constance.

'I would, and have,' revealed Helene. *Perhaps a trifle smugly*, she thought. Of course, she went up there! She didn't just rely on the plants that Eugene brought her, and they were at their most potent if gathered in the dark.

'Stones are important,' she emphasised. 'They're ancient things and have souls too. Look how short the life of a human is compared to a stone.'

Helene collected stones. Her bedroom was full of them. Usually small enough to be held in the palm of her hand, they were all shapes and sizes. She liked the flat ones best. Some were richly patterned, like oil-painted miniatures, like several transparent paintings placed on top of one another. Others looked like maps. Jean said that one of her favourites looked like a bad skin condition, so she tried to keep them secret after that.

Usually, when she first picked them up, they were wet and looked beautiful. They were like little worlds into which she could gaze, but after a few minutes, they would dry, dust over, would look flat. Helene thought that they were going into hiding because they had been disturbed, like the starfish and sea urchins which curled up, or withdrew, when she touched them. She promised herself that one day she would liberate the stones.

Helene had a theory that everything was fine if you obeyed the rules. Daemons were our higher – or lower – selves, and we should look out for them. The *deildergheists* were only trying to take back the border stones, but the forces which really haunted the burial places were the death deities who guided the souls of the dead in the afterlife. She knew all this by instinct.

Jean seemed to be fascinated by it all as well. When she talked, he would sit there and listen. He gave her the impression that he believed it, but as Helene said, it wasn't even a case of belief or disbelief – it just *was*.

She had to admit to herself that she rather enjoyed laying the legend on thick for Joseph, who in spite of all his protests of scepticism, often looked worried at what was being said.

'Hmm... great family, aren't we? You two... blessed with wild imaginations... overemotional personalities, and me? I'm too smart for my own good.' Helene thought his chin looked squarer than ever.

'Tell you what, Big Brother,' said Jean, 'first one of us to turn up our toes contacts the other from the afterlife, eh?'

After the meal, the sparring between the two eldest brothers continued. Robert excused himself to read, while Helene helped Constance clear away, wash, and dry. When all was done, Helene fondly patted the sleeping Balzac and retreated to her room to write her diary.

She had kept a diary since she was ten years old, the year their father died. Was it really fifteen years to the day when she first started them? She tugged open the deep bottom drawer of the walnut chest which stood in her bedroom. There they were, all fifteen of them in maroon linen-bound covers – except for the year when the stationers in Boulogne had sold out, and she had to have dark green.

When she was little, Helene used to wonder how this monumental piece of cabinetwork had been brought into the house. Her dad had always told her that they had built the house around it, and sometimes she still believed it.

Who had made it? She wondered about the men who had felled the tree, sawn, planed, stained, and polished the wood. Who had made the little dovetailed joints – her father had called them – which held each drawer together? What kind of lives did they lead, and did they go to church? She had a hunch that the chest of drawers was a bit like the tumulus, full of secrets and thoughts.

Constance knew she kept the diaries and, at first, wouldn't allow a lock on the drawer. That was only fitted after Aunt Icie arrived, because she thought it would encourage *real* self-expression. None of the boys knew about the diaries – so far, that was.

Helene spent a lot of time on her own. As the only girl, perhaps unsurprising. Her closest brother – age-wise – was Jean, and there had been a time when they played a lot together. That stopped suddenly because of Joseph. It was all right – he'd said – for her and Jean to play "together" but not "play with each other". Joseph implied that Jean had done more than just show her his "thing", but she knew he hadn't. Joseph had just grinned that funny grin, and that had been the end of the matter. After that, Jean never spoke to her without sounding humorously polite about everything.

When Helene was older, she'd explored her own body; her new, and sometimes alarmingly painful, breasts. The tours she embarked upon were both nocturnal and diurnal. She examined, delved into, probed, and burrowed her "unmentionable place" – as she had once overheard *Maman* referring to it – with the rigour and regularity of a school project. What she expected of these excursions she wasn't exactly sure; it felt nice, and she left no stone unturned – in fact that was the limitation, for as time went by, her inner physical world proved less interesting to her than the outer one which surrounded her.

She began thinking about her dad again. She missed him every day.

She remembered lying in bed in the days after his death, her knees drawn up while she thought about other people who had died. Where did they all go to? If, for instance, all the people who had ever lived in the world were still here in their bodies, there wouldn't be any room for living people.

Of course, they were cremated and buried, ashes and bodies mouldering down. That's what stones were; that's why she liked them. They were made from the bones of dead animals that had been pressed together millions of years ago, but that still didn't answer the question as to where their souls had gone.

One day, she decided that she'd worked it all out. Whilst their bones had become part of the rock the planet was made from, their souls became part of their loved ones who were still alive. It must be true because she *was* becoming more like Arnaud.

Before writing up today's events, she revisited her very first entry – ever.

14 September 1924

We needed to make a sacrifice. It won't bring Papa back, but it might give him protection wherever he is. I made a time capsule – reliquary I think Maman called it – using a tin which had had biscuits in, given to us by our Aunt Icie one Christmas. I asked Joseph if he wanted to put something in the capsule, but he said he was too busy on the farm.

We buried the "reliquary" in the top of the old burial mound which overlooks the sea. Maman knew about it, but we didn't tell her what we'd put in it. Robert put his painted wood spinning top in the tin. I think it was very brave of him; he is only six. I put my best doll in. Jean is only two years older than me, so he isn't as busy on the farm as Joe. He really surprised us by putting his Jerusalem cross in the tin. It's a small wooden cross with silver dots on it. Mum said they were mother of pearl. He said he hated it because it reminded him of the time when he was convalescing after German measles, and Aunt Icie took him on a trip to Bruges and made him kneel and kiss a glass tube which had Jesus's blood in it.

I told him he couldn't put the cross in the capsule because it was sacred. He said that was good because the burial mound was sacred as well. I said that the whole point of this was that it should be a sacrifice and that if he hated the cross then it wouldn't be a sacrifice. He said it was a sacrifice because it had been a gift and a lot of thought had gone into that. He put it in all the same and we agreed that it's a secret. Then we climbed back down to the farm from the tumulus; it's very steep but I ran some of the way.

CHAPTER 4

THE POWER OF THE MOUND

'Do you remember reading about Dr Theodore Meulne and how he almost turned Le Vieux Vicente into a tourist attraction?' asked Helene, as she and the family sat around the scrub-top at a late breakfast the following day.

From where she was sitting, Helene could see the curve of the tumulus where the nearest of its two stone berms seemed to be absorbing the late morning sun. Beyond and seawards, the cloud was piled high into limitless sky, and though dazzling at its summit, it appeared so dark at its base behind the mound that it gave the impression of having been somehow artificially tinted. The storm was perhaps still a way off, but to Helene, the tumulus looked like some animal about to raise itself on its front limbs and move closer to her.

A daring thing to do – talk about it openly, Helene thought; it was a kind of taboo. Alright, it was part of their lives; they could see it every day; it was in their thoughts, and Jean had no qualms about bringing the subject up, but somehow, to discuss it over the breakfast table seemed to risk inviting it into the house, just like poor Eugene had unwittingly done the previous evening.

Joseph was right about starting a *gîte*. The crop sharing wasn't going to get any better, and Le Vieux Vicente could be an asset. It was on their land, so why not use it?

'Almost certainly the tumulus is four thousand years old,' Helene continued, quoting in a mock academic voice, 'and at least thirty important personages – most likely chieftains and their queens – are buried there. With your idea of turning the farm into a *gîte*, Joe, it would be an ideal attraction.'

To Helene, none of her brothers looked enthusiastic – in fact, Jean looked decidedly odd. There'd probably been another argument with Joseph that morning while they were blocking up the hole. The spats were getting more frequent than ever. Perhaps he was ill, sickening for something as *Maman* always said.

'I'm not sure that the general public is ready for Le Vieux Vicente,' contemplated Jean aloud. 'Meulne made a right hash of it,' he continued, croakily. Jean was doing what he always did: trying to give the impression of someone who knew what he was talking about when he never did.

'In what way? Come on! More explanation needed,' demanded Robert, cheekily parodying their eldest brother.

'He'd studied the subject all right, found similar burial mounds in Brittany, and came up with a convincing theory that there were at least thirty bodies buried there – perhaps thousands of years apart. Then he spoilt things by press-ganging various locals – including the priest – into trying to dig out what he referred to as "treasure", and if that girl hadn't hurled herself off the cliff—'

'It wasn't her fault she'd just been jilted,' Helene intervened.

'Ooooh, it wasn't just false love, you know – it was the *energy* of the place,' continued Jean, lowering his voice and apparently recovering somewhat from whatever it was that had happened earlier. 'Spoooky, it works well for some, but obviously not for others.'

Helene was feeling that Jean was missing the point here; all this history was good. It didn't matter if it seemed to him like a pastime for the entertainment of the middle classes.

'Look, I know we're covering old ground here,' she persisted as Jean sniggered at the metaphor, 'but what's really important is that we know that at least seven of the burial chambers still have the bodies, plus whatever they were buried with. That's because each time they interred somebody they stuck a great big stone in the entrance so it couldn't be moved, and there are seven of those so...'

'Quite so, quite so, good for Papa, when he made Joe and I block it up.' Jean was smirking and gently slapping the table with the flat of his hand as if he was seconding a proposal at a village meeting.

'People would be fascinated by a place which they thought was haunted,' she persevered. 'Also, what about the skeleton that was found when Dad was digging out the chalk for the new front gates?'

Robert was too young to remember all that, but the others did. It had been the talk of the village for a good while after the event, and Arnaud never missed an opportunity to say how the two policemen who came to "view the body" had said that "foul play was not suspected", before calling the museum to finish digging out the skeleton.

'Foul play?' Arnaud would thunder melodramatically. 'There'd been plenty of foul play all right but about four thousand years ago!' He had been convinced that it had been the pickaxe of one of his helpers which had decapitated the skeleton, and separated the hand from the arm, but the museum confirmed that the remains were the victim of what they elegantly referred to as a "ritual killing".

'Then there was that incident years later when we were all grown up, and went along to the Chateau Musee Citadel to see the reconstruction in a glass case. Because *he* was all crouched up in the hole, he – the skeleton – looked quite small, but the museum people had written his height on a card and he was really tall, exactly the same height as Jean!'

Over the years, practically everybody who'd worked on the Fourniers' land had turned up lots of "odds and ends" as Arnaud called them. The more interesting ones had gone to the museum; some sat in wooden crates in one of the sheds, whilst others had simply been thrown away or used as rubble for building repairs.

Helene could never understand why Jean was always suggesting she collect the old bits of pottery that were found. Surely, they had "*human* political significance", he said, whereas stones were stones? That was just the point for Helene: the stones didn't belong to anyone, and never had. They were free, and they were more ancient than any of the prehistoric "things". The thought of having pieces of cooking pots in her bedroom gave her the heebie-jeebies, and unlike her brothers, who thought that the pots belonged to an era of long ago, to Helene, four thousand years ago was "just like yesterday".

'You could be a guide, Amber,' continued Jean, 'but you'd be talking into thin air because nobody will come around here; you've got to look at it from the visitor's point of view.'

'Especially as we'll probably be at war this time next year,' wailed Constance.

Oh, for goodness' sake! thought Helene. *Why does Mum always have to put the dampers on things?* Yes, everybody in the room knew that, but that was exactly one of the reasons that they all needed a project to work on together.

Joe had been dead silent.

'Folk will come. They'll be the same types as go cycling round Germany… but count *me* out as keeper of the keys to the "tumour".'

Helene could see him glancing down at his watch.

'Oh, Joe,' she was laughing, 'we thought you'd be leading the bidding for that job! Seriously though, that *deildergheist* legend is compulsive. They're not just soulless creatures toiling away at tasks they can never achieve, you know. They've learned to take out their frustration on the community, in mischief or worse. Anybody could be one, hiding away.'

'Yes, even Joseph could be one.' Jean raised his eyebrows in the direction of the doorway through which his brother had just disappeared.

'Don't joke, Jean… and anyway, *deildergheists* were never children. They don't develop or grow; they just stay the same forever.'

'I could name a few politicians like that,' smiled Jean.

'I bet that Joe really believes all this. He *always* clears off whenever we start on about it,' Jean whispered.

Helene had been reading about a man in England who had recently come up with a strange idea.

'They're called ley lines. Imagine you've got several natural features like waterfalls, and you look at them on the map. If you can draw a straight line through at least three of them, you've got a ley line, and it's really important because anything or anybody on that line can have a special power.'

'It sounds like a parlour game.' Even Robert hadn't heard of this idea.

'But lines are just geometry on paper; they don't exist

in nature; anyway, there aren't any waterfalls round here,' insisted Jean.

'Look, I've proved it,' shouted Helene, jumping up and standing in front of the window. 'If you stand on the tumulus, right behind you is the Pointe des Galets; in front of you is the stone ford which crosses the stream at the end of the dairy meadow; then there's the Healing Stone, La Vielle Vache, and beyond that Moulin de l'Hermitage. They all line up, and what's more, the sun rises behind the windmill hill and sets dead over the Pointe. I haven't even looked at a map; I don't need to.' Helene could feel moisture tingling on her top lip.

'If you get several of these lines converging, then it means it's a real place of power, magical.'

'You haven't mentioned the stone circle,' said Constance

It was true; perhaps that was on another ley line, with the magic pool. Helene hadn't thought about that one; in fact, the less she thought about the stone circle, the better. It wasn't one of her favourite places – she hated even walking past it. But the pool was special – Joseph had discovered it and shown her when they were children.

'Power can be good and bad,' interrupted Jean. 'You've got to look at it from the visitor's point of view; we wouldn't want them going away thinking they'd been gripped by demonic powers, particularly if they are all like Joseph,' Jean continued, serious now. 'So, you're saying it's haunted, Amber?'

'I'm just saying it's got *place memory*,' Helene replied, matter-of-factly.

'Oo-err,' Jean mocked again.

'It just means that a place has the power to absorb events which have happened there and to store them.'

'Then, several centuries later, somebody terribly

imaginative and sensitive like me comes along, and hey presto!' smiled Jean, waving both hands in the air like a street minstrel.

'I think what Amber's trying to say,' interjected Robert, 'is that somebody with the right kind of reception can see or hear these things – a bit like a wireless operator receiving a signal...?'

'Yes, a receiver.' Helene was nodding furiously.

'And so, our down-to-earth, practical-minded eldest brother couldn't possibly be a receiver, whereas our middle brother with the wild imagination and idealistic politics could well be. Ever *seen* anything?' asked Robert of the smiling Jean, who pretended to hit him round the head.

'Perhaps the rusted tractor remains at the bottom of the cliff are on another ley line?' Jean couldn't resist the comment as Joseph reappeared and hovered, looking puzzled, his eye still on his watch.

'I think you need to look at things from other people's point of view,' continued Jean, glancing sideways towards Joseph, tongue firmly in cheek. 'You may have trounced Thibout in your competition to see who could plough closest to the edge, but it wasn't worth losing your tractor.'

'You're pushing your luck, Jean.' Helene suddenly felt that she needed to be on her own. Nobody seemed to be taking the conversation about the *gîte* and the tumulus seriously except Joseph, and he looked as if he was about to deliver one of his brickbats. She seemed to be on the edge of a dangerous dialogue. Why did she have to prove herself about the ley lines and the *deilderghiests*? Truth or legend, it didn't make any difference; it was all important to the success of their business. She felt emotional.

The others could clear up the breakfast, so out she went into the dry, cool air of the remains of the morning, across the yard, between the great bulk of the grain store – running now – straight through the walkway of the old dairy sheds and across the meadow, pausing only to take care over which of the granite stones she stepped on as she crossed the stream. She was perspiring, part emotion, the rest exhilaration. Right! No going the easy route; wool pullover, baggy cotton shorts, her legs could take it! She strode through the clumps of golden bracken leaves – not yet crisp as they would soon become by the end of October – and she grasped the stems, first with one hand, then the other, pulling herself up the steep slope. As her feet found dryer ground, her bare legs brushed rosebay willowherb, some still in flower and standing proudly, other plants lying almost flat after a night of rain. Soon she was at the summit, gulping the air, could smell that intoxicating bitter acid scent of the plant – fireweed, it was known as in the old world – and turning to look at the tiny farm buildings below her. She laughed. It was amazing. She had done that little walk – her tumulus rush, she called it – hundreds of times, yet every time it was different.

She sat down and rested her back against the honey-coloured rock, spread out her bare legs, and looked at the damp, sticky seed constructions clinging there. Eighty thousand per plant she had once read, would you believe it? Where did they all go to? Yet there never seemed to be any more nor fewer plants on the hillside.

She was glad to be out of that kitchen – away from *Maman*, bless her. She'd never felt close to her. Her mother was scared of the past, and frightened of the future, whereas Helene loved both – particularly the past – but then she believed that everything went around in a circle anyway.

Sometimes, as the only other female member of the family, she felt lonely. Over the years, she had begun to make potions out of wild flowers, bark – all the stuff that

Eugene brought her. She'd no idea how; it just seemed to come to her. She had her testing methods, putting a tiny piece of leaf on her tongue to see if it was bitter or burning. The next day she'd do the same, but this time she'd swallow it. She kept notes, strictly private, locked away in the drawer of the walnut chest in her bedroom. Thibout was her guinea pig, and if he had a stomach ache, Helene would find a cure, like the fireweed she had just run through. That worked well – you could eat it raw – and Thibout was still alive so...

She liked to look after Thibout. She wanted to look after Joseph, but there seemed to be no way she could.

As she lay against the wall of the tumulus, she imagined herself as an ancient apothecary. She often had a weird picture of herself surrounded by pots and potions, and the further she drifted into the fantasy, the more she felt as if she'd been dipped in some sweet syrup of magic.

As she shut her eyes, she could see that she was standing in a large room. In the centre was a pile of blackfire burning on a stone hearth, and stretched out not far away on a miniature landscape of wool fabric was Balzac – well, it looked like Balzac, a Balzac from an ancient era.

She opened her eyes. In her haste to get out of the farmhouse, she'd forgotten to call him. He was still in his basket, poor love, and a bit slow. She returned to her dream, allowing her eye to explore the phantom space.

She could see rough-hewn timbers, resting on wooden pegs, each twice the size of a man's finger. There were shelves, upon which stood row after row of fired sticky earth containers, some no larger than a woman's thumb, others the girth of a man's chest. Most were covered with a strip of cloth smeared with animal fat and secured around the neck with a skin thong. There would be aconite – used as a hunting poison – and containers of wood tar used as treatments on folk with infected wounds. She must wake up!

Since her father died, Helene began to find solace in Le Vieux Vicente, but she hated the coldness which often clung to the hillside there and the mists which enveloped it. She liked Thibout, fruit, the dark earth, dark nights of which she had no fear. She hated brevity, shallowness, lies, human sleep – animals never really slept, except Balzac of course. As she closed her eyes, she had a wild idea.

Growing around the tumulus were clumps of small mushrooms with a double "s"-shaped stalk, a whitish bell-shaped head, and a tiny nipple on the cap. Arnaud and Constance had always warned that these belonged to "the poison group", and she'd left them alone, but Jean's friend, Raymond, had recently insisted that they weren't poisonous and could induce a "visionary experience". He hadn't tried them but that's what he had heard.

Helene set about gathering a small number. At first, she contemplated eating them there and then. She'd got as far as trying one herself years ago, but it tasted too bitter, so she'd spat it out. She'd left them alone after that, but now an unseen voice was speaking to her, urging her, *Come, try me!*

When evening came and she was preparing the meal of sea bass stew – courtesy of Thibout and Amaury – she lightly fried in butter just four of the dozen she had collected and ate them. She had hidden the ones she hadn't used; she certainly didn't want Constance finding them as she arrived in the kitchen to prepare the vegetables.

The floured sea bass sat in its fish kettle waiting for water to be poured around it – gently so as not to break the skin. Constance arrived, and the two women bustled about, tidying up and setting the table. The vegetables and fish would only take twenty minutes so they could be placed on the table just before the lads arrived. Robert was already sitting at the table, quietly reading.

Helene had no idea what effect the mushrooms might have, other than Raymond's vague description. Almost an hour had passed since she had consumed the four tiny fungi, and nothing seemed to be happening. The bass was now simmering gently inside its kettle whilst the vegetables were roasting in the oven. She glanced across to the table where Robert sat and laughed. She fancied that his hair seemed to be tied back in a pigtail; he looked like an eighteenth-century footman, and a cheeky one at that, she thought as he appeared to wink at her. She winked back. At the same time, she was conscious of strange flicking movements at the edges of her vision. It seemed as if all the parts of the room at which she wasn't looking directly, were full of some frantic activity.

It was rather like one of those dreams she sometimes had when she discovered a room in the house that she hadn't known existed before. The dream usually ended with her waking up and thinking that the unknown room had not been a pleasant place to be.

All was now ready to serve, and they were just waiting for the boys.

'You seem happy enough,' suggested Constance. The comment seemed to Helene to be loaded with unexpected meaning – hostile. Her mother was jealous and trying to provoke her. Helene was seized with an urge to fly into a flaming row with her. As she tried to control her feelings, she looked closely at Constance and, for the first time, thought how beautiful she was. Her dark, copper hair was swept backwards from her head in an enormous topknot, like a picture she'd once seen of Queen Nefertiti, nostrils dilating; her eyelashes seemed to be flicking and fluttering.

'Oh, I'm fine.' How trite! She glanced across to where her gabardine mackintosh hung from its peg by the door – it seemed to have acquired the exquisite finish of chamois, and thoughts of immense importance were almost certainly concealed within its folds; then, as the vision changed, it appeared to be no more than a giant piece of tripe dangling there, ready to be boiled in some huge vessel and served with onion to a crowd of hungry farm workers. The notion that this object was ever meant to be worn as a protection against the rain made Helene want to giggle hysterically.

Who was this coming racing into the room? She was seized with an urge to laugh – Jean? He seemed to resemble a giant hare. Flat feet, exaggerated long shanks, haunches, and the floppy white hair moving up and down in such an inexhaustible tangle, he looked like he'd grown large white ears. Jean, a hare, and so lustful-looking, she sniggered. His nose enormous, flattened, whilst dark nostrils twitched, scenting impending food.

The *attacks* – as Helene had already decided to call them – were coming in surges like the waves of the sea. The intensity of the vision would build, break, and roll away.

She had lost all sense of time, but as she glanced at the grandfather clock, she could see that less than two minutes had passed since she had looked across and seen the "cheeky footman" seated at the table. So, time went around in a circle, did it? Well, it certainly didn't travel in a straight line.

Helene had no idea how long this experience was going to go on; would it get any worse? She could excuse herself; Constance had now taken over duties as waiter. But if she retired to her bedroom, what would the landscape be like there? What horrors might be lurking inside the chest of drawers next to the diaries or the stones? She thought of Le

Vieux Vicente. *I have eaten of its forbidden fruit, and I am in its grip until it decides to release me.*

No, she would tough it out down here, where there were amusing *characters* to look at.

A flurry of activity behind her made her turn; it was Joseph. *He* looked normal at first, but as he removed his stout canvas jacket with its deep, upturned collar, it was as if the beast inside was being released. The muscles of his neck seemed to have swollen to gigantic proportions. Flexors, extensors, and rotators bulged. Dark bangs of hair became glistening horns. He looked like a Jacob ram being paraded at the Cambrai show. It wasn't funny, just horrible. She suddenly had an awful feeling that this is what it must be like to go mad. She had entered a world of psychosis, but the dreadful thing was that Joseph – or whoever this creature was – seemed to belong there permanently. The "Hello, little sister" seemed to contain the dark subtext, "I've been expecting you for a long time", as if this *hell* was his natural territory into which she had innocently strayed. Every thought, each tiny thought she grasped at, *he* seemed to have got there first; this was *his* world, and he could read her thoughts.

For what seemed like eternity, she sat, eating nothing, perspiring, trying to smile, and most important of all, avoiding the eyes of the Jacob ram. Gradually, the attacks became less intense, the waves began to ebb; and she knew the dreadful experience had peaked.

As she and Constance finished the clearing away of the debris of the meal, Helene at last admitted that she hadn't been feeling well. She did not say why. Never again would she underestimate the power of nature. *Imagine*, she thought, *if I had eaten all of the dozen I had gathered.*

Into the compost bin went the residue of the infernal fungi, well out of the way of Balzac, who incidentally – as she had glanced towards his basket during one of her paroxysms – looked very handsome indeed, rather like the Egyptian god, Anubis.

She wondered whether the window through which she had looked in upon this strange and violent phantasm was one of truth. Or was it distortion? Nothing to do with reality – either way, that vision of Joseph had upset her.

As she escaped to her room, she began to search for comforting thoughts. It was then that Aunt Icie came into her mind. Out came the diaries…

14 May 1926

Today Aunt Icie arrived here from Amsterdam. She's come to live with us and to teach Jean and Robert and me French, German, English, and Dutch, and Joseph too, if he'll listen. She was married to Mum's brother, but he was killed in the war. She has a new little baby called Otho. Mum says she's adopted Otho, but I think he's our aunt's baby, but no one seems to know who the father is or was. I think it's the real reason why she's come to stay with us so she can bring us all up together. So Otho is our cousin, but he's too young to play with us, even with Robert. He is very white.

Away went one maroon-covered volume, and out came another as Helene skipped on.

6 November 1934

I feel that Mum sometimes resents our Aunt Icie; perhaps it's little Otho? But Mum seems to love looking after him while Icie teaches us. I know that we children are country people, but we're not like Mum. She's felt like an outsider looking into her sister's life of middle-class sophistication. In Amsterdam, people generally speak at least two languages, and Mum only speaks French so feels like a provincial. What on earth attracted our cosmopolitan aunt to Mum's brother? I think that the answer is simply the truth: that Aunt Icie saw in Uncle a kind, generous, and honest man and, as I understand, he remained so up to his death.

I know that our aunt often feels frustrated by her life here – apparently barren of culture – where an "argument" is seen not as an intellectual thing but as an emotional row. Where "ideas" are seen merely as a list of tasks to be done; keeping would-be idle hands out of mischief.

Aunt Icie has set about creating an intellectual world for us children. It wasn't intended to exclude Mum. Aunt Icie's world isn't just of the intellect; every part of the education she gives us is given with love. I think that Mum has stood by and watched us emerge with minds – not like our Dutch tutor but of our own. Somehow, it has been no longer of Mum's doing – beyond her control – and I think she can't accept that.

The fact that Joseph – to a certain extent – has missed out on Aunt Icie's enlightened thinking, has acted as a kind of bond between him and Mum. Aunt Icie on the other hand has never been able to get to grips with Joseph.

'He's a bully; he's arrogant; and I fear that there's real malice in him,' she said to me today.

7 November 1934
Otho has been sent away to prep school near Amsterdam. Nobody knew Auntie was planning it; her brother just turned up at the farm today and took him away. It was horrible!

4 November 1936

Today we received news that Aunt Icie has married again – is it really six months since she left us? She's married a Jewish man introduced to her by her brother. Robert, Jean, and I jumped for joy. For one purely selfish reason, it could mean trips to go and stay with them. For some reason, neither Mum nor Joe has mentioned Icie's name since she left. Icie said that Otho is getting on well at boarding school.

She began to write that day's entry.

2 September 1939

Today a number of immigrant workers arrived in the area – first Czechs, then Poles. Jean says Poles are good workers. Joseph says they are troublemakers.

Anyway, believe it or not, Thibout and Amaury Giroud have taken on the Poles!

"Daddy" Giroud says to me:

'Lobster and crab are fetching better prices at the moment; this will give the boys more chance to take the boat out; the Poles will help work the farm and we'll still take our crop share from Fournier.'

I think that one of the Poles, Zbigniew, likes me. He's certainly good-looking: blond, high cheekbones. Joseph is furious. Jean likes the idea.

CHAPTER 5

THE BIRTHDAY PARTY

Jean didn't know how he'd got through the rest of the day. It had helped being with the family – even though Helene had gone off in one of her moods.

As he stood in the stubble of the wheat field, he kept visualising the scene, over and over again. Had he missed something? There's a rational explanation for everything. Joseph had been taking a risk in holding him so far out over the cliff edge; the two of them could have easily both gone over. You don't endanger yourself like that as a prank.

Whatever the answer might be, he couldn't share it with the others... *do you know what Joe tried to do to me?* That, of course, was all part of it. To *tell* would be family disloyalty at its basest, plus it was he who was the excitable, overimaginative sibling, the fantasist, the outsider. Could he let Raymond know? It wouldn't help matters either; no, he was on his own in this. It seemed as if Joseph had a diplomatic immunity.

***

That evening, Jean was sitting in the kitchen with Robert and Constance. Helene was hard at work preparing Robert's birthday supper. Joseph was expected shortly.

Mother and youngest son were doing all the talking – he animatedly, she with a fidgeting nervousness – while Jean felt drawn down into the swamp of his own gloom. He welcomed this supper, if only to sit in the company of his siblings. He was going to wait and watch Joseph's every move. The answer to his question would be in Joseph's body movements.

The bizarre event had also made Jean realise that, somehow, he must take a grip of his life, start to control it, shape it, be the master of his own destiny – even if he made a mess of it, it would be his doing, not someone else's. He stared at Constance's worried face as it mouthed to Robert across the table, like two faces in a silent film.

Helene was preparing pheasant – a special recipe of her own. Jean was doing nothing. He needed time, was feeling exhausted, and he had a cough. He hoped that Joseph would not come just yet.

The gently pulsing light from the kerosene lamp burning behind Helene's head gave Jean the peculiar feeling that his sister belonged to the past which she so often talked about, as if she were a priestess about to offer up a sacrifice. He felt himself begin to perspire, and as he pulled the back of his hand across his soaking top lip, he realised he was being drawn into one of his visions. The figures in front of him had become part of a huge gathering of people, and there was a communal feeling of apprehension.

All fell silent, and Jean watched as the priestess of his vision dispatched a number of tethered animals – piglets and lambs – threw the entrails onto the shadowards Bonfire of Renewal and the carcasses into the sunwards conflagration. Unable to move, the ancient Jean watched as holy men examined the entrails of the eviscerated animals for traces of the gods. Nothing was saved, for this was a sacrifice; the feast would take place shortly.

The feeling passed; Jean felt himself calm; and once again, everything seemed to be back in the present. He studied his sister as she took two fresh snipe which she had plucked and cleaned. She placed the bodies on one large, cream-coloured plate and the livers of the birds on another. Then, using her hands, she removed all the flesh, passing it through the steel mincing machine which was attached to the end of the scrub-top table. To the mince she added a little beef, lard, pepper, and salt and – still kneading it between her fingers – gradually fed the whole concoction into the body cavities of the male and female pheasants.

'So... you're off to agricultural college now, instead of university?' Joseph grinned at Robert as he arrived and took his place at the table. 'Why don't you come and work with us?'

'Especially as there's going to be a war,' prompted Constance, as she helped her daughter by cutting two enormous slices of bread, each larger than the female birds. The two women worked in unison taking the snipe livers, butter, two anchovies, a handful of capers, and a dessert spoon of Dijon mustard, and using the mix to cover the bread slices.

'If you come and work with us, you won't have to go into the army...' The logic sounded potent; to Jean it sounded like Christ being tempted in the wilderness. *Let the kid make his own mind up, will you?* Joseph was staring at Robert, his eyes dark brown liquid discs.

'What about building construction? You could do that at college. It would be another string to your bow. It would stand us all in good stead. Imagine it, eh, when we start that building business, you and I – we'd make a great team!'

A great team? A wave of nausea passed over Jean. It would be a combination worse than chalk and cheese – more like arsenic and the human body. *Leave him alone, will you? Stop trying to persuade all the time. He's a creative boy with a great future. He doesn't want to be menaced by an ignorant bigot like you.*

'Your dad would be proud of you if you stayed and helped. University's la-di-da, not for us. You could carry on with the work that Dad did on meadow grass... make a name for yourself. You'd be living here, in God's country. You couldn't wish for better. Hmm...' he broke off suddenly, 'you know, I'm too smart for my own good. I've just caught that fertiliser supplier trying to con me.'

'Oh, you mean the one you were telling us about last week – he's going to help you revolutionise production?' asked Helene as she unwrapped a large, soft, yellow cheese and shook it free of its cloth.

'He's one of those Czech fellows that arrived last year, isn't he?' Jean heard himself say as he recovered from another bout of coughing. He was desperate to keep up with the action as Helene transferred the enriched slices of bread onto the backs of all four pheasants and inserted them into the oven.

'The less said about Czechs, Poles, Romanians the better,' rumbled Joseph. 'Too many immigrants in France...'

'Dad hired a Welshman, way back before the Great War, and a Chinaman, would you believe, so he once told me,' said Helene.

'That was then, and *they* went back home. *These* folk settle here, marry our women... that's the rural areas – where Europeans come – but cities, different story with nig-nogs from West Africa. Right now, it's difficult to find labour, so there're plenty of jobs for them, but soon there won't be.

They'll be taking *our* jobs, and they breed like mad. Mark my words, before so long there'll be more West Africans, North Africans, and Arabs in France than there are white folk. If everyone stuck to their own country, we wouldn't have any problems.'

'Your friend 'Mr Hitler' doesn't seem to agree with that idea.' Jean felt a sudden rush of energy.

'Germany was owed Sudentenland, and Austria has always been German in spirit!'

'There should be more tolerance for migrant workers,' said Jean.

'That's just the kind of liberaliste view I'd expect from you, Raymond and co.'

'Look Joe, there's nothing wrong with having an empire. We lost most of our American and Indian colonies to the British, but practically the whole of West Africa and large parts of Southeast Asia are French. We've done a lot of good there.'

'Spread the French language,' said Helene, 'and the Catholic religion.'

'That's what I mean. It's been all "give" at cost to us – except to you and your friends who go on about exploitation.'

'Joe, many French industrialists, and folk in general, benefitted from cheap labour and dangerous conditions in the colonies. It made life easier for everybody back home. We're not giving them handouts; we're paying them back. It's only right that we should offer them a home here.'

'You know, Jean, you should bloody well go and join the Quakers!'

Jean could feel the air being pushed out of his lungs and his fists clenching under the table.

He watched Helene take a respite from the oven and put the finishing touches to her floral arrangements – seasonal wild flowers of blue thistle, sea campion, yarrow, and heather with a twist of honeysuckle threaded though it – strange but *very* Helene. She returned to the stove, leaving Constance, who stood twitching at the strand of honeysuckle.

'All right, back to that Czech fellow before I was rudely interrupted. Being a foreigner is only part of the problem. He's been seen interfering with little girls. If I had a daughter, I wouldn't let his type anywhere near her. All men caught doing that should be castrated immediately, and I'll operate the tongs! Are you going to stop that coughing, Jean?'

'He can't help it,' shouted Helene as she slowly whisked some flour into a container of beef stock and placed it on the hot plate.

'Right, watch!' Without warning, Joseph darted from his seat and, before he knew what was happening, Jean felt the tingle of a strand of hair being snatched from his head. Almost in the same action, Joseph leaned over to where the largest loaf of bread was standing like a small monument on its wooden board. He hacked a modest slice of the stonebake and ripped it in two. He took the long strand of Jean's blond hair, placed it between the two slices of bread, and clapped his hands together, the bread between them.

'And for my next trick…' He snapped. Giggling, he made his way over to Balzac's basket. The collie opened one eye in somnolent suspicion as Joseph pushed the hair sandwich towards the dog's grinning mouth.

'Eat well, you hound, "may *you* be sick and this boy sound"!'

'What about Balzac?' protested everyone, but Joseph persisted.

'It'll work; you'll see.'

Once again, Jean felt as if he was locked inside his own world.

'You really are mad, you know,' he muttered, barely hearing his own words. The others laughed, but it wasn't a joke. Joseph grinned his mirthless grin. There really was something bestial about Jean's elder brother.

Constance was adding cloves and milk to a bowl of breadcrumbs to make bread sauce. Jean leaned forwards, trying not to cough.

'You haven't given up the idea of university after the ag. college, have you? Imagine living in Paris, Rob!'

'Oouh, ooogh,' intoned Joseph, sounding like a bad ghost imitation, the corners of his mouth forced down. 'Paris! The rat race, eh? Sharks, fast boys.'

Jean gave yet another sigh and sat back. It was happening again, the ancient Jean – or whoever this person was in his body – appeared to be witness to some arcane feast. A large and oafish individual was forcing himself into Jean's mind. He appeared drunk and was being supported by two stewards. Slung round his neck – like a giant rigid nosebag – was a sticky earth-fired jar containing a syrupy amber liquid, which was sloshing about against the walls of the drinking vessel.

The eye of the oaf came to rest upon a wicker cage which had been placed upon the rush-strewn floor and contained a flock of tiny birds – perhaps quail. The yellow-beaked, black-headed birds were pecking at everything which was thrown into the cage.

Without warning, the oaf lunged at the cage, pulled open the tiny hatch within the side of the basket, and with a movement puzzlingly deft for a man so drunk, extracted the nearest quail and held the little pulsing bird close to his face… Jean must be feverish, his cough getting the better of him. He was going down with something…

The mysterious revellers of his inner vision seemed unremorseful in their enjoyment of this performance. The oaf opened his mouth, bared his teeth, turning full circle as he did so.

What in the sun's name was going on? The ancient Jean hadn't expected this. Was the thug actually going to bite the head off the tiny creature? But the tyrant's exploits appeared to be too much for him, and he pitched forwards abruptly. The quail's life was spared, and the entire contents of the drinking jar gushed onto the floor. Jean wanted to intervene, but he couldn't. He could hear his own voice shouting inside his head, *Who am I? Where am I? Am I human?*

Still within his Bronze Age vision, he could see stewards emerging, bringing in steaming chunks of meat resting in shouldered sticky earth-fired bowls, sufficiently broad at the rim to delve into with hands and deep enough to accommodate the fat...

At last, he broke free.

'Amber, how's that new chap of yours? Zed something... can't pronounce his name.'

'Zbigniew – it's pronounced Sbishek. He's fine, working hard like all of us.'

The birds were now roasted; a bowl of herb salad, a spelt and rye loaf, and two cream bowls containing butter were placed on the deal-topped table. When the pheasants were brought, Helene added her final touch: two pheasant tail feathers and half a dozen Florida oranges, cut into segments and arranged around the edge of the dish. Jean saw Robert smile, heard him gasp; oranges were a rarity in the village, let alone the Fournier household.

'That murder in Boulogne, the woman who was raped and then thrown into a canal. They've got the Pole who did it,' announced Joseph.

'Why a foregone conclusion that it would be a Pole?' breathed Jean, again barely audible. His voice felt flat and tired.

'You take a look at the *Wanted* notices outside the police station; all foreigners!'

'Who's made them into criminals?' Jean was feeling emotional now. Constance looked like she was going to speak but didn't.

'Yes, go on, blame the French people for that; it's everybody's fault except the person who does the crime.' Joseph must be angry now; he was rarely sarcastic.

'No, Joe, I'm not saying it's we – the people – who make the criminal; I'm saying it's we – the people – who are responsible for them. That's our lot. We have to learn to cope with it. That's how civilisation evolves, isn't it? Stopping them coming into the country or deporting them isn't the answer.'

'Jean, do wipe that grubby mark off your cheek before addressing your mother.' Jean did so, blushing shamefully.

'If you put the same enthusiasm into farming and estate management as you do to entertaining your mother and sister with your lopsided ideas, we wouldn't have anything to worry about. You know I'm really looking forward to this meal.'

He knew it was rude and selfish of him, but Jean couldn't take any more. He had to get out, get away from Joseph. He rose with as much self-control as he could muster and walked towards the kitchen door.

CHAPTER 6

AUNT ICIE

As Jean stormed across the farmyard in the withering light, he thought of Aunt Icie.

In the midst of this disaster, it was her memory which gave him comfort. It was she who had shaped his later childhood, held the family together. They had been lucky to have her.

As he began the slow climb to the tumulus, the clumping of his great feet, and the tinkling plash of water against the granite stones, began to still his fear. The tu-whoo of an early tawny made him smile, while the picture in his mind's eye of Icie with her cropped blonde hair and dancing eyes made him laugh with joy.

He laboured up the slope, recalling Icie's going away party when the whole family took part in a farewell evening of entertainment.

They had decided they would all dress up as famous characters from French history. It was agreed that nobody except Aunt Icie would know who each had chosen to be. She would help make the costumes, and the others would have to guess who was who.

As everybody gathered and busied themselves for the event, there was an air of anticipation – not just for the celebration to come, but what about Joseph? The tractor disaster of a few days earlier seemed to have taken over his mind. He wouldn't speak, and when he did speak, he was rude to everybody – even Constance. It seemed to have developed into a kind of illness – nobody had seen him all day. What was going to happen that evening? What, if any, character would he play, and would he turn up at all?

Once the meal was over, the scrub-top table was pulled back, and an area cleared as a kind of stage. One lamp was left burning. The costumes were all hidden in everybody's bedrooms, and each person went off to change as their turn came.

There had never been a shortage of space at the farmhouse. There were six bedrooms, so everybody had one each. Even though he was the oldest, Joseph had chosen the smallest bedroom, so small that no one else could get in there when he was installed, so he was always there alone.

First to appear was Aunt Icie, and as the general mutterings and chat hushed, all eyes focused on the "stage".

As the room became silent, a human foot, clad in a very long, pointed shoe – skilfully crafted from paper – glided into view a metre above the floor, followed by what appeared to be a white stick at head height. Next, a gloved hand appeared, grasping in it a rather fine rapier – a piece of kitchen equipment as the hand guard – and a garden cane, with what looked like an oversized lump of putty on its tip, acting as the safety button. As Icie's head finally emerged, all could see that what had seemed to be a white stick was really a long false nose which she held up in her left hand, concealing her real one.

'Pinocchio!' shouted Robert.

'Noo!' scoffed Jean. 'He's Italian anyway, and since when did he go around fighting duels with rapiers?' That was the clue, and as everybody chorused "Cyrano de Bergerac", Icie triumphantly held up the nose and took a bite out of the end of it, revealing that it was made out of pastry.

Next was Robert, who had decided to appear as Harry Houdini and had already sprinted off to his bedroom. Icie took her place with the rest of the audience as they waited for him.

'Are you all right, Robert?' Helene called as the minutes ticked by. There was so much clanking and rattling from the variety of old chains and padlocks which he had collected from all over the farm that day, that by the time he arrived under the kerosene lamp dressed in combination underwear and shackled in a mass of metalwork, everyone had guessed who it was.

'He'll get blood poisoning from all that rusty rubbish,' complained Constance.

Jean hadn't liked to say at first, but it had to be said…

'But Houdini was Hungarian, surely?' There followed an intense debate as all challenged the still-bondaged Robert as to the validity of his act.

'I know all that,' he smiled smugly, 'but I'm Jean Robert-Houdin whose tricks and name Houdini copied!' Nobody seemed at all convinced, but it had all been very amusing.

The interval gave Constance plenty of time to dress and appear as Henriette Marie. Everybody said that she looked wonderful in the huge brocade curtain she had gathered round herself and pinned with the help of Icie, who had acted as handmaiden. Together they had devised a daringly low neck and draped lots of braid round her from the house needlework collection. The chains even made an appearance, but this time they were very fine ones and had been kept inside the house so sparkled in the lamplight, a bit like the strings of pearls they were meant to be. It took the audience a while to guess, though having Balzac proudly trotting along next to her on a length of the sparkly chain helped.

Now it was Jean's turn as d'Artagnan. There was no hesitation from the audience who cried "One for all, and all for one!" before he had barely arrived on the stage dressed in an old leather jerkin which had belonged to Arnaud. It didn't really look like the doublet it was meant to, but the white scarf wound round his neck as a stock, and the oversized wooden sword helped the general effect, though the real stroke of luck was finding a small stash of items under the floor in one of the outbuildings, including a three-cornered hat. Everybody collapsed laughing because it was full of holes, and Constance was convinced that rats had nested in it.

Helene would have needed Icie's help, and even the two of them must have struggled to tie a large metal cooking dish over her chest to form a breastplate. Joan of Arc seemed a virtuous choice, and as she and Icie arrived on stage gathering the old geometric patterned curtain around her, and grasping the long wooden pole to which had been tied a brightly coloured scarf, Jean shuddered at the thought of being a martyr.

As the applause died away, everybody looked at one another. Was that it? Nobody quite dared speak. Then the kitchen door banged, and a figure stamped in and onto the stage, a face scowling under improvised bicorn hat. Everybody laughed as it thrust first one gloved hand, then the other, across its chest, deep into Father's old trench-style coat, unable to remember which hand it was that the self-appointed emperor concealed in that way.

Jean had thought that it was an odd choice – corny but rather sad.

'Deeply unlucky, I should say,' he'd whispered to Helene as Joseph shambled off.

The simple medium of invention, a few modest props, and the help and love of Aunt Icie had helped to create a gentle entertainment – a far cry from the *Guignol* that had emerged this evening. Jean wondered how events had seemed to mark their lives as a family. The death of their father and the burial of the time capsule seemed to signify the end of their early childhoods. Aunt Icie's farewell party represented the final days of their teenage years. What event would mark the close of their young adulthoods?

Refreshed by both walk and memory, Jean reached the tumulus and placed his hand against a chunk of the honeyed stone, now almost luminous in the twilight. He would walk round it – just once – then back to the farmhouse. He could handle Joseph now. There might even still be some pheasant left for him.

As he walked along the seawards side of the mound, he noticed something dark on the concrete surface of one of the blocked entrances. He knelt, peered closely in the almost vanished light. He found himself looking into black space, so infinite he could not comprehend its beginning or end. It was a hole "big enough for human men to wriggle in through" or, thought Jean, as he felt a sickening thrill, perhaps to wriggle out through! It had happened again.

CHAPTER 7

THE CRUCK BARN

It was a misty afternoon, and Jean and Robert were sitting at the kitchen table. Helene was standing at the stove stirring blackcurrants in a large copper pan, while Constance was sitting at the table bookkeeping.

Jean watched as Joseph marched in and out of the kitchen, fetching documents for his mother from where they were stored in his gatehouse office.

Jean was thinking about the news that Germany had invaded Poland the previous day and that France and Britain were at war with Germany. What was going to happen now; was this a rallying call? Three days had passed since that awful evening on the clifftop when Joseph had tried to kill him, and there they all were, still going nowhere – except for Robert. At last, he was off to agricultural college tomorrow in Cambrai, not the Sorbonne he had so much wanted, but he could apply after he'd finished the course. After months of dallying, someone had made a decision – bravo! It would do him good to get away – even in this uncertainty.

'The Poles started it,' Joseph snorted as he joined them at the table. He said he admired Hitler for standing up to people and for having a vision for the future. 'They attacked a German wireless station.'

Jean had gleaned a slightly different story from those who frequented the Bar Tabac.

'That's German propaganda – they're masters at it. The Germans were dressed in Polish uniforms... but that's not all; the Russians have attacked Poland from the east.'

Russian communism was the thing for Jean. Though his view was based upon what he'd heard from others. Nevertheless, he voiced opinions, if nothing else but to try and deflate his elder brother.

'To have had a social revolution, and then to do a deal with Hitler, is pernicious to democracy,' said Jean, feeling grand for one short moment.

'I bet you're a closet pacifist.'

How far that man is from the truth, thought Jean as he recalled his own efforts, when he had talked about going to Spain, joining the International Brigade to fight the fascists.

'How can you say that, Joseph? Remember Spain?'

'But you fluffed it, like always. You just couldn't organise it!'

'And thank God he didn't,' said Constance. 'Now you've got the pleasure of arguing with your big bother instead of lying dead at the bottom of some Spanish ravine.'

Jean couldn't quite believe it, but the fact was that, in spite of Raymond, and his other friends in the village, he just hadn't had the right contacts to get there.

'The farming life keeps him on the straight and narrow.' Constance didn't look up from her bookkeeping.

'Those blackcurrants smell delicious,' shouted Robert with overexaggerated enthusiasm.

'They're blackcurrants and gooseberries; there weren't enough of either to jam separately this year,' returned Helene, as she began to pour the dark, viscous liquid into creamy-coloured two-kilo jars. 'Zbigniew says that the Russians are as bad as the Nazis; his family have lived in Kashubia for generations. They've been invaded from both east and west.'

'It's a bit like that round here,' said Jean. 'Think of the number of hostile armies that have tramped up and down this coast.' "The Fatal Avenue"[1] some historian or politician, he couldn't remember who, had once called it. He thought about his own little Field of Mars at Pointe des Galets, that in its own way might have been a training ground for military manoeuvres over the years. Mind you, he'd stopped calling it the Field of Mars since he heard of Hitler's creation by the same name at Nuremberg.

'Mosely and the Astors say that the real enemy is Stalin, not Hitler.'

'How on earth do you know all that?' Jean never failed to be surprised by Robert's well-informed remarks. He felt proud to see his younger brother constantly questioning life and sometimes a tinge jealous of him. He always seemed to come out with the remark that Jean himself would have liked to make.

'He reads the newspapers,' Helene smiled, 'which is why he's off to college.'

'He's about the only one who does,' said Jean. They'd never even taken a newspaper at the farm. He picked up all his snippets of news from the Bar Tabac and intellectual Raymond.

Balzac grinned across from his basket as if agreeing with Helene, while Jean fancied that when his elder brother spoke, the animal would drop its head and appear to abandon itself to sleep.

Balzac had other ideas. Yes, he loved the tall mistress with the amber eyes. He was a little wary of the tall tailless male with white curly hair and big feet and distinctly suspicious of the other two-legged male with dark red hair who had once kicked him.

'Balzac, *Balzac*, Bal*zac*, *Balzac*!' they would shout, but that was just *their* name for him. *He* knew who he was, even if they seemed to have forgotten who they were. He was *Hound* from an ancient earth, who wanted and needed meat, would run with Amber-Eyes. Sometimes even as far as the Dead Place where she would show him the stones and they would look for smelly plants which would make him jump and dance. There he had seen *those* things – the dead *twolegs* who could walk – which Amber-Eyes could not see... well, almost never. But the dark, red-haired *twolegs* who had once kicked him could see them... almost always.

*****

'Ag. college, all right, all right, but can we change the subject?' demanded Joseph. 'We need to talk about the farm.'

Trouble coming, thought Jean.

'We've got nine buildings on this site, and we're only using three of them. We could have a thriving business here. I want something worthwhile to leave to my children.'

'Ooh hark at him; you generally need a wife first before you can produce children, you know,' smiled Jean.

'I've more chance of getting married than you,' snapped Joseph, launching himself to his feet, the legs of his chair screeching on the tiles. He turned on Jean, and in a terrible moment, he also was on his feet and facing Joseph. 'Spending all your time with Ray-*monde*,' said Joseph, exaggerating the last syllable.

For a moment, the two men were clumsily locked together, like stags in a joust. Jean's hands were holding

Joseph's forearms – almost beseechingly – while there was that grip on his own upper arms, digits digging into the soft muscle. He could smell the other man's sweat, and something else.

A gentle, high-pitched wail, like a siren that's been muffled with cloth, was coming from the end of the scrub-top table. Constance was leaning forwards, staring at Jean, her knuckles thrust into her mouth. It was Jean who gave way, his arms dropping like a dead weight. For the second time that week, he left the room without saying where he was going.

It was an infantile exchange for two grown men, but it was a sore point. Jean twenty-six, his elder brother twenty-eight, and neither of them had really had any serious girlfriends. The remoteness of the farm and the nature of the work made it difficult to even meet members of the opposite sex, let alone develop relationships.

Outside the kitchen door, Balzac was grinning up at him from his basket, but this time, the fur of his snout was drawn back to reveal teeth the colour of old china clay, set in gums which glistened pink and black.

Jean needed time for reflection. He *had* to get away from The Dark Night. His mother was getting him down as well; how could she be so cold all the time? She was as cold as Amber was warm, but he wasn't sure where he stood with his sister, except he knew that he loved her. He knew he loved Raymond as well.

As Jean wandered away from the farmhouse, he felt puzzled. When you've grown up with something, you tend to take it for granted, seeing only what you need to at the time.

He was in the middle of the farmyard now. Perhaps what he wanted in life was a craft; maybe he wanted to make things?

He had a vision of himself as a craftsman – a metalman – smelting, casting, forging. How easily things could inhabit the mind, yet once they left it, how difficult it became! Jean couldn't believe what he was seeing in his mind's eye…

Two imaginary boys from that ancient world stood at either side of a stone vessel and were flexing their thigh muscles as they grasped lengths of willow pole three times the thickness of a man's thumb. They steadied and, using all the deftness they possessed, lifted the giant stone bowl, with its fiendish-looking white contents, clear of a furnace. As he continued to stare, the ancient Jean saw the white mass in the crucible gradually turn to a fiery orange. Then a metalman spoke, as if he was a priest or a wizard.

'This is where we look through a window into the next earth. The gods are watching. They decide the outcome, for these men are holding the sun's blood.'

The two young apprentices tipped the crucible so that its contents slowly disappeared inside the heated mould. Jean broke into a fit of coughing just at the thought of it. How could something which started life as stone be turned into a liquid like bubbling milk? Burrrgh, burble, blurrgh, blood… and then become the sun's blood? He could almost feel someone thrusting a cup of the honey-coloured liquor at him, and he resumed his breathing as best he could. He gazed again and soon the mould was cool enough for two assistants to carefully lower it into a trough of water.

'Urgh.' The prehistoric Jean fell into another paroxysm of coughing, as the air was filled with hissing and spitting. A cloud of steam surged out – rising higher than the worst cooking accident he'd ever seen – and up to the wooden rafters. The two assistants were already tapping the mould while Jean could see fragments of dried, sticky earth fall to the floor. There it was at last, The Leader's sword, still too hot to touch and lying innocently against the dark *earthblood*.

More water was poured over it; the metalman was soon able to grasp it in his hand, and he held it aloft in the moving firelight.

'Near perfect,' he declared triumphantly.

Jean looked around himself. Here he was back in the here and now, a sort-of farmer, but not a very good one, and one with hazy ideas about politics. The funny thing was he hated the idea of politicians… that certainty about everything. All they spent their time doing was persuading other people, rather like Joseph in fact. How could they be so sure about things? Some of them would start off well; then they'd just do what the rest of their party wanted them to. Priests as well; how could they be so perfect and pious and know the answers to life?

Fair enough; you couldn't really have a dithering dentist or a doubtful doctor. Neither did you want a genius in either profession, with one great success followed by nothing. The professions had to know what they were doing. It was all down to training. It was the bigger questions which interested Jean. But what was *he* going to do? He just wasn't ready to decide. There was nothing wrong with that. He would be like an archaeologist; they didn't go rushing around digging up everything in sight. It was a science, a discipline of waiting for ideas to mature and technology to improve. Yes, he would wait… after all, he didn't want to burn himself out.

Who am I? What am I? Joseph might well mock – "If you don't bloody well know who you are by now…"

Where do I come from? The questioning voice in Jean's head persisted. *And where is my home?* It was the Jean of the modern world that was asking the questions, but it was the ancient Jean which seemed to be supplying the answers: a beehive-shaped structure of rough stones, heaped high in upon themselves until the forces within them become so strong that they create a space, tall enough for a man to stand up in, and of sufficient diameter to enable him to lie down, and to sleep. Folk around the Bronze Age Jean lived in houses, and in so far as this stone construction provided him with shelter, kept him out of the wind, and safe from prowling wild beasts, Jean had to agree that he too lived in a house. But his real home would be always within his mind...

Back in the twentieth century, Jean felt as uncertain as ever about life. Sometimes he thought it might be better to be like Joseph. 'The past isn't important; it's the present which counts...' he would say, '...so keep your mind on the job, will you!' Joseph was always saying how everything in the world got better every day and that Bronze Age man was stupid.

But that couldn't be right; otherwise, in another four thousand years, the Josephs of the future would say that the Joseph of the present was stupid? It wasn't as if evolution meant that things automatically got better; it just meant change, but too slowly for Jean. No, Bronze Age man was just as intelligent as Jean and Joseph; he just hadn't discovered as much. It was all about discovery, uncovering things.

He made his way over to the cruck barn and stood outside the door. The family story was that this was the site of a large house built in the seventeenth century... probably true, as the family had owned all the land including the rather grandly named Chateau des Galets, and Pointe des Galets, for centuries. After the revolution, the chateau was confiscated by the State and a number of peasant families were housed within its walls but so badly mistreated it that, within a few years, it had to be demolished. After further years of State ownership, Arnaud's grandfather bought the land back from the Government for a token sum.

Jean's eye travelled backwards and forwards between the gatehouse and the medieval cruck barn – the only two remaining parts of the original estate. The gatehouse chimneys had been fashioned to look like castle turrets, and even in the mist, the whole composition appeared luminous and charged with a special energy. The building seemed to be full of light and – as if it were impatient at being held in a kind of suspended animation – might combust at any moment.

He kicked open the door of the cruck barn. Like every other door on the holding, it was painted green and hadn't received another coat since Arnaud's accident in the war. Through a combination of weather and distress – received at the hands and feet of petulant farm labourers – it had acquired the patina of fine oxidised copper.

Arnaud had stopped using the barn for grain storage and threshing after the war, so only planks, a length of hurdle, and various building materials which Joseph had collected, stood there.

At one end of the barn was a gallery. Its height was twice that of Jean, but way above that, the roof ridge was the height of six Jeans, and some of the supporting timbers in the roof were so wavy that, as a child, he had been convinced that they were trees and still growing.

Joseph had once calculated that there were over three thousand tiles in the roof, and Jean could remember men working on ladders all summer almost every year, until it became difficult and too expensive to get the labour.

There was no waterproofing felt so, as he looked up, he could see each tile, in glowing terracotta with the local maker's stamp on the clay. Half closing his eyes, he could imagine that he was inside a huge, luminous, three-dimensional mosaic, rather like a gigantic version of the tiny icon Aunt Icie used to have on her bedroom wall…

Much as Jean loved Icie, he thought she had overdone the religion thing. It had put him off for life. She'd been brought up in the Nederlandse Hervormde Kerk – Dutch Reformed Church – while Constance had never given them any religious instruction, and Arnaud never mentioned it. It might seem highly improbable to an outsider, thought Jean, but the Fourniers have well and truly slipped though the net of Roman Catholicism. It wasn't as if there had been apostasies in the family, just indifference. Joseph wasn't interested; Helene had a belief all right – she talked about what she called "the God within". As an aspiring communist, Jean saw himself as an atheist, but if there was a "God within", was it within man or the world without? Helene had once said – he couldn't remember it exactly, but it was something like – "the spirit" – whatever that was – "slept in stones, breathed through plants, was dreamt of by animals, and was awakened by humans".2 It was a bit of a strange saying to fathom, but he'd thought about it a lot.

As Jean stood, his feet firmly planted on the milk and lime floor, it seemed to him that everything was moving except the barn and the neighbouring buildings. He could feel the warm air passing through every tiny aperture in the roof and walls. Though there was no wind, he could hear a hiss in his ears, as if he was aware of the smallest particles in the air crashing together in their frantic rush through life, while the barn and all its parts lay inert – immovable. Sometimes even he, with his restless craving for change, would have liked to have been able to freeze his memories in time just as he and his younger brother and sister had done all those years ago when they buried the biscuit tin in the tumulus. But somehow, he knew that things were going to change. He and his family were going to join those mad molecules of air, jumping and dancing in their journey from past to future.

When he emerged from the cruck barn, he caught sight of Joseph standing outside the farmhouse kitchen door talking to a man. It wasn't the usual machine supplier he had seen before – perhaps this was his son or an assistant. He decided to walk round to the rear of the house and go in through the back door. It would mean that he could return to the kitchen without having to walk past Joseph.

Taking his time, he entered through the lean-to wash house. He was about to step back and rejoin the others in the kitchen when he noticed Joseph was still outside the door, the machine man opposite him. He paused to listen; Joseph had his back to him but was clearly audible.

'I can get that cheaper from a bloke in Calais,' insisted Joseph.

'No, we checked the market and ours is the cheapest; we're prepared to take a small loss because we sell a lot of them, but that's it; we can't do it any cheaper.'

Jean knew what was coming next. Joseph's righteous indignation was mounting to anger – it was mock anger of course; nothing Joseph ever did contained genuine emotion; it was he who was playing the machine man, enjoying controlling those around him.

Jean hovered in the passageway, and he could see Joseph's face now, a caricature of umbrage.

'We've all got families to feed,' the man went on, while Joseph leaned forwards slightly and raised both his hands, palms upwards.

'I'm a humble man,' he incanted softly, both eyes almost closed, his expression one of carefully controlled torment, as if he was confiding his most intimate thoughts and inviting the machine man to do likewise. Then it came, what Jean knew would eventually come, what always came. Joseph leaned even closer, until his nose was practically touching the other man's, and began in a gentle whisper, 'I tell you that I can get those parts cheaper elsewhere.' He continued in a voice full of pain, ending with a tiny sob, 'I swear to you on my daughter's life.'

It always worked. The ignorant simply believed him, while those who knew him better just sighed and let him have his own way. Jean didn't know whether to laugh or cry. Quietly, he stepped back into the wash house, closed the door, sat on a chair, and laughed.

When he eventually joined the others, the conversation had returned to the threat of invasion.

'Hmm, the *Ligne Maginot*… best set of fortifications ever built.'

Jean was just in time to add, 'But it stops at the Belgian border. If the Germans come, that's the way they'll do it, through neutral Belgium.'

'But what will they actually do when they get here?' asked Robert.

'Give the country the revolution it deserves.' Joseph smacked his hand down on the scrub-top.

'But you have to look at it from the human point of view; the Nazis are subduing the people, not freeing them. What really counts is a better, fairer world for the people,' insisted Jean.

'But people are not really human beings. That's just where you've been going wrong all these years.'

Jean knew that the pair of them could go on like this for hours.

'This country is run by old men,' snapped Joseph.

Jean burst out laughing again. 'I'll agree with you on that point!'

EPIGRAPH

This ae nighte, this ae nighte,
Every nighte and alle,
Fire and fleet and candle-lighte...

... If hosen and shoon thou ne'er gav'st nane
The whinnes sall prick thee to the bare bane...

... If meat or drink thou ne'er gav'st nane,
The fire will burn thee to the bare bane;

This ae nighte, this ae nighte,
Every nighte and alle,
Fire and fleet and candle-lighte...

Dirge, anonymous. First collected by John Aubrey and recorded as being sung in 1616 but believed to be much, much older.

CHAPTER 8

A DEATH IN THE FAMILY

The mist of the early afternoon had vanished, and as the evening tantalised with a watery sun, Helene thought that Le Vieux Vicente seemed to have become a stage whose richly coloured scenery was a sky the hue of gun metal. Constance said the mist had just been a heat haze.

The stillness seemed like that which might occur after the closing speech in a play just before all is overwhelmed with applause. But in this theatre, the acclamation came sporadically, in the form of undulating rolls of thunder.

Everyone seemed on edge, and Helene had that feeling she often had before a storm, a mixture of excitement and fear. As the backdrop deepened from gun metal to charcoal, the kerosene lamps were lit, and the focus for her shifted from hillside to the Fourniers' kitchen. As the five of them sat around the table, the talk was awkward and every window and door open wide.

Helene felt as if they were sharing a box at the theatre and that the real action was still taking place outside. Every few seconds, the soft glow of the room was invaded by a flash of unearthly white light. Through the open window,

Helene glimpsed the tumulus, like the body of that animal she knew so well in her dreams but was always unable to describe. A crisp white fretwork of light silently appeared high in the sky and reached down. As it did so, it seemed to twitch.

She recalled the time as a child when she had blundered into one of the farm sheds just in time to see Arnaud administering the death blow to one of the elderly dairy herd. Now, as then, she felt fear and shock.

'It must be right overhead,' said Jean amid the continuous bangs and crashes. How strange it was that he spoke almost in a whisper with all this noise going on. Then Helene saw it, a disc of white light like an enormous shooting star. Robert saw it as well, yet all at the table rose as one and advanced towards the open door. The room was filled with an intense white light, and Helene put her hands to her ears as she heard a loud thump; she had to swallow to relieve the pressure in her ears. For a moment, she was unable to breathe; it was as if all the air had been sucked out of the room.

The thunderbolt appeared to have struck the bluff at the southern end of the tumulus and several small fires seemed to be already burning among the still-dry bracken and long grass.

As the rain came like ghostly drapes being drawn across the hillside, the temperature in the kitchen dropped. Joseph and Jean moved in unison to shut the windows and door.

'Where's Balzac?' The basket was empty – both internal doors off the kitchen were shut so he couldn't be in the house – and everybody agreed that he'd been there when they began eating. 'He must have slipped out when we were all watching the storm.'

'He's a big grown-up dog; he'll be alright,' Jean tried to assure her, but Helene didn't agree.

'That's what I'm worried about. Let's face it, the thunderbolt frightened us, so what's it done to him? Anyway, not to put too fine a point on it, he's an old dog now.'

Jean and Helene put on waterproofs, lit four pressure paraffin lamps, and searched the yard, but no luck. The door was left open, the washing-up completed; Helene wanted to search further, and it was Joseph who suggested they should form a search party. Odd – she remembered him once kicking poor old Balzac. Constance wasn't keen, didn't want to be left on her own. Robert offered to stay but Joseph insisted that they needed four in the team.

Helene knew exactly where their search was going to take them, as she imagined Jean and Joseph did also. She was worried about Balzac, but she knew as well as her two older brothers that the three of them had been drawn by the power of the tumulus and the meteorite, or whatever it was.

It was late when the four of them set off, clad in waterproofs and each carrying the Tilley lamp which he had lit before searching the yard. Joseph's plan was that they should spread out and walk in a line some forty metres apart directly up the hill to the tumulus. He and Jean would take the steepest section in the centre. Robert would take the easier climb to the south through the wheat field, while Helene would follow the only path to the north.

The sky had cleared, and a wind had arisen. Helene crossed the stream, could see the tiny glow of the three other lamps away to her left, and as she tiptoed from one glistening knob of stone to another, she imagined Joseph and Jean splashing straight through it.

'Balzac!' she shouted into the murk over to her right.

'… zac!' came a shout from over to her left, and 'Bal…!' as the first and last syllables uttered by the other members of the party were eaten by the wind.

This was another world, a prehistoric one, and it seemed that Helene was reliving a journey. The late evening earth was cool but her feet warm, clad in thick animal skin, packed with sheep's wool. She knew that her ancestors had not only discovered that wool could prevent the foot sores that such a walk could inflict, but the effect of compression and sweat upon the wool over time could produce a kind of cloth. It was such a cloth that the prehistoric Helene wore wrapped around upon her trunk, stretching down to the knee in the form of a close-fitting vest, fastened at either shoulder with a bronze pin. On her head was a cap of animal skin, whilst wound around her shoulders and arms was a cloak of the same pressed wool, this time daubed with animal fat to give some protection from the rain.

Ancient Helene relished the prospect of a journey, particularly at night. A light snow on the ground was best; one could keep going all night in the pale light with that dirty yellow sky that looked like sheep's wool that had been dipped in weld stems dye. But this was the beginning of the rutting season, and the air was warm and full of a wild mix of scents. The half-eaten moon would have to suffice as a guide.

Slung across her left shoulder was a long skin bag containing her sharpstone-tipped arrows, while around her waist was a thick band of animal hide which had been treated with ash and the juice from trees to make it soft and durable. She envied the others with their bronze buckle fastenings in the form of snakes. She would make do with a simple double-loop knotting.

Firmly back in the present, Helene was pushing ahead; she almost felt she was walking too fast. Way over to her left, she could see the tiny speck of Robert's lamp coming and going. The two lights in the centre of their formation had dropped back and, at times, seemed to be barely moving.

'Bal… Bal… Bal…' she could hear like some infernal echo.

Helene stopped. It was almost as if the four of them were somehow incomplete, inadequate. A new thought occurred to her. Less than two hours ago, she had felt that *they* were the audience watching a play; now it was clear to her, they had become the players and were being watched, directed even. The tumulus itself was the audience and they must play up, play on, bow, indulge in all manner of acts of obeisance, if only they were going to justify their presence on this hillside.

She had an awful feeling that her ancient self had suddenly been drawn into some ceremony and that she had become one of a mysterious pathos on its way to a burial. The sounds of water and melodious voice had given way to grunts, and every member of the strange ancient cortege was being tested. There were far easier routes to the place of the dead, but the group *had* to follow straight, along the line of power. As she began to climb the slope, the miasma seemed to cling to her body, and she could no longer even see the torch which must have been burning no more than a few paces in front of her. There was chanting but punctuated with coughing and the rhythmic creaking of a woven casket. Perhaps the power was beginning to work, for as she stared ahead of her, the mist seemed to be drawn aside, and she experienced the bizarre vision of a casket being hauled almost vertically in front of her. At its top, the pale feet of a dead woman were visible, while at the bottom were coils of blue-black hair spilling between the thongs of the coffer. At last, ancient Helene could see burning torches, and this time, they were in the hands of the masons standing either side of the entrance to the burial place.

She pinched herself; she must concentrate and stay in the here and now, for at last she was at the summit. She reached the northern end of the tumulus, and the tiny fluorescence which had drawn level with her at its southern end would seem to indicate that Robert had arrived there also. The two specs of light in the centre were rocking backwards and forwards; it looked as if those who carried them were making little progress. Helene imagined Joseph and Jean having to pull their bodies up the steep slope by grasping handfuls of bracken and grass.

As a deathly white moon made an appearance as if from the wings of a stage, she could see that the air was full of floating rosebay willowherb seeds; launched in the stillness of the air before the storm, they were now greedily seeking any surface on which they might settle and propagate. Because of the intensity of the rain, the seeds no longer roamed the air in a cloud; they were glued together in clusters the size of Helene's fist, and three of these had settled against her upturned collar.

It was Robert who found him. As Helene stepped onto the area of whitened stone, she saw her youngest brother squatting, his lamp wedged between chalk and earth. Two paces away from him was an object the size of a baby's cradle and shaped like a giant coffee bean. It was balancing almost vertically. It must have been rock, but it looked like steel that had rusted away, revealing a mysterious black space within.

As she struggled to take in the vision of the huddled figure of brother and alien rock, she could see that between the two lay another object. It was Balzac.

She knew at once he was dead. He was lying so beautifully curled up, with his hair soaked by the rain so that he looked like an exquisitely coiled rope lying on the deck of a well-ordered ship bound for somewhere wonderful.

She thought of her father, his last two painful years spent mostly in hospital and the visits that Constance had made backwards and forwards which had ended only when she arrived one morning to be told that he had died in the night.

For a moment, she felt the clap and crack of anger within her body; a fulmination from a distant and primitive world where something like this had taken place before. He was dead. Of course he was. That's how this whole thing was bound to end; drowned just like the father of her ancient self had been. His saturated body had been brought home to her to be cremated, the ashes packed into a fired sticky earth container and buried out in the Neolithic Urnfield. Who was left to do that now?

But her anger was only an ancient memory, and she began to calm. It was as if Balzac was an old man, perhaps the prince of an ancient province who, after a long interval – of unintentional absence – had answered a special signal and returned to his palace to die peacefully.

For a moment, Helene thought that they might bury him there. Then Robert and Joseph made a cradle for the body using Joseph's waterproof, and the four took the gently sloping pathway through the wheat field back to Chateau des Galets.

'We'll have a little funeral for him.'

'Of course,' said Jean. Helene could hear what sounded like a slight humouring in his voice. She looked at him.

'We have to give him back, you know; we don't own our pets, just as we don't own our children, when we eventually have them.' She smiled. 'And we don't own our parents, so we need to give them back to wherever they came from. That's what the committal is in a funeral service.'

She must sound like a priest – laying down the law! – but poor old Jean looked rather like he was out of his depth.

'Because we're told so little about death before it happens, people think that a funeral is something held in an atmosphere of grief. But grief is violent, and to *give back*, you need calm. Remember some of those village funerals? I mean, a tragic death is a tragedy – a child, a person dying well before their time, or by accident, murder, or taking their own life – but so often these weren't; they were simply folk who'd lived to a ripe old age, yet how agonised folk seemed to be! Sobbing and wailing on one another's shoulders?'

'You're right, and then somebody or other would cry out that *he or she had been taken from them*, as if they had been robbed.'

'Nobody *owns* anybody.'

Balzac dying suddenly made Helene want to tell Jean about how she was feeling about their search and the tumulus. 'Do you remember Aunt Icie showing us pictures of paintings and sculptures and telling us that it wasn't really the artist who was creating them, it was the spirit working through the artist? I know that we're not *artists* and we aren't creating a work of art, but what she was saying was that some things that happen are beyond our control. I had this feeling that when we were sitting round the table watching the storm, we were looking at a play but that after the thunderbolt we'd become the players, and our audience and director was Le Vieux Vicente.'

Jean nodded.

'I thought that too, and I've started to wonder whether it's working for our good or whether it's trying to harm us; maybe Joseph is right. Did you notice how calm he was when we were up there?'

***

As Helene lay in bed in the pre-dawn, she felt that this might be the event which marked the end of their young adulthoods.

Robert, at eighteen, didn't really count in her calculation as he was off to college tomorrow and they wouldn't see him for a while.

Helene had once likened all the family members to parts of a human body. Robert was obviously its head, she had said, Jean its soul; she had hopefully suggested that she might be its heart. But when she came to Constance, she couldn't think of anything, and what was Joseph? Jean had suggested – in Joseph's absence of course, and very cruelly – that he was its bodily fluids. 'Flesh and blood!' she had corrected him forcefully.

Joseph had been uncharacteristically peaceful throughout the search for Balzac, particularly as they'd been right up to Le Vieux Vicente. But it was untypical behaviour, for of late, his whole body seemed to be changing. His jaw, his fists, the way he stood still seemed to signal confidence, but she knew that those eyes, dark, liquid – and mesmeric as others seemed to think – were really looking for reassurance and that she was the only person who could give it.

The altercations over the supper table were worsening. Her feelings of hero worship for him were still there, but there was a new, incomprehensible feeling that something extreme was happening to him which she was unable to identify. He seemed reckless though he did not always take obvious risks, ruthless but was not always manipulative, desperate but by no means at the end of his tether.

Towards morning, as she slept, Helene dreamed that she, Jean, and Joseph were all floating in the air like kites. Instead of string, they were each attached to the earth with the flesh of their umbilical cords. As they floated, rain began to fall in sprays of red and green, and suddenly, she became aware that Joseph's cord had broken and that he was floating away and out over the sea. She was helpless, and as he passed her

– grinning his unhappy grin – he raised his hand as if to beatify.

She struggled awake and began to write.

CHAPTER 9

OCCUPATION

18 May 1940

Dear Aunt Icie,

We heard the news about the occupation of Amsterdam and very much hope that you are all right.

The Germans are very near here now – at Cambrai I believe – and British troops are protecting us, although I'm told that they are really Welsh Guards.

Everybody has been talking about turning the farm into a gîte to take paying guests. It's strange, as you know how few people come here. Joseph says that it would be like the Jugendherberge thing in Germany where everyone goes off on cycling or walking trips. Jean doesn't think much of the idea.

You'll be delighted to hear that Robert still wants to go to university in Paris, although just now as a stopgap he's gone to agricultural college in Cambrai if that doesn't get closed down soon. Who knows what will happen now? Joseph actually thinks a German occupation might be a good thing.

I've become very fond of a young Polish man called

Zbigniew. He's been working for Thibout. He's of a good family and is on a working holiday to extend his farming knowledge. Joseph hates him; I don't know why he's like this about Polish people; he doesn't really know any.

I've learnt some new Chopin. Daddy Girard still lets me play when the boys take the boat out.

Do let me know how you are, and give my love to Otho – it will be his fourteenth birthday soon!

All my love,
Your little Helene.

***

26 May 1940

Daydreaming, and pipe in mouth, Jean was wandering through the farm buildings at Chateau des Galets in the late afternoon shadows. He ambled past the old milking sheds where Arnaud had once kept the small herd of dairy cows.

How bitter the argument had been when Joseph sold off these cream-rich cattle in favour of more abundant milk producers, but the local suppliers rejected the milk as inferior, so he had to cut his losses and sold what was left of the herd. The sheds had long since fallen into disuse.

He continued through the paddocks, where Bertrand and the rest of the ploughing teams were grazing, and on through the tall, covered way between the haylofts and the threshing barn.

The wall of the barn was constructed of lightly blushing brick and shiplap panels, gently silvered over generations. There were no less than four openings into its loft, all at different heights; each door had long, tapering iron hinges, and every entrance was secured from the outside with a fat timber wedge knocked home through a wooden handle. At seemingly random points, iron nails the thickness of human fingers had been hammered into the shiplap, and a variety of working tools were hung against the wall – a pickaxe, a shovel, a pitchfork, a hacksaw – almost as if left to petrify.

Jean always shuddered as he passed this point, remembering his fateful trip to Bruges with Aunt Icie when he had stood bewildered as she showed him an entire wall festooned with prosthetic limbs and crutches abandoned by euphoric pilgrims who had supposedly undergone miracle cures.

What a relief to pass this place and walk out into the sunshine of the meadow, unchanged for centuries – bird's-foot-trefoil nestling oxlip, cornflower complementing sunny buttercup, while in the damper areas towards the stream grew orchids, spiky mare's tail, and wild garlic. He became so engrossed watching a white butterfly hovering around patches of mugwort and meadow clary that, at first, he didn't hear Joseph coming up behind him.

'The bastards have gone, and they've taken Daddy with them!' yelled Joseph, as if he was the medieval town crier announcing some crime against the community. Thibout had always made no secret of the fact that if the Germans came, he, Amaury, and Daddy would flee to Cornwall. There they planned to make a living fishing in Looe. If not, there would be other useful work to do, and as Daddy said, 'The Germans will take that much longer to get there.'

'They took three Welsh Guards with them in the boat; there were hardly any evacuation craft. It's difficult to believe, but they say that the British got four thousand troops off, though thousands more Tommies are still here heading for *Dunkerque* – some of our chaps too. They'll never get them all off!'

***

The speckled underbelly, wings, and the three black bands round the tail identified the bird which was swooping over the rosebay willowherb of the hedgerows as Helene cycled along that early afternoon. The sparrow hawk has no other predator in this habitat, and it preys on the weakest songbirds, so only those with the best escape tactics survive. Helene marvelled at the beauty of this creature as she pedalled along the road between Chateau des Galets and the nearby port.

It was now some four months since the invasion – the official start of the occupation – and the Germans hadn't been near the farm, so Helene decided to make the short journey into the port to see the conquering hero for herself.

She did not share the disdain of her brother Jean, nor did she feel the trepidation which her mother did. Perhaps Joseph was right about this invasion; it could provide opportunities for them all. Either way – she was experiencing an almost palpable excitement.

Several kilometres before the road began its descent into the port, the land on either side levelled out to give a panoramic view from sea to inland horizon. Helene always enjoyed cycling along this stretch; she loved the sense of freedom and space. The huge sky was full of activity. Over to her left, a weak sun was gently illuminating fields of celandine and meadow grass, while to her right, and over the sea, the same light source was reflecting off the water in giant pools of silver. Straight ahead of the handlebars of Helene's bicycle, the sky seemed to be the colour and texture of smoky velvet, like a vast coat with a dark tail which seemed to sway slightly and threaten to touch the earth.

She was fascinated by this phenomenon; it reminded her of a rare visit the three youngest children had made to the cinema in the early days of Aunt Icie. In one of the films they had watched, Buster Keaton is shown running away from a tornado. The camera shows him from the front, frantically running to escape the advancing "twister". The tornado inevitably overtakes him, but by a cinematic trick, he is unharmed, though still left desperately running but this time absurdly trying to catch up with it.

As she came out of her daydream, she saw that the lower section of the swaying grey "tail" was in fact a column of army trucks wobbling from side to side. As it got nearer, she could see that at the front of the column there was an open-topped jeep containing four soldiers, the driver and passenger soft-capped, while the two rear-seat passengers were wearing those funny "coal scuttle" steel helmets.

Looking straight ahead – with not so much as a sideways glance – Helene was never quite sure whether it was the uneven road surface, or merely her own lack of concentration, that sent her pitching over the handlebars and onto the road.

She swayed on her knees for a moment, reeling from the shock, but the advancing pain seemed to be anaesthetised with embarrassment as it dawned on her that she was being stared at by sixty or so helmeted troops. The column came to an abrupt halt.

'Are you hurt, *m'amoiselle?*' The perfect French of the captain – wearing a uniform with gold ciphers on the epaulettes – was anodyne yet welcome.

'Did any of our vehicles touch you?'

Helene's shaking head triggered a heel-clicking response as the captain about-turned and marched back towards the jeep. As she struggled into a vertical position, and picked up her undamaged bicycle, he turned and looked at her. It was a curious look, as if he'd recognised her from somewhere.

'Is that *your* bicycle?'

'… Yes.' Without acknowledging her reply, he joined the lieutenant in the rear seat of the jeep.

The question made her feel queer. She was going to say, "Well, actually, it belongs to me *and* my brother Jean", but something made her change her mind.

She needed to revive herself before continuing and suddenly had a wild idea. She would go for a swim. She knew a place, a small cove. The beaches were still open to the public; she had no swimming costume, but so what?

Why should her eldest brother be the one to take risks, court danger, driving tractors too close to the cliff edge, making enemies of his suppliers, boasting about ducking and diving on the black market?

Instead of getting back onto her bicycle, she walked, turning off the road onto a rough track which led down to the sea. She pushed the machine, putting the flat of her hand gently against the leather saddle to try and stop it bouncing on stones which were half buried in the track. Way over to her right in the distance, she could see the soft curve of the roof of Le Vieux Vicente. No one would see her. Nobody would come.

She always had in her mind's eye a picture of a special place by the sea. Everyone must have! Each time she thought of cove and sea, it was this one image that came to her. It was a place well concealed behind blackberry bushes, high up against a sheer rock face.

Enfolded in her Bronze Age imagination was a wide platform of purplish-hued stone. It was just like the colour of an *earthblood* floor after fire ash had been raked away. The patterns on the rock resembled the ripples which form on the surface of water after it has been disturbed by rising fish. The marks were elongated and pointed towards the sea as if they had a voice; they seemed to say: *Come! This is how it is done.*

No matter how high or low the wandering water lapped against the platform, it would always be simple to carry a boat, set it down, and push off into the deeper water. In her mind, Helene would walk to the edge of the water and stand, the soles of both her feet feeling the coolness of the rock beneath them.

From Helene's inwards eye, the light on the flat sea's surface looked so powerful the water looked as if it was frozen. The wandering water was at its lowest point, and she could see the edge of the sloping rock platform, while beyond was a watery earth whose form and dimensions were indefinable other than by myriad colours and lights moving to infinity.

Helene looked up to where sky met sea, where sea was at its bluest, sky at its lightest, and in the very centre of her vision was a cliff, black at its base, and gold along its top edge, the home of seabirds which appeared like whitestone dust blown across an *earthblood* floor…

Back in the here and now, she reached the end of the path, and as she looked down, she felt a twinge of dismay. The tide was coming in. Somehow, she hadn't expected that. Today was nothing like the place of her mind's eye.

She spotted the way down onto the beach. There were two stones – *ceremonial*, she thought – lying side by side, brown and covered with a yellow latticework of lichen. They were very like another smaller pair she had taken last year and which now stood in her bedroom on the walnut chest of drawers. Helene thought they looked happy and welcoming, and she felt a pang of guilt. Why were these two stones here and the two she had taken, there? Perhaps they didn't belong in her bedroom, and she should return them so they could be, once again, a group.

She lowered her bicycle into the mat of plantain which covered the edge of the rock, and over she went, abseiling, but instead of ropes, she was grasping great handfuls of long grass mixed with bracken stems. As she slipped down the final metre of the live green wall and stepped onto the rock, she heard a hollow thud. The still sparkling pools she had gazed at during her last visit had turned into hungry culverts, greedily sucking in water, only to disgorge it seconds later.

It was a marine feeding process, never-ending, and after each course, it seemed to get hungrier and noisier. The sea had sounded loud from the end of the path, but down here with her back to the green wall, she was aware of its power. Every few seconds, there was a giant crash, followed by more sucking and hissing as the water was pulled back over a surface of sparkling black and purple pebbles.

Swimming seemed like madness, but for the time being she was mad, held in a state of temporary psychosis by this unforgiving watery ritual. She thought of her experiment with the mushrooms, but she had ingested no fungi this time. She glanced up at the bluff. No one would see her; the only person who ever went up there was Jean, and she would be very happy for him to see her now, mistress of her own destiny.

Over her head came the pullover; off came the double-laced shoes; she tumbled out of the trousers and tiptoed across the biting sharpness of the beach. Then the first white wave hit her – spraying everywhere. Soon she was swimming in open sea, and she turned to look back at the waves – dark where she first rode them, then gathering white edges as they rushed towards the now distant patch of beach where she had undressed moments ago.

What *was* going to be become of her and the family? What about Joseph and Jean? When they were younger, the sparring seemed to help – as if it was a preparation for the bigger struggle in life – but now it was beginning to look like a fight to the death.

Without warning, a glistening velvety head appeared in

the water close to her, then another, and another. She must swim back.

Once again, she glanced up at the bluff, but the mist had come, and the tumulus was hidden from view. She had swum out too far. She pulled forwards with her arms, but it was no good; she didn't have the strength to get back. She called for help but all that came out was a squeak in the face of the roar of the water around her.

Perhaps she was losing consciousness, and that strange sensation of being bumped, first in the small of the back, then the buttocks, then the balls of her feet, was part of the process of drowning. She had lost control, but the comforting feeling of the bumps continued until her body broke through the violence of the surf and she felt the sharpness of pebbles digging into her back. Almost caught by the under draught of the wave, she managed to turn and crawl across her agonising pebble bed to where her clothes lay.

After she began to feel better and had scolded herself for swimming out too far, she dressed and prepared to climb the wall of grass to where she had left her bicycle. The mist had cleared and she noticed a figure standing on the tumulus. Tall and blond, it must be Jean. Then she remembered Jean had set off with Joseph with the cart less than an hour ago.

Puzzled but invigorated, she wheeled her bicycle back up to the road and ran with it before leaping onto the saddle. Her bike tyres were really bouncing; she had mended a puncture yesterday and they were pumped to perfection – Jean would tighten the chain. After all, it was his bike as well – half was anyway – they shared it. Both of their bikes had got so rusted over the years that he'd had this idea of making one machine out of the good remaining bits of both of them. So, it was quite distinctive: brown leather saddle, black frame, dark green front forks, dark green pump.

'On, Balzac, on!' she shouted as she began pedalling hard. Comical to others perhaps, but Balzac was still very much alive in the form of her spirit guides. She was excited now. Her thoughts coming, surging like the waves from which she had just escaped... where *had* that walnut chest of drawers come from? The tree which it had been made from – what forest had it come from? If it had never been felled in order to be made into this repository for her stones and diaries, then would it be still growing somewhere? Once trees got made into furniture, people forgot about them, standing in nature, packed in forests, waterlogged in swamps, lonely in fields. The tree might well have died for all they cared, but it had just been given a new life. Wood made into furniture wasn't dead; it was still very much alive.

Who was that standing on the tumulus? It was that man they had found buried and curled up by the front gate with his head and hand struck off. The one that they had sometimes joked was Jean's ancestor. He should have been carrying his head. Not likely! Ghosts weren't naïve, not like people.

Her mother had looked so beautiful that evening after Helene had eaten those mushrooms, so why could she have not seen all that before? Why was *Maman* looking so worn out now? Was it because she always did things out of a sense of duty and never from the heart? The garden behind the farmhouse – her mother would only plant and water things; she would never prune or clip. Helene did that; she wasn't frightened of cutting through green stems, seeing them fall to the ground, gathered up for compost, to moulder down. It was part of life and death, the never-ending cycle, like the feeding process of the sea.

Had the seals really saved her? She had survived, just like Joseph was doing, only he was stockpiling surplus grain, exchanging it for meat, then selling it to people for inflated prices, and Jean was forging food coupons and selling them. It was all survival; only the fittest would do so. Why did she have to ask so many questions in life; why didn't she have all the answers, just like Joseph always did?

In the town, the main street was crowded, with groups of people standing on the pavement. Helene wheeled her bicycle through the market square, past the front of the church. It was here where the guillotine used to stand. She knew that because there was a shop opposite, and in its window was a photograph of the last public execution to take place there – *Not that many years ago*, she thought grimly. There were hardly any cars about so lots of places to leave her bicycle. Not surprising, because the Germans had all the petrol. She remembered to take the bicycle pump with her; they were always getting stolen.

She joined one of the groups of spectators. There were several groups of soldiers, a sergeant, a corporal, and a helmeted captain like the one she met earlier, armed with a pistol in a belt holster. A number of private-ranking soldiers carried rifles over their shoulders.

Among a group of officers was a captain wearing a black tunic displaying a red enamelled Iron Cross with an SS runes ring and lightning bolts. *French army uniforms aren't a patch on these*, thought Helene as she looked again at the officer's cap, decorated with white braid and a cap badge bearing the image of a human skull. *He's not bad-looking either*, she thought. *His blond hair and high cheekbones, not unlike Zbigniew.*

She became aware of a band playing, and very soon, marching at medium pace and in threes, appeared a column of helmeted soldiers. Two tenor trombones, eight B flat cornets, one B flat flugel horn, and two euphoniums were moving forwards; each man had a fine music stand clipped to the instrument he carried before him. Twenty-four players in all made their way past *the charcuterie, boulangerie, patisserie,* and bank, pumping out lively Bavarian marches.

People were smiling and started to clap their hands as the column filed past, and Helene found herself doing likewise. An elderly man standing next to her spat conspicuously onto the granite cobbles at the feet of one of the players.

'Fancy spoiling things,' she found herself saying aloud.

Like lightning, two men in shako-style caps, with brass horse tail plumes, appeared from nowhere and manhandled him backwards while Helene watched. No one else seemed to notice. The two policemen were joined by two SS guards who knocked the old man to the ground with the butts of their rifles while the policemen dragged the stunned body away.

CHAPTER 10

THE STONE CIRCLE

The smoky grey velvet tail in the sky had disappeared. It had been replaced by a feeble sun, and Helene thought it made the bandsmen look sickly, as if they were made out of wax. She had thought of going to the police station to complain about the way the old man had been treated but thought better of it. He could have been a wanted criminal – just because he was old didn't mean to say he was good.

Most of the troops had gone, and the people who had been lining the streets were drifting away. She noticed something lying on the pavement; it was a silver fob watch. Before she could move to pick it up, one of the green-uniformed policemen passed in front of her, swooped down and, with a single movement, transferred it from its place on the flagstone into the left breast pocket of his tunic.

As she retrieved her bicycle from the market square, she saw a man standing looking at it. He was short and stocky, and dressed in one of those funny black leather zipper jackets.

'Is this your bicycle?' Perfect French but she knew he wasn't. He was wearing a navy beret – but all wrong – and the cigarette he was smoking wasn't French.

'Yes!' This time she nodded emphatically. He watched her as she replaced the dark green pump in its holder; then he seemed to lose interest and wandered off. Of course, that was it! It was market day; she hadn't bought anything and he was wondering why not. She was glad when he'd gone.

Her mind was still moving fast. Too much seemed to have happened for her to return to Constance and the farmhouse kitchen just yet. Only two hours ago she had fallen off her bicycle, perhaps come close to drowning, and why had that old man been so brutally beaten?

She needed some time for quiet contemplation, to ask questions, maybe receive answers. As she was wheeling her bicycle back out of the port, she decided to visit the magic pool. She hadn't been there for years. It was Joseph who'd shown her the spot – odd really for someone as down to earth and practical as him to make it into a special place; Joseph did have his moments.

She remembered her first visit to the pool alone. That's when you first start noticing things for yourself, rather than having things pointed out for you by someone else. It was then that she felt she'd been there before, in another life. The ancient Helene had felt the warmth of the sun on her neck – she loved the open country, but best of all was the dappled shade of woodlands. Here, unlike moor or cliff edge where the air was never the same for more than a moment, she was able to enjoy the stillness of the forest. The heady constructions of an air livened with the scent of bark and fallen leaves as they mingled and mouldered down into the *earthblood*.

She could remember gazing at the rocks on the forest floor, overgrown with algae and fungus. She envied the two plants living luxuriously side by side, supplying one another with the enriched air essential to produce intensely coloured lichens. Here she could really breathe. It was an air so calm and still that each redolence had the time and space to act on its neighbour without being carried away by wind.

The cloudless sky gave her the feeling of something bluer than anything she had known. Trunks of the trees around the clearing hinted at a darkness approaching black at their bases, rising through sullen purple to capricious green and culminating in a shock of fiery foliage. On the forest floor, an unknown distance away, she could see patches of brilliant orange, yellow, and green light where an old tree had fallen and left a hole in the roof of leaves, and the sun was pouring in.

Her heart was pounding with excitement and just a little fear. Right at the centre of the clearing was a pool. It was still and silent, and within its immeasurable depth was the answer to Helene's question. She could look at its surface and see the reflections of clouds and those of her own face. It was true; the ancient Helene had studied her own reflection, and she knew that here she could feel strong, be herself. She must ask her question, and as she examined the strands of grass and flakes of leaves which cast a black pattern on the surface of the motionless pool, she began to utter the words...

Helene still had to walk past the stone circle, but she felt emboldened by her vision of the pool. The sun seemed to have regained some of its strength, a pale orange disc dipping into the sea and turning it white – it was almost as if she was witnessing events in some cosmic foundry. She would just have time to reach the pool and return to the road before darkness.

What a glorious ride back it was going to be, the lights of the port on her left and the dark bluff of Pointe des Galets over to the north! Then she could settle down for the evening with her own calmer thoughts.

She hauled her bicycle off the road and toiled up the hill. The gorse on either side of the track glowed as if it was on fire, and again her spirits were raised. Then she saw the topmost tips of the stones. The brutality of the place! They looked like black teeth – premolars, upturned with the roots facing skywards – worse still, smashed teeth, the consequence of a giant fight or perhaps sudden contact with a monumental jackboot. Why was that old man beaten like that? In a few minutes, she would be back on her bicycle, freewheeling past the circle towards the gentle copse, the silvery pool, and the answers which she so badly needed.

There was a human figure by the circle, between two of the stones. Helene could see that a barbed wire fence had been stretched round it, in front of which stood a helmeted and great-coated sentry, motionless. What right had he? Even if she hated it, this was her space, and someone had invaded it. She reached the top of the hill and mounted her bicycle, ready to ride past him.

But something was different – at first, she couldn't spot it, then she saw it – there was a railway line that hadn't been there before. It appeared to run from the direction of the port right into the centre of the wood and then just stop. Worst of all, the pool had vanished. Where there should have been visible the glint of light on water between the trees, there was only a white blotch. The pool had been filled in with crushed chalk.

The sun had gone completely now, and she felt cold. Her mission no longer had any purpose, and all she wanted was to get back home.

'Halt! You can't go any further!' There was no *mamoiselle* this time. The voice came from a German captain, but it wasn't the nice-looking one she'd seen in the town, nor was it the one who had appeared after she'd fallen off her bicycle. This figure seemed to have come from nowhere. Then she saw the jeep and the helmeted head of its driver.

As the captain glided up to her, Helene desperately wanted to run, but the air had become thick, as if she was standing on the bottom of a pool clad in heavy boots, able only to wave her upper limbs.

'What are you doing here?' the voice snapped, and as the man's head turned to look down the valley and towards the wood, she could see that what she at first thought was a young man – twenty-five years old, perhaps – had the neck and ears of an ancient creature.

She struggled for a reply, but each thought which came to her seemed trite. It was dark now. Home should have been fifteen minutes away, but she knew it might as well be an eternity.

The face moved closer, and there was a smell of decay. She tried to look away from the strangely vacant eyes, towards where the sun had been just minutes ago, towards Le Vieux Vicente, anywhere except…

A lean hand groped its way along the rear pillar of her bicycle until it found what it was looking for: the pump, the dark green pump. It brought the object between their faces – handle facing upwards as bony finger and thumb closed in on its shaft. Helene wondered whether she might lose consciousness as she saw the object begin to gently wave in front of her like a metronome.

The claw-like limb fumbled for the small metal ferrule at the tip of the handle and pulled, withdrawing the fabric-clad pumping valve. Then, almost as if in an act of synchronicity, the creature held the pump like a telescope to its vacant eye whilst the headlamps of the jeep flashed on. The small void in the pump handle was empty – Helene was carrying no secret messages there.

'You can go,' croaked the voice.

CHAPTER 11

A BLACK MARKET

It was the morning after Helene's encounter with the Nazis. She was standing washing up at the kitchen sink while Constance dried the pots. The two brothers were sitting at the table. It might well have been mid-August, but the sky was still dark, and it was already mid-morning.

Helene was making far too much noise – she'd already chipped a dinner plate – as if her strange experience of the evening before had taken something away from her, stolen her dexterity and exchanged it for a kind of brute clumsiness.

When she'd returned from the stone circle, she'd said nothing to the others, just got on and cut slices of cold boiled ham from the joint she'd taken from the meat safe and served them with buttered leeks, potatoes, and pickles from her pantry store of preserves.

But with her last night's diary entry written and asking questions – but receiving no answers – she must ask again, this time of those closest to her.

'What's happening at the magic pool?'

Constance looked blank. Jean looked amused.

'Don't tell me. They're holding some pagan ceremony

up there, youths and maidens passing to and fro wearing flowered headdresses, their heads top-heavy with strange compositions of poppy, mallow, meadow clary, and marjoram flowers.'

'I'm serious, Jean.'

But Helene too grasped that precious glimpse into the ancient world where yellow flowers could cure a failing human liver, where wort would only calm a fever on midsummer's eve. Helene's ancient self could see that folk had gathered motherwort, fennel, comfrey, borage. But she also knew what yellow bile was; black bile, phlegm, and that fireweed placed on a pus-filled boil would draw out the poisons. In her prehistoric mind's eye, she could see two bonfires, one sunwards of where she was standing, the other shadowards where the holy man was standing. The air was redolent with a mix of scents as the Helene of the ancient world tossed armfuls of aromatic mugwort, chamomile, and thyme into the shadowards bonfire.

She and her Bronze Age party withdrew to the edge of the crowd. Helene had full view of the first of the torch-bearing stewards. Each wedge of massed humans contained within its midst individuals each carrying a flaming torch so that within the assemblage of several hundred, sources of light gave out symbolic patterns which would continue until sunrise in the form of special signs arranged in the shape of sky fire…

'No, Jean! Even if there were any rekindling festivals, they won't be holding them *there*; they've filled it in!' Jean obviously didn't know, unsurprising really, it wasn't somewhere he normally visited… but what about Joseph?

'Don't you care, Joe? They've cut down parts of the wood, and there's a railway line running there from the port.' Joe was just sitting there not saying anything.

'It's not my fault,' he eventually said. Helene could hear that click on the roof of his mouth.

'I thought that as it was your special place, you might feel something about it.' Maybe he did, just didn't want to say, and yes it was true, it wasn't his fault and there was nothing they could do about it. Helene began to feel sorry for him.

'Look, I've got to go and tell the Poles what to do today and meet some people,' he said, getting up and walking to the door. 'I've set up this network for food in the village. The Nazis are putting the screws on supplies; it needs a local bloke to organise it. I said I'd do it.' He was making it sound as if nobody else wanted to.

'They'll come and ask you to collaborate, you know,' said Jean, 'the Nazis, I mean.'

Joseph exhaled so his top lip puffed out and wobbled. It looked funny; Helene had never seen him do that before. Then there was that click again.

'They won't ask *me*,' emphasised Jean. '*You're* the boss. Don't tell me what your answer will be.'

The kitchen door was standing open, and Joseph went out into the still-dark morning, making stamping noises with his boots. As he passed the open kitchen window, he leaned back into the room for a moment. 'We've got to think about the future... everything's changing now. We can't stay stuck in the past.'

'Well, the version I've heard,' said Jean as the thump of Joseph's feet disappeared, 'is that he's started this meat syndicate – he's treasurer of course. He calls it a co-operative, but he controls everything; nobody else has a say. Everybody who wants to get meat has to put in so much money a week. Didn't you know, Amber, doesn't he tell you anything?'

'I knew,' volunteered Constance. 'How do you think we got the ham? The price was good.'

'Yes, for *us* it was; that's because the Fourniers' weekly contributions are fixed, he's made sure of that, but everybody else's fluctuate every week. Over the six weeks he's been running this thing, he's hiked the contributions every week.'

'That's because the Nazis control the economy,' said Helene. Somebody needed to speak up for Joe.

'Yes, they're pushing meat prices up all the time,' added Constance.

'True,' agreed Jean, 'but Joe's raising the prices *before* the Nazis do. He's trying to be one step ahead of them. Local butchers won't speak out because they don't want to rock the boat. Also, he's giving them a handout, a proportion of the surplus cash he makes every week. All right, the Nazis are causing inflation, but people like Joe make it worse.'

'Are you saying my Joe's dishonest?'

'Look at the facts, Mum; he's not telling you the whole story. He's a man who likes to have secrets.'

'You're the secretive one, my lad. You tell crazy tales for everybody's amusement to hide your own weaknesses and to conceal your own nasty thoughts. I'll have no secrets in this house!'

Helene watched in amazement as Constance lifted up the tea towel she was still holding and cracked it in the air as if it was a whip, threw it to the floor, and flounced out of the room in the direction of her bedroom. Her dun-coloured print dress gently licked around her legs as she departed, as if the garment were attempting an apology on behalf of its host's violent actions, and to its Cinderella-like companion now lying in a damp, twisted knot on the floor by the sink.

'The story's even worse than that, Amber,' continued Jean, apparently unmoved by his mother's fit of temper. 'He's not paying the Poles anymore with grain from the harvest – they're subsisting on food only now. He holds back their crop share and swaps it for cheap scrag-ends from local butchers which he sells on to people in neighbouring villages. I'm surprised he hasn't been beaten up for what he's doing, but that's the thing with Joe; people won't stand up to him, so nobody speaks out. Mum probably knows that; that's why she's angry, because she's frightened.'

'So, what are *you* going to do, Jean?' Helene was confused. The Nazis were a bad lot; that was obvious to her now because they'd filled in the magic pool. Jean might think that Joe was playing at being a gangster, but someone needed to take charge.

'I don't know… I've got a few ideas but—'

'But you don't want to share them. Mum's right about you – you *are* secretive! I'll tell you what, though. You and I are going to have to take over the running of the farm. I've seen it coming since Thibout and Amaury left. Whatever Joe said about them, he trusted them. He doesn't trust Zbig and his men; look how he didn't want to take them on in the first place. It was Thibout who hired them, and now they're gone, Joe's been landed with the Poles. Meanwhile, he's losing interest in the farm!'

'It's not what I want to do.'

'I know, Jean, but at least you get on with Zbig, and he'll take orders from you. Joe hates me spending any time with him. He says that he and I are going nowhere, and when the moment's right for Zbig, he'll just clear off.'

Helene looked through Jean's floppy pale hair into those blue eyes. She could see that something had just sparked there.

14 December 1940

My dear little Helene,
I do hope that this letter finds you all in good health

and that you weren't surprised that it was delivered to you by courier. It is no longer possible for us to send letters through the post.

Terrible news – Otho has been kidnapped by the SS and forced to join the German army. This was two months ago, and we haven't heard a thing. He's only fourteen; we are just praying.

If you can get the materials for your project to convert parts of the farm into an auberge, I think it would bring you all benefits.

The Germans have put an absurd exchange rate on the mark versus the guilder. So, things the Germans buy from us are very cheap for them, but things we need to buy from them are very expensive.

Life here is becoming difficult. Simon is no longer allowed to play recitals. The Germans haven't banned concerts, but they won't allow Jewish music to be performed, and anyway, Jewish pianists are forbidden to play. Not only that, but Simon also isn't allowed to travel anywhere, even to use trams; nor is he allowed to own a pet. We have had to find another person to look after our beloved Siamese.

Don't be surprised, my little poppet, if your Polish man has disappeared one morning. Like us, he has lost his nation, but his countrymen are escaping and finding their way to England. There are many Poles gathering there with a passion to join the invasion force which one day will liberate us.

Please destroy the letter once you have read it. My loving wishes to you all for Christmas; here's hoping that 1941 finds us in better circumstances.

Your loving Aunt Icie

CHAPTER 12

GUARDIAN ANGELS & VOICES

'We're damned if we do and damned if we don't,' moaned Joseph as he sat with his mother at the kitchen table. A year had gone by since the Nazis had arrived at Chateau des Galets, and Joseph was not happy.

Great things should have happened – for him of course, perhaps even for his family – but now it was as if a wall had arisen in front of him. He must break through it.

'Are you listening, Mum?'

'I told you,' Constance insisted. 'You really believed that the Germans would bring some good, didn't you?'

'Well, so far, they haven't. We're subsidising them.' It was plain enough to him. 'We're paying higher Government taxes. Instead of getting the best market for the crops we're producing, the Germans are forcing us to sell at rock-bottom prices. Where land is required for German building projects, tenants are thrown out, owners offered returns for giving vacant possession but with no legal agreements.'

'We know all this, love.' She didn't sound very sympathetic.

'We've just got to lower our expectations and take a cut in production. We're not the only ones. Zbigniew and the Poles who took over Thibout's work are feeling the pinch as well.'

Sod them! thought Joseph.

He was itching to start building, but what and where? All available building materials were being consumed by the Germans. He looked at Constance; then she suddenly gave him *that* look and said what she always used to say to him when he was little.

'Things *will* get better, poppet, and don't forget, you've got a guardian angel, you know.'

Guardian angels? That was what Joseph feared. He didn't like the idea of something – or someone – who would watch over him, prevent him getting into "scrapes" as his mother, and Helene, might suggest. After all, what was wrong with his self? From that space in his head would come thoughts; he would act; what he did would affect other people. Why could it not be as simple as that? Yet it was from this cave at the front of his head that unwanted voices sometimes came. It had been like this as long as he could remember.

There were lots of them and, usually, he could follow what they were saying, at other times not, for occasionally they appeared to speak in foreign languages.

As he got older, Joseph had realised that the voices were of those who were no longer living. He knew that because they would always ask him – not by name of course, they didn't seem to give a damn about Joseph Fournier – if he could speak to someone on their behalf. It was always a relative, son, sister, a mother.

Only that morning he had been troubled by the voice of somebody by the name of Daniel who told Joseph that he was the father of Isabelle. As Daniel's voice whined away, it claimed that Isabelle was not in fact *his* daughter but was really the daughter of Edouard, an actor with whom his wife, Josephine, had had a secret affair. Isabelle had found all this out after her mother Josephine's death, but then Daniel had died before explaining it all to Isabelle. Daniel – it appeared – was desperate to tell Isabelle that he loved her, that it didn't matter, because in death, all children – no matter who had begat them – were equal.

What Joseph found particularly disturbing was the fact that Daniel's voice had been blethering on to him for twenty-eight years – since Joseph was four – and that it was some years later that he even began to understand what was going on. The problem remained unsolved and seemingly unsolvable. Perhaps by now Isabelle was dead, but Joseph doubted it. Logic told him that if that was so, then Daniel would no longer need to trouble Joseph as he would be able to speak to her himself.

His mother was making him sound fortunate. He grinned, but he knew it was a cheerless grin. He looked up and saw Helene at the door.

'Your machine repair man's here, Joe.'

'About time too.' He looked at his watch – 1102 hours – it was another morning wasted...

Now it was just the two women sitting at the table as Helene took the chair Joseph had just vacated.

'I'm worried about Jean,' whispered Constance.

'Jean? Don't you mean Joseph?'

'No, *he's* all right,' snapped her mother, clenching her teeth, 'a down-to-earth lad, sound as a bell. No, I'm worried about that dreamer with big ideas going nowhere; his father praised him too much, held Joe back. We've never been firm enough with him; his birth was a miracle; we were just pleased he'd survived; we just let him do what he wanted.'

Helene heard footsteps in the lobby. Jean must have come in through the wash house, to avoid Joseph probably.

'I think Jean's involved in something…'

'Mum!' Her mother hadn't heard Jean enter the lobby. Helene took her mother's hand and squeezed it, stared at her, shook her head, speaking softly, 'Mum, Mum.'

'I found some photographs of people – head and shoulders—'

'Mum, please—'

'Folk I've never seen before. They fell out of Jean's bag. Joe says he's forging food coupons—'

'Been seeing spooks at the tomb of Lord and Lady Muck again, have we?' Jean was there, standing in the doorway.

'No, I was just thinking about what Mum was saying to Joseph about guardian angels,' said Helene.

'Oh, don't talk to him about those; you'll have him throwing salt over his shoulder, kilos of the stuff. Remember how he was when you dropped that five-franc piece and picked it up when it was *tails up*. You'll have bad luck all day now,' he chortled, mimicking his elder brother's "now you've gone and done it" voice. Constance leaned forwards, pushed herself to her feet and walked out of the room.

'Wait a minute! Guardian angels, they appear, do you a favour, then they bugger off, that's it, isn't it?' Helene laughed. It was quite funny, in a down-to-earth sort of way. How unlike Jean.

'It's a bit more than that. They can save people's lives if they think that they're not ready to die yet.'

'So, do you think we've lived a life before, Amber?' asked Jean, sitting opposite her – in the seat their mother had just vacated – his face mock serious. 'You know that feeling when you're so sure that something's happened before, it's so intense, and then it's gone, like a dream that you can no longer recall when you wake?'

This reminded her of the talk they'd had after Balzac

died, but she still wasn't sure whether he was playing her up or if he was genuine.

'I don't *think*, little Big Brother, I *know* – we've not only lived before, but we've also seen, heard, touched, smelled, tasted, *and* dreamed before.'

'I've never thought about death before,' said Jean. 'Dad's death, I don't think it made much impression on me – grieving, that is, whatever that is.'

'Thinking about death isn't necessarily morbid, you know; it's just a process every living creature goes through. We're never taught about death – I mean, everyday death. Not Jesus's death or the martyrs – those are the only deaths Aunt Icie ever mentioned to us, so we never know about it until we experience it, and the first time most people do that is when their grandparents die. I know that Mum and Dad's generation lost lots of fathers and brothers in the war, but with our generation, it's never talked about; we grow up listening to people either joking about it or practically bursting into tears as soon as they so much as see a coffin.'

'And Balzac, what happened to him, do you think?' asked Jean.

'He has another life too.'

She suddenly took hold of the sleeve of Jean's guernsey. 'Look, Jean, I've heard from Aunt Icie. It was actually before Christmas, and I didn't want to mention it. If we think things are bad here, it's nothing compared to what they're going through there, but the worst thing is that Otho's been press-ganged into the German army. It's what Mum feared might happen to Rob, but Rob's old enough for conscription; Otho's still a child! I think it's because Icie probably refused to let the Hitler Youth get him.'

'He's perfect for them, looks-wise anyway.'

'Don't say that, Jean!'

Jean was never really bothered about Otho – Helene couldn't remember him ever taking any trouble with him – seemed indifferent really. Rob hadn't; he was lovely with him – even though there were six years between them. Rob saw him as his "little brother". With Rob being so bright, the two of them got on really well – Otho was very creative, liked drawing and painting. They wrote little plays together and performed them for the others to watch – except Joseph; she couldn't remember ever seeing Otho and Joseph together.

'There was something wrong,' she spoke aloud this time.

'What, with Icie and Otho?'

'No, with Joe and Otho. The way Otho was suddenly packed off to boarding school and the way Icie left not long afterwards. I haven't told Joe about this latest piece of news.'

'Otho had to leave sometime, and Icie couldn't stay here with us forever. We had eight glorious years of her education…' *He's missing the point, again*, thought Helene.

'Let me introduce you to the Fourniers.' Jean raised his hand and, in mock music hall voice, 'Gentleman farmers with a strong peasant streak, as visible as the fat in rashers of streaky bacon. Old money? Yes, but just a little sparse these days. Inbreeding? Possibly, over the centuries, and certainly plenty of skeletons ready to get up and start dancing. But wait! The family are finally starting to evolve and, after millennia of eccentricities, bigotry, and a tendency to old folklore, they're becoming arriviste—'

'Shut up, Jean. You're quite right – with some of it anyway – but what I'm saying is there was something strange about it all. I mean, why send him when he was eight years old? It wasn't as if he was going into the navy.'

'Who knows exactly what goes on in the inner life of Joseph?' asked Jean with a mock shudder. 'He's never had any really close friends, and he works all the time. Which reminds me, you know how you were saying that I should take over the running of the farm? Well, *he's* just come up with this plan for us to produce vegetables – kitchen garden, not for sale – it's to "keep our weekly food bills down", he says. But what I say is, who's going to do the work? It won't be Joseph; he's too busy wheeler-dealing and generally putting people's backs up in the village. It'll be you, me, and Mum, as if we hadn't got enough to do already. But that's his idea – it's not really about making ends meet; it's all about keeping the three of us with no free time. He's told me *you're* "up to something".'

'What!' Her voice was high and indignant.

'Nothing specific, but that's Joe: suggestion, intimation, inference, speculation. Always avoids direct confrontation – manipulates his victims into retaliating out of sheer emotional exhaustion, so then *they* look like the aggressors.'

Helene remembered when they were little, how when Joseph completed some task or other and would sit or stand and stare, Arnaud would demand to know what he was doing. Joe would say he was "thinking" and Dad would explode, 'Well get on and bloody well *do* something!'

Joe did it with *Maman* now. She'd finish her bookkeeping, household tasks, and just sit and stare into space, no knitting, no embroidery, no dressmaking, and – God forbid – no reading, and Joseph would ask her what she was doing, only this time when she answered that she was "thinking", he would always ask rather warily, 'What are you thinking *about?*' It was as if it somehow scared him. She would never say.

CHAPTER 13

AMBITION REALISED

Joseph was gazing out from the window of his gatehouse office at the newly widened road. He was trying to focus his eyes on a small grey-green two-part blob which bounced up and down in the distance.

His watch told him it was 0932 hours. He liked his watch – inherited from Arnaud – and it felt comfortable to know the time. He would often look at it when he was troubled by his voices. It always seemed to help.

Within a few seconds, Joseph had identified the blob as the forms of motorcycle and despatch rider. As he saw the machine disappear under the gatehouse, heard its engine roar beneath his feet, he rose and watched from the window opposite as it rocked to a halt by the farmhouse door. The rider did not need to dismount. Joseph could see Helene holding out her hand as the corporal thrust a manila envelope at her.

'It says that Captain Luft and Lieutenant Traugaut will visit Chateau des Galets at 1100 hours on 13 May, and would M. Joseph Fournier be so good as to make himself available for interview. No reply necessary,' read Helene.

Joseph experienced a sudden cramp in his bowel; he must get to the toilet without delay. Christ! So, this was it. They were coming to question him about dealings on the black market. Somebody had squealed. Most likely some of the beef and lamb he'd acquired had been too well hung, and this was how its recipients were getting their revenge.

Why didn't they just turn up and arrest him? Why make an appointment? They were smooth though, the SS; Joseph knew it. He'd heard stories. They would question him obliquely. Find out what else he knew; put pressure on him to *shop* others.

'It's tomorrow; lucky I'm free,' he palpitated. He would have to watch his step. These people might be foreigners, but they weren't seed suppliers or local wheeler-dealers. There was another problem: tomorrow was *the 13th*. 'Oh Lord,' he said out loud, 'that's the day witches meet; this could be the devil, but there was no saying no.'

***

'It's the dishy one I saw in town a couple of years back, but I don't think much of his sourpuss friend,' smirked Helene as she burst into the kitchen the following morning.

'There are five of them actually, but the ones sitting in the front are drivers and things,' she added excitedly.

Joseph had spent a bad night. After hours of lying awake, he decided on a plan to deny everything. He peered out of the kitchen door and could see a figure standing in the middle of the yard, boots crushing coltsfoot which sprouted between the chalk *galets*. The captain had removed his cap and was staring up into the vast blue sky.

As soon as he saw Joseph, he snapped the cap back onto his blond head and, clicking with his heels, he inhaled through his nose, perhaps rather too quickly as Joseph caught him exhaling with pursed lips.

'M. Fournier, delighted to meet you.'

'Bweeawp.' The gastric turmoil of the night once again visited itself upon Joseph, and he turned away to try and disguise the belch.

The impeccable manners made him feel queasier than ever. Luft's lieutenant was standing with his back to both his captain and Joseph, scrutinising the corporal, driver, and two lance corporals standing by the front of the jeep, who had already lit up cigarettes.

Three cigarettes all lit from the same match. That's bad luck for a start, thought Joseph, glancing at his watch. It was 1104 hours.

He had a ghastly vision of himself spreadeagled over that miserable piece of hurdle he had been storing in the cruck barn, Traugaut holding his arms from the back, whilst Luft thumped him in the stomach. No, he had to keep calm. It would be questions. He could cope with them. He couldn't see Luft as a bare-knuckle man.

Oh God, he abruptly recalled the cigarettes. *That's* why they had lit three up at once. They would follow him into the barn and all hell would be let loose.

'Captain Luft, if you would like to step this way, please,' Joseph suggested cautiously. The polite formality was catching, but it didn't seem to be working in Joseph's favour.

As the three men entered the vast, glowing space of the cruck barn, Joseph was visited by the uncommon idea that they were walking onto the stage of a theatre and that someone or something had programmed them to engage in a dance, involving choreography which would produce perfect geometry. Exquisitely sinister.

The captain took up a position directly under the apex of the immense roof, whilst his lieutenant rhythmically paced around the barn's perimeter, hands clasped behind his back.

'These are all hand-made and individually stamped tiles – a very beautiful piece of art,' enthused Luft, tilting his face to the roof. Joseph hovered opposite the *hauptmann* and wondered how and where he was going to fit into this strange performance.

He felt more disadvantaged than ever. The captain appeared to have chosen the high ground from which to launch his enquiry. The floor of the barn sloped, and though he and Luft stood no more than three paces apart, the captain's mouth was several centimetres higher than Joseph's, and every time it opened, the sound it made seemed to pass right over Joseph's head. Joseph wondered whether he was going to be sick.

But there seemed to be another force at work, something preventing him from pitching forwards and vomiting. It was curiosity. There was something familiar about Luft. It was not the shouting kind of recognition of the street, more a feeling as if Joseph had unearthed the root of a familiar crop which had been sown thousands of years previously and in the wrong field.

Joseph was familiar with this sensation. Throughout his life he had been aware that there existed *other* beings. When he was little, Constance had said that having imaginary friends was just part of growing up. He'd never told Jean or his father about the voices, but he told Helene when they were older. She'd said that he should listen carefully to them because he might be psychic. Joseph was appalled; he was as sane as the next man. He was annoyed with himself for having even mentioned it.

His siblings boasted of "visions" as Helene called them, while "glimpses" was the label which Jean used to describe his experiences. They seemed to take pleasure in what they could see, but the two of them were as mad as bats. Helene was a girl so bound to be fey, and Jean, well, just listen to what their mother had to say about him! The last thing Joseph was going to do was to admit to anybody what was happening to him.

Joseph's name for these *things* was "cracks". He relished the slightly obscene inference, but it was no joke. There was something terrible about them – more like a crack in the sky and a hand reaching down... he'd got the idea from Aunt Icie – not that she ever used the term "crack", but she was always going on about something she called "the thin places". The way she saw it was that there were two worlds – the world of God and the place of people – and between them there was this wall, but it was more like a skin than a wall – a membrane, she called it. Sometimes, you could get a glimpse into the world of God but only where the membrane was thin, so you always had to look for the thin places, she said. Joseph didn't see it like this at all. He wanted to keep away from the thin places because what he saw through its "cracks" disturbed him.

Joseph stared at the SS captain in front of him, and instead of being pulled over into the abyss of physical sickness, he felt himself peering through one of the "cracks", drawn into an ancient world. The sun's strength! Supposing Luft knew all about his black marketeering? It sounded like he might have done, but then the man before him was a master at making folk feel guilty, feeling as if they'd said or done something wrong. Not only was his way of speaking strange, but it seemed loaded with other meanings. What did he mean by "art"? The art of deception perhaps, or was this

Joseph's guilty conscience? Joseph felt he knew this man of old, that talk with him was risky. Words uttered in innocence – but with insufficient forethought – could put one under scrutiny, even land one in serious trouble. Luft was a kind of hunter – but in a very genteel sense of the word – more of the mind than the body. The likes of him hunted deer with packs of hounds, but Luft would never stick an arrow in anything; somebody else always did that. No, like Joseph, Luft had never killed or even injured anything; he was a man of thought, and those who didn't know him might even say a man of peace. Luft's was the kind of mind which never went in pursuit of the obvious. So, folk who wore fabrics dyed with the most recently discovered intense colours, who had the loudest voices, or who laughed with the wildest laughter, were of no interest to him. Life was not black and white to Luft; it was an infinite number of shades of grey. The "crack" closed.

A gap between the roof tiles was transmitting a lozenge-shaped shard of sunlight onto the floor directly between them.

'M. Fournier,' began Luft, 'you have a reputation in this area as a capable manager. I also hear that you have ambitions in the building industry.' He paused; Joseph stared, mesmerised. Luft continued with his little speech.

'You may have heard of Organisation Todt. Its task is very simple: to make the west coast impregnable to invasion.'

The single lozenge of light cast onto the lime-finished floor between the two men had been joined by three smaller versions of itself. The lieutenant began his third circuit of the barn.

'Your expertise would be of great value to the Third Reich – and to France of course – its Empire, and the benefits to you and your family could be enormous.'

Joseph found he was looking straight at Luft, who was standing like a megalith. Joseph began to perspire, quietly, in the knowledge that he was being closely observed. At first, Luft stared back at Joseph, then his gaze shifted above Joseph's head, out of the open door of the barn. His eye seemed to be searching for something. It settled upon where Joseph knew the burial mound was.

Joseph looked for clues in Luft's expression. The eyes were like those of a wolf, but it was impossible to know whether this creature had just made a kill or not. Was this a trick? Was he expecting Joseph to refuse, and if he did so, would he be arrested and punished? A bizarre thought came to him. What if Joseph declined the offer, wanted to remain loyal to France and the French people? As long as he emerged from the barn alive and punishment-free, then the family and the other folk in the village would assume that he had agreed to do whatever they had asked, even if he hadn't.

They were clever, these Nazis. Walk out of that barn without being arrested, and nobody would believe he'd said "no". In fact, they wouldn't need to bother arresting him; he'd be under a death sentence from partisans who had drawn the only conclusion possible. That would be his punishment. He was fucked. There was no going back now.

The pacing lieutenant had drawn level with Luft and, without waiting for Joseph's reply, the two of them heel-clicked *Heil Hitler* in unison and stepped through the open door out into the sun.

'This area will once again be prosperous, you mark my words.' Luft smiled and pursed his lips as he and Traugaut marched to the waiting jeep.

CHAPTER 14

DO WHAT THOU WILT

It was afternoon when Jean returned to the farmhouse kitchen. They were all there – except Robert of course – just standing there, Joseph sitting at the scrub-top looking as smug as hell. Jean sat down at the table opposite Joseph.

'You're bloody mad, you are, working for the *sale Boche*.' Constance was right behind Joseph, trying to look as if she was protecting him. But *she* couldn't take care of a rabbit. Her posture was vertical, but there was something temporary and unsatisfactory about her stance, like the odd, tall, slim stalk of meadow grass which survives the scythe for a few moments, only to keel over without the support of its neighbours.

'It's collaboration! I know you've been talking about it, but I didn't think you'd actually do it.'

'It's survival,' reasoned Helene. 'As an employee of Organisation Todt, he can buy things at non-inflated prices, and we can actually buy petrol again. There'll be benefits for all of us.'

Jean could feel Joseph's gaze on him. His hair was no longer flopping into his eyes; it was shining, combed straight back and held by some kind of pomade. His chin looked squarer than ever. There was a definite line of a moustache on his upper lip.

'Well, you have to look at it from the point of view of the ordinary humble man,' he said, imitating Jean. 'It isn't the card which life deals you that counts, it's how *you* play it. We can all sit around complaining and idealising, or we can do something with it. So, what are you going to do, little brother?'

Jean felt shocked. In some ways, he couldn't help respecting what his brother had said, but he knew in his heart that Joseph had decided to follow false gods.

'Well, don't show your face in the village; somebody's liable to shoot you, and it won't be a Nazi.'

Jean stood up, stood down from the table… looked at Helene.

'You and I need to talk, Amber.'

Helene rose, followed him. A bold move for Jean, but it didn't necessarily mean that he and Helene were in accord. She had leapt to Joseph's defence, though she was prepared to talk, so that was something. The tumulus seemed the obvious place for them to head for.

Jean banged the outer kitchen door with such force that he could see the latch had failed to engage; it swung back inwards on its hinges, shuddering. He needed to cool down, keep a clear head. This talk was critical.

The Germans had only just requisitioned the land at Pointe des Galets for something or other. Signs had been posted along the pathway by the wheat field saying so, but no fences had been erected, and they were free to walk on the land which had belonged to the family for so long. The last time they had done so was the night Balzac had died, and now this could be the last time they would do so for some time to come.

Jean was calming down; he even felt quite nervous as the two set out, he wearing his beloved guernsey pullover and cavalry twill trousers in spite of the cloudless sky and gentle breeze. She in grey corduroy trousers and a home-knitted pullover, out of the top of which peeped the white, rounded collar of a cotton blouse. Jean was carrying a new – he had to admit, rare – addition to his wardrobe, acquired through Raymond who had described it as a Canadian-style bomber jacket. He wasn't quite sure about the colour, and another friend of Raymond's had referred to it as being "jaundiced". He could see Helene eying it, but she didn't say anything, so perhaps she approved after all.

It was one of those days when everything seems hopeful yet uncertain. The sun coming and going behind an expanse of wild-looking cloud, and Jean's eyes had no sooner adjusted to dullness when the next moment they were blinded with powerful light.

In the areas off the path – too steep to be scythe cut – he could see curling bunches of big fat comfrey leaves and, already, signs of their tiny blue flowers. Every few minutes there came the ratcheting screech of a cock pheasant, and sometimes one would strut in and out of view on the path ahead of them, with its scarlet head standing erect, its gleaming green yolk and shiny black underbelly.

'It's no surprise to me what Joseph has done…' he began.

'It's survival,' repeated Helene almost mechanically.

'What, telling lies about people?' He couldn't tell her the truth about what he was doing. 'Look, I know there were a lot of brave chaps in the French army in the war… but our new civilian generation has never really been tested; folk of Dad's age were called upon to give their lives in the Great War and, in a way, Joseph has answered that call, but I'm worried that he may be wrong. I suppose what I'm saying is that however strong one thinks that one's principles are, they can be no more than theory. It takes a crisis to put them to the test.'

'The Nazis have principles,' said Helene. Jean turned. He wasn't sure whether this was an argument *for* or *against*. Her eyelashes were fluttering as she spoke. It was a rare Helene mannerism but unequivocally the sign that she was making what she thought was an important point.

'Yes, but I'm not sure that Joseph will get on with those principles because it won't be him who's holding them; he'll be working to somebody else's. He thinks he's made a decision, but the decision was made for him by that captain. You know what he's like – likes to give people the impression that he knows what other people are thinking, but it's bluff; he relies on making massive assumptions about people. These Nazis may be governed by principles, but they're not Picard businessmen; they're not wheeler-dealers. Joseph will find himself out of his depth. For Christ's sake, he could have said no.'

'If he had done, we probably wouldn't have seen him again.'

'You know that might not have been a bad thing for everybody, including Joseph. If the Nazis had executed him, we could have all mourned him as a hero, whereas now everybody thinks he's even more of a shit than they did before.'

'Jean, that's a terrible thing to say, and you know it.'

'The question for me to answer is: what am I going to do now?'

'Jean, you don't have to do anything. Just get on with your job.'

'I know it might sound pompous, but I want to be master of my own destiny; I need to make some kind of a move.'

'Life isn't a game of chess, you know. The real things that happen are often beyond our control.'

But she's wrong, thought Jean. Life *is* a game. It's a series of forced moves, and one needs to learn when to resist those forces and when to give in to them. Joseph had got it badly wrong; he'd humiliated everybody; he was living life seen through a fog of jealousy, so thick it had driven him to try and kill Jean. Well, the time had come; the worm was turning; and Jean, for one, was going to get his own back even if he paid for it with his life.

'I mean, do you know what he's really up to? He's not just breaking the Nazi rules by hiding grain or swapping it for rancid meat which he gives to people in exchange for their life savings. He's dismantling farm machinery and selling the parts to "fences" who supply partisan groups. He doesn't care which side he's on! He's even pimping for women in Boulogne!'

'Don't be so hurtful, Jean. You've no proof.'

She was right. He had not – did not – but right now, he hated his brother so much he would say anything, even if only part of it were true.

As they arrived at the northern end of the tumulus, Jean noticed that the long grass which normally grew on its roof had been close scythed. Its smooth, pale green surface looked to him like some kind of heavenly miniature sports ground, and he had a peculiar vision of a troupe of young men, clad in white singlet and trousers, leaping up onto its pristine surface and performing the most exquisite of callisthenics.

Helene said she thought that the stones looked so pale and clean, the whole thing might just have been built.

'How *can* it be four thousand years old?'

'That's what everybody says. Hold on, you're supposed to be the one who can see into the past,' said Jean. It was difficult for a twenty-nine-year-old man to believe such a thing was so old. He could no more picture that than he could imagine the universe or the continuum of space and time. It was impossible to take it all in. He laughed, glancing at Helene. Yes, she *had* taken it in all right. It wasn't a case of her believing it or not – it just was!

They walked on into the south wheat field, keeping to the cliff path, and Helene looked into the distance, towards the Moulin d'Hermitage.

'People say to one another, "Are you happy?".' She sounded fierce all of a sudden. 'Happy?' she repeated, shouting. 'What does *that* mean? You know, I think that you, Joseph, and I have all tried to be too self-sufficient. We've all relied too much on our isolated lives, when what we really need is other people. That's what happiness is – it's neither contentment, nor a frisson of joy – it's something inbetween, indefinable really.' She lowered her voice slightly. '*He who binds himself a joy does the winged life destroy; he who kisses the joy as it flies lives in eternity's sunrise.*'[3]

Jean thought the verse sounded familiar but weirdly foreign – perhaps it was one of Aunt Icie's sayings.

'There'll be new ones coming along,' she added abruptly. She must have seen Jean's puzzled look. 'I mean children, families, we'll have them someday; they come and go; time passes in an instant.'

'Do you sometimes think that everything's been planned out for us and that there's little we can do to change it? Do you think there's somebody out there overseeing the whole lot?' asked Jean, pausing and raising both his hands as if he had just unearthed a conspiracy.

'Not in the sense that they're offering eternal damnation for some, and salvation for others, I don't,' Helene replied. 'I think we *can* change – not just our view of the outside world, but I think we can even change our personalities. We're all given a set of tools and, like artists, we have to work, developing our ideas with ever-changing media. No matter how carefully we plan and try to live our lives to a code, nothing is certain.'

'But that's just a process; I really want *things* to change, particularly here.'

'*Do what thou wilt*,'[4] said Helene as if she had thrown down a challenge. Jean thought he'd heard that phrase before as well.

'You mean do whatever I like?'

'No, it doesn't mean that – think about it – it means do what you're meant to do; find out what it is, and *do* it. Set the world alight.'

'What, you mean the spiritual world?' asked Jean. 'I'm not sure I know what it is...' Helene gave a laugh, which would have been audible out in the bay below had anyone been out there to hear it.

'The spiritual world, we're living in it right now!'

As they turned to walk back down to Chateau des Galets, Jean could feel more questions burning away.

'If you really commit yourself to a cause, do you have to have proof that it's right? I mean, how much of that commitment should be duty to one's country, and how much of it should depend on self-determination?' Jean dropped his outstretched hands in exhaustion and looked at Helene. She was smiling, standing firmly on that continuum, somewhere between the late Bronze Age and a future which, to him, seemed completely uncertain.

PART TWO

Secrets Uncovered

CHAPTER 15

A SECRET UNCOVERED

November 1941

Joseph climbed into his Wehrmacht issue four-wheel drive Citroen and pulled out of Chateau des Galets onto the newly widened road. He barely recognised the landscape.

Since his recruitment into Organisation Todt (OT), the road had been extended with a swathe of crushed chalk, designed to move a lot of vehicles and supplies quickly. It was now early November and the clouds of white dust which drifted behind the convoys of lorries were sometimes barely discernible from the mists which hung about the slopes. Open trucks and mechanical diggers toiled up the escarpment, carrying building supplies for the new fortifications at Pointe des Galets.

Much to his delight, Joseph's first task for Organisation Todt was to supervise the removal of part of the old burial mound. He was only sorry that the intention wasn't to raze the whole thing to the ground.

As a man who always liked to control everybody and everything around him, he couldn't help feeling uneasy about his present position. For a start, his instructions did not come from Luft or Traugaut; they came in written form signed by the secretary of staff, General Mezger.

Cut tumulus (to the stated dimensions), and ensure clear site, it said.

That was it. No explanation, no notion of what installation was to be placed there, and worst of all, no sight of any drawings. It was like being asked to complete a jigsaw but only being handed one piece at a time.

Joseph swung the Citroen into the dusty space which was once his wheat field; he could see mechanical diggers devouring the south-east corner of the burial mound. He glanced at his watch. It was 0800 hours.

The work which was taking place was a neat job; a team of men with kango hammers had removed most of the stone, while the diggers picked up the rubble. Joseph noticed that all the entrances to the tumulus, which he and Jean had helped Arnaud to block up all those years ago, had been reopened. He also recalled the holes that had appeared so mysteriously.

The thought that anybody – well, anybody on the site, which had now been made a secure area – could wriggle in there gave him the creeps. What had also given him the willies was the fanciful notion that – and he blushed as he recalled Helene telling him – tumuli represented the human female sexual organs, while standing stones were quite obviously phallic. It was no coincidence, Helene had insisted, that folk were buried in the foetal position; it was symbolic of a further period of gestation, in preparation for the afterlife. Christ! Well, this demolition was going to be symbolic all right; he would make sure of that.

He'd been particularly on edge all morning. In that cave at the front of Joseph's head, Edouard had been nagging on about Isabelle again, and this time, somebody else – a woman by the name of Henriette – had also trespassed into his cerebral territory, claiming that she was the sweetheart of Jules, who had been killed fighting a duel with Oscar, his rival for her love. Henriette, who said that she had died of tuberculosis shortly after the duel, wanted to say sorry to Jules and to tell him that all love was equal in death.

As Joseph walked through the still-rising dust and up to the newly truncated wall of stone, he was puzzled by the sight of an old biscuit tin. It had taken a mauling from one of the diggers, but *that* looked like a spinning top, and there was a doll – its face smashed in – lying among the debris. But the sight of a small wooden cross nestling against the detritus sent his pulse racing. It was *the* Jerusalem Cross.

Aunt Icie's brother – Joseph's godfather – had made Joseph the gift of a tiny silver cross; beautiful, but it never measured up to what he'd given Jean. What the hell was it doing here discarded and forgotten? He bent down to pick it up and felt a surge of blood to his head.

One of Joseph's subliminal "cracks" had opened, and he felt himself helplessly peering into it. Instead of the dusty midday, he found it was night; he could feel the vivid pulsing light of pitch torches, and the group surrounding him – no longer OT labourers – were staring down upon a female body prepared for burial. The flesh of the face – although skilfully painted and shadowed – looked distant, while in contrast, the one-piece deep violet-dyed dress worn by the dead figure hinted at having a life of its own.

Two objects conveyed the impression of floating above the body. One was a bracelet, encircling the left wrist in the form of a bronze "S", whilst standing out from the throat was a braided bronze necklace with two concentrically placed inverted horseshoe shapes, terminating in delicate spirals.

Joseph felt his heart thump; the face of the queen seemed oppressively familiar...

The ancient Joseph could see masons entering the mound carrying their torches and pulling a sled bearing the queen's body – for it *must* be a queen – and stopping at the first chamber on the landwards side.

He watched as the two men carefully lifted the body from the casket. In the confined space, and hemmed in by slabs of stone, this was not easy. The dead one was silent, but the living grunted and gasped as one of the men took an animal skin – the coat of a fur-backed beast – and began to envelop the corpse with it.

After lying in state, all trace of stiffness seemed to have vanished from the deceased, and the masons were able to wrap the body into the protective layer of fur, fold it into the foetal position, head facing towards the sea. Jars of grain and berries were placed on either side of the head, and the masons began the task of sealing up the chamber.

As the "crack" closed shut, Joseph walked back to his jeep and looked across the valley. The fog had cleared, but he was barely able to take in what he was seeing. The ground in the distance by the Healing Stone above Chateau de Galets gave the appearance of having been stripped of foliage and was now an expanse of white chalk. Timber huts had been erected with barbed wire stretched around them. Columns of men were disembarking from trucks and being led into wired compounds.

Joseph looked at his watch; it was 0920 hours. He would return the Jerusalem Cross to Jean without delay.

***

Jean was sitting with Helene at the scrub-top table. It was early evening and the light had gone. The kitchen door was closed, the stove lit, and there was a chicken pot-roast in the cast-iron cooker. They did not expect Joseph for supper.

'Zbig's going to see Joe to speak to him. There's something going on at the Healing Stone Camp. It's to do with all the men they've brought in to work on the coastal defences.'

As his hand reached into the pocket of his jacket, it could feel the Jerusalem Cross his brother had returned to him earlier that day. He counted its sixteen tiny external boxwood points, pressed his thumb into the small low-relief figure of the dying Christ. He found it unexpectedly comforting.

'I feel guilty,' sighed Jean. 'Zbig's been telling me for ages that those blokes aren't being treated properly; Joe says they're being paid, but I know for a fact that they're not even being fed decently. Some of them go missing every day, but I can't do anything; I'm just a bloody farmer. I was going to speak to Joe about it this morning when he got back from site... but something else cropped up.'

'Too late now, Jean! I'm worried what Zbig will do; he burns on a short fuse.'

'I'm not sure that Joe can do anything either.'

'Maybe not, but someone needs to tell him all the same.'

'We could do with Joseph spending more time on farm management.'

'You need to tell him that as well, Jean.'

'We all relied on Thibout more than any of us let on to one another. He was really good with briefing Zbigniew; I get on with him all right, but he needs more supervision. Nobody knows as much about farm management as Joseph – or as much as Thibout did – and not to put too fine a point on things, I'm getting busier with other activities.'

'What! Coupon-forging? Just watch it, will you, Jean? Raymond and those other people have got more experience than you.'

'No, we're working out a fairer food syndicate system; don't tell Joe, though.'

'Jean, be careful; Joseph's playing at being a gangster. Things are bad enough between the two of you already without you setting up in competition with him.'

CHAPTER 16

DANTE'S INFERNO

Joseph tried to pull himself together. It had been months since the "crack" with Luft, but the prescience at the tumulus had been so vivid that he was feeling close to exhaustion. Jean was to blame, of course. If he hadn't so maliciously discarded the Jerusalem Cross for Joseph to find like that, then he wouldn't have fallen victim to another "crack". The shock had brought it on.

He sat on a wooden chair perspiring, trying to breathe deeply. Order was what was required. He must leave chaos behind and return to the world of normality and the work which he so loved.

At last, the cave in his head was silent, and he began to look around at the room – a space which had been used exclusively by him since Arnaud had died. It was the Chateau des Galets Farm registered office; all the records were kept there, but recently, it had become Joseph's den. Nobody other than him went up there. Nobody wanted to.

The building was an odd one. Four brick towers all at forty-five-degree angles to the road. Angles were the whole idea, because whoever had built it wanted to be able to have a view full circle. The space between each pair of towers had been infilled, leaving in the centre a bridge under which all who came to the chateau had to pass. And it was this bridge – a space measuring some five metres square – that formed the room in which Joseph now sat.

To his left was a grubby, cream-painted door which led onto the landing. An open tread timber stair led on down to the ground floor and thereafter out under the bridge where the gates had once hung.

The lobby on Joseph's right was where the farm records were kept, in a row of awkwardly proportioned armoires, also painted a dismal shade of cream.

His mother was a good bookkeeper. Shelf after shelf of red ledgers – and stock books – but Constance never ventured up here; Joseph would always take the relevant books to her – there were rats, she said.

To the left of the red ledger shelf was a row of maps, meticulously stored like books, and Joseph took refuge in thinking about them. Michelin maps had been a passion of his father, so much so that quite inexplicably after the Great War, he had acquired a set of the new maps which described the battlefields. A collection which had been published even *before* the armistice had been signed.

Map number 301 Pas de Calais and Somme (62) was the area upon which Chateau de Galets appeared, and Joseph had grown up with that reference 62/C3 1*38/50*45 stamped in his mind. Merely repeating that code to himself could sooth him.

It wasn't as if he took the slightest pleasure from the thought of "the landscape". Walking, joy in the gentle acoustic of water courses, delight in the dappled shade of a copse was of no interest to him. What appealed to Joseph about the maps was the fact that they represented order.

The idea which brought him the most satisfaction was that of subjugating nature – with all its unruly awfulness – by imposing upon it a regular grid.

He found stimulation in graphic keys, symbols, and the legend which adorned each sheet, which was why – in spite of his nervousness about his new job – he was delighted to be issued, by Mezger's office, with a set of the new Michelin maps which had been prepared in Germany ready for the invasion. Joseph was quick to identify that they had been based upon the 1938 editions but had been skilfully adapted. He noted that certain economies had been made, for instance he could see that between sheets 54 and 60, the gap in the French version had been filled in. Translations had been made, though imperfect. He noticed that the equivalent of the Michelin 55 was referred to as a "4 blat – which is part of the batch entitled No Frankreich". The blue hatching so prevalent on the French versions to depict the sea had been omitted, and a redesign had been carried out on the folding of the maps. Joseph sat back in the wooden chair. He was troubled by a new thought. Why had he not noticed it before? The French versions of map 62 had never shown Le Vieux Vicente, but the new German map did.

Their surveyor must have visited the site before the invasion. It was the same story with the magic pool; there it was marked on the new German map – it didn't say "magic", of course, just "spring", but Joseph couldn't even recall anybody apart from Helene who even knew of its existence.

Since he'd been working in the OT, he'd taken to sleeping in the gatehouse. He needed to be on his own. But the main reason for partitioning himself from the rest of the family was that he knew he was no longer welcome in the main farmhouse.

He looked down at his watch; it was 1620 hours. Darkness began to crawl round, and the scene outside looked ragged. If he had looked behind him, he could have seen out of the other window to where the land climbed northwards towards Le Vieux Vicente. He preferred not to look that way at the moment.

The tail of his eye caught the cast-iron stove, but it was giving him little cheer. He had been staring, trance-like, out of one of the four windows, watching truck after truck rolling along the road to the construction sites. Lorries carrying tons of steel reinforcing rods, bags of sand and cement, came toiling by, loaded with row upon row of batching cement mixers.

A thought crept into his mind, ill-fitting at first but, like his new OT uniform, he would have to get used to it. He had been disturbed by what he could see happening on the site of the Healing Stone. Every day, more men were being brought in. Some were taken off to work inland, but several dozen were marched past his window daily before dawn, and they would return in the dark, some wearing overcoats to protect against the late autumn chill; others just wore their tunics buttoned up. Most of them looked thin and gaunt. He knew there was a job to do, but why did men have to be brought here from so many different countries?

He sat apprehensively, for it was about life in the Healing Stone Camp that Zbigniew and his three countrymen were on their way to see him.

The four Poles lived in the cottage which Daddy Giroud had rented from the Fourniers before he and his two sons made their escape to England. It may not have been luxurious, but Joseph knew it was a far cry from the conditions which the new foreign workers were being subjected to.

'These men, they are not being paid,' snapped Zbigniew, his large domed forehead furrowing as he thumped on Joseph's desk. There were only two guest chairs in the office, and as he had made no attempt to fetch more, all four visitors stood, while Joseph sat in his chair, feeling bewildered and glancing down at his watch. The seconds seemed to pass very slowly.

'The payments are held up by the Reichsbank,' he lied.

'There is barbed wire around the camp.'

'Hmm, that's to stop people getting in,' said Joseph. 'There's a lot of racial prejudice around here against people from Eastern Europe.'

'Why to bring them all from Poland, Czechoslovakia, and Romania? Why not to use German labour?'

'There are French workers there.'

'Absol-ut-ely there are!' exploded Karel, one of the other Poles. 'They are Jews; we know as well as you do that German law is that every Jew to living in France is be intern-ed; this is internment with forc-ed labour.'

The four men stood back from Joseph's desk.

'We to have nothing do with your regime.'

'Huh, what are you going to do?' reasoned Joseph. 'You can't work the arable holding on your own; the Germans control all the supplies; you'll starve!'

'Wait to see,' said Zbigniew, frowning as he and the men stamped out of the office and thundered down the timber-boarded stair out into the cold evening.

✳✳✳

'What is there to do on an arable farm in November?' was the question Joseph heard himself ask as he stood in the yard, alone and in the darkness of the following morning; 0530 hours, his watch told him. 'Stack onions, sort sugar beet, check the wheat seed drilling equipment is working.' He was astonished to see Zbigniew and two of the other Poles already doing just that, working away by kerosene lamps. So much for their posturing of yesterday evening!

He had to admit to himself that he was quite pleased to see them. For one thing, he couldn't work on the farm now; he had better things to do, and you couldn't get the labour – so many men under the age of thirty had been carted off to work for the Germans in the Fatherland… so where was Jean? Off with Raymond, no doubt still forging food coupons. Huh, why didn't they go into the meat business like him? Grain for meat and meat for real money; he was doing well now; if only he hadn't got rid of the dairy herd – free petrol, a salary from the OT, he was going to be a millionaire! Hell, though, that had been scary when Luft and Traugaut turned up to see him that time. He would have to watch his step…

The roar of an army jeep prised him out of his thoughts. In a further instant, the yard was full of jeeps and shouting soldiers, sub-machine guns at the ready. Christ! Joseph felt an explosion of perspiration. This really was it. The Poles must have discovered the bags of grain he had set aside for resale and twitted. What harm was he doing? It was his grain to do what he liked with, and it was only equal to what he had to give to Thibout and Amaury as crop sharers before they'd buggered off. He was in a panic.

But the soldiers didn't even look at Joseph. He stood forlornly in the approaching dawn and watched the three Poles being dragged, then bundled – one into each of the jeeps.

The officer in charge caught sight of him.

'You!' he barked. 'Yes, you!' Joseph was blinking; he must look surprised. 'Come here, immediately.' Joseph froze. The order had an odd effect upon him; his feelings dodged between indignation and fear. This was his patch, and some damned foreign dog was ordering him about, after he had voluntarily given him the benefit of his skills and expertise. Bloody cheek!

'Lie down on the ground!' screamed the captain, ripping a Luger P08 from its holster and pointing it towards Joseph's head. This time, Joseph found he really was unable to move. The air around him seemed to have become thick, denser than his own body. The captain came stamping across the yard, and Joseph felt the barrel of the Luger butting behind his right ear. This was it, his punishment for stockpiling grain… but why were they arresting the Polacks? It was *his* grain. A thought came to him: *where was the fourth Pole?*

'Where's Karel?' blurted Joseph. He didn't care; he was probably no more than seconds away from being dead.

'Gone to flame field,' he heard Zbigniew mutter from one of the jeeps before being ordered to "Stuff it!".

Oh, for crying out loud! Joseph hadn't done stubble-burning for years. Arnaud had always enjoyed a good burn-up before the ploughing season, but one of Joseph's suppliers had convinced him that using herbicides would be cheaper and more efficient.

The point was that starting a field fire – even a controlled one – was illegal; they could all be shot on the spot. As Joseph sat in the rear of one of the jeeps – bouncing over dark earth, then speeding across pale chalk towards the wheat fields – his heart was pumping with fear. Even if the *Boche* hadn't found out about the grain, he was going to be shot for burning stubble, and it was all the fault of those bloody Poles.

The sky was beginning to lose its shiny jackboot blackness and was dissolving into cineral dinginess as the small convoy of jeeps rattled over the chalk, then one after another, they lurched along the edges of the wheat field.

Wedged in the back of the jeep, Joseph could smell it before he could see it. For a split second, he was almost comforted by the sweet aroma of burning wheat stubble. Then, above the heads of the driver and captain, he saw it, a long twisting mass of black smoke, and below, the pale land being devoured by a low wall of orange flame.

The four vehicles rammed to a halt, and Joseph was pushed out onto the soil and manhandled to a spot a few metres clear of the jeeps. The *hauptsturmführer* and two helmeted corporals with sub-machine guns followed. The remaining soldiers stayed holding the three Poles in the jeeps.

There was a break in the smoke, and there, standing on a patch of dark space surrounded by flame, was a grey boiler-suited figure with its back to the assembled group. Karel was leaning towards the distant bluff, his arms slightly extended but hanging limp, as if held in limbo. Just visible above his bowed head was the dark, dull curve of the remains of the roof of Le Vieux Vicente.

As if it had suddenly been brought to life, Karel's body started to twitch then turned to face the gathering – arms outstretched like Leonardo's Vitruvian Man. *He's pleading with them not to shoot*, thought Joseph. But Karel seemed to be in a kind of trance, as if his body were no longer his own. First, the right outstretched arm descended through an arc, disappearing behind the back, and as the left arm followed suit, the right knee was raised.

Joseph watched, appalled, as the man then stretched his body backwards in a crab-like posture while making circular motions with his hands in front of his stomach. The Polack had clearly gone mad.

As the earth beneath it glowed and burned, the figure raised itself into an upright position and its hips began to gyrate. This was obscene; he must be possessed. Joseph turned and stared at the captain. Out of the corner of his eye, he could see Karel was now stamping with both feet into the dark, carbon-laden earth.

Nobody spoke. It almost felt to Joseph as if he had given the order *himself* as there came two clicks, followed by a rush of fire from both weapons. The grey figure spun round twice, sank down, splashes of red mingling with black earth.

As Joseph was pushed back into the jeep, an unseen voice seemed to mutter a credo: *limbo, greed, lust, and anger; limbo, greed, lust, and anger; limbo…*

'There was a breakout at the camp last night by some Poles. They were helped by somebody on the outside. One of our guards was injured,' said the *hauptsturmführer* in almost conciliatory tones as, minutes later, Joseph was pushed out of the jeep at the farm gate. The captain seemed calmer now, as if soothed by the killing. The four jeeps disappeared, taking with them the surviving Poles.

CHAPTER 17

HELENE STANDS UP TO JOSEPH

It was the evening, after the arrest, and Joseph was in his office. He was sitting awkwardly because he was irritated by a voice in his head. It was a man called Kurt worried about a butter dish, a family heirloom which he had evidently broken quite by accident just before his death, thus depriving his daughter of this supposedly valuable piece of porcelain. Kurt was a bloody nuisance; he'd been on about this butter dish for years.

But Joseph had more on his mind than Kurt. He had not seen his sister since Zbigniew had been taken away, and it would be a very angry Helene who he was expecting to arrive any minute. As he shifted his position on the wooden chair, he tried to imagine the sort of questions she was going to ask him, and how he was going to answer them. But he had to remember that whatever she asked, it would be the product of an overemotional mind.

Why on earth get involved with a Pole anyway? She and Jean made a right pair, and it fell upon him, as the oldest and most responsible sibling, to deal fairly and justly with them. That's what this war was really about, fairness for ordinary working folk, discipline and order; somebody had to keep order. What was more, she didn't have to deal with the people he had to. He was sure she was up to something. Well, if she was caught, she would just have to take the consequences. It was 1759 hours – so Joseph's watch told him.

He heard the door bang in the entrance lobby downstairs and the sound of Helene's footsteps. Why was it that *her* elegant little feet had the skill to transfer weight from heel to toe, whilst lanky great Jean walked everywhere on his heels? Chalk and cheese was probably the answer. He grinned. He was still grinning when the battered cream-painted door swung open and continued opening until it gently bumped the rubber doorstop.

Helene, dressed in a three-quarter-length boulder-coloured mackintosh buttoned against a turtleneck wool pullover, remained firmly but elegantly poised directly over the threshold. Her face, backlit by the lamp on the landing, seemed to have changed from the relaxed horizontal set it assumed when she was producing apple puree and transformed into an alarming vertical condition. The front wave of her hair, normally hanging leisurely over her forehead, was now reaching upwards, while her neck curls hung low, clawing the epaulettes of the mackintosh. There was a fragment of something adhering to her left cheek.

'Welcome, little sister!' bawled Joseph. 'I gather that you and Jean have been doing sterling work clearing the old dairy ready for that *gîte* we are going to open. By the way,' he added, 'do knock in future, we're supposed to for security.'

Ooooh, we're really in for it here, thought Joseph, *but why get so upset over a Pole? I mean, look at the mess they've got us all into.*

'I can't believe that you don't know where they've been taken.'

'Hmm, they don't tell me anything,' Joseph replied truthfully. 'They only tell me what I'm meant to be doing on the morning I'm meant to be doing it.'

'Men in that camp have been beaten; others fall sick and just disappear.'

'Into hospital – you've got a crumb on your cheek by the way.'

'There *are* no hospitals here; you know that. What I would like you to do, Joseph, for *me,* is to go and see Captain Luft and ask him where Zbigniew is. Jean hates what you're doing; Mum's worried that local people will come and set fire to the farm because of it, so just do this one thing for me, will you?'

For a moment, Joseph's eye escaped Helene's stare; it fled through the window and up to the Pointe des Galets where it settled apprehensively on the moonlit tumulus. He felt as if he were being forced to ask it for help.

'I want to help you, Joe. You're not right, but you just won't be helped; you're breaking, and you need mending, *badly,* before it's too late.'

She turned, walked away, leaving the door open against the rubber stop where it had come to rest.

Suddenly, Joseph felt deflated. Everyone was against him it seemed, but he wasn't stupid; it wasn't difficult to see why. He began to feel as if he was contracting some sort of virus, a mess of things was nagging away at him.

For some reason, Aunt Icie and her grim little son came into his mind. *He* knew why the boy had suddenly been sent away to boarding school all those years ago.

He had always hated the sight of the blond little cuckoo. It started first as a game. Joseph would come back from the fields and find the pale little shaver playing adventurously far from the farmhouse door. Why did he have white eyelashes and funny porcine eyes? With his pink, powdery skin, he looked like a little pig.

'There's a big giant coming to eat you!' Joseph would growl right in the boy's ear as he hurried past. That soapy, milky smell! The three-year-old would moan in terror as he fled towards the safety of the kitchen.

When he was older, it was Chinese burns; no one seemed to notice the inflamed skin on the boy's arms – anyway, the redness always went away after an hour or so.

Joseph was a law unto himself. Constance assured him he was being responsible; after all, he was running the farm single-handedly while his siblings were being luxuriously educated by Icie. He was keeping order, and regularly punishing this little interloper was part of that reordering, an essential component of keeping control.

One day, when the boy was eight years old, Joseph caught him throwing stones into one of the water troughs by the old dairy sheds. It was the day after the disaster with the tractor, and he decided to take the little blighter to the brink.

As he held his head under the water, the boy's arms and legs kicked out, catching Joseph in the crotch. For that he gave him five more seconds, and as he looked at his watch, he listened, fascinated by the aquatic yodelling coming from the struggling body under his right arm.

The evening sun cast a human shadow across the water trough. There was a figure standing behind them – it was Aunt Icie...

Joseph knew that things were wrong, not just with his job and his family. It was him as well. He knew that he had to make an effort, but it was going to be difficult because he certainly wasn't going to give up his job with the OT. Helene *had* got under his skin so he *would* go and see Luft. After all, somebody had to keep order in the family.

***

Helene felt strangely energetic as she walked back over to the farmhouse. Several things were running through her mind: the manila envelope which had arrived for Joseph, her talk with Jean soon afterwards. She knew she hadn't given him the answers he was looking for – after all, she didn't have any; Joseph was the one who had an answer for everything. Jean would find what he needed soon enough. Joseph wasn't going to change – she should have seen that long ago. But if he wouldn't, then *she* would. She knew what she had to do now.

CHAPTER 18

JEAN DOES "AS HE WILT"

'He's brooding,' said Helene.

It was several weeks since she had confronted Joseph about Zbigniew's arrest, but nobody had heard a thing. Joseph had shut himself away in his office and on his various building sites. As Jean and Helene sat opposite one another in the farmhouse kitchen, Jean tried to think of something reassuring to say but couldn't.

'Do you think he'll *ever* go and see that *Boche* captain?'

Helene seemed to be looking at him queerly, as if she knew the answer but wouldn't say.

'What we need, Jean,' she was ignoring his question, 'is more help with the farm. Joseph's doing this deliberately – not getting in replacement helpers – it's a plan to tie the two of us down so we've no free time.' Why should Helene need more free time all of a sudden? Jean was suspicious. 'What about taking some of those poor men out of the Healing Stone Camp?' she continued.

'Good idea, but we still need two experienced managers to

do Joseph's job, and where are we going to find them? Even if we can get labour, but we need bosses as well; neither of us is putting in anything like the hours we need to run this place properly. I'm busier than ever with the syndicate now.'

'I don't know what *you're* meant to be doing with the syndicate because nobody seems to be benefitting from it except Joseph.' She seemed testy.

'All right, Amber! Why don't *you* ask the *Boche* captain yourself? You seem to be seeing plenty of one another. You're sailing very close to the wind.'

'He got me a job at the Hotel de Ville,' she was trying to justify herself. 'I can't ignore him.'

'What! No wonder you want more time away from farm duties. Amber, the farm needs production and management, not extra cash. It's time spent on the business we want, not paper money that's losing half its value every month.'

'I'm sorry, Jean, but I can't work all hours on the farm. I don't want to end up like Mum, spending the rest of her life in mourning, doing housework, accountancy, never going out, never finding friends.'

So that was it. Jean could see what was happening now. This was all Joseph's doing, intended to drive a bigger wedge between Jean and his sister. How furious he must have been to see the two of them, apparently in accord and getting on well, as if a bond had been forged between them, and made even more special by Joseph's collaboration with the *Boche*.

It must have been Joseph who had asked Luft to find Helene the job at the Hotel de Ville; it was designed to break that bond and leave Jean on his own, struggling to work the farm and unable to work on whatever secret activities Joseph thought he was doing... and it was common knowledge that Luft and Helene were seeing one another. Jesus! It was a trade-off; Helene was beholden to Luft now. His brother didn't care that people might think she was an SS whore.

If only Jean could say to Helene what he wanted to say – share his secrets – but he couldn't. He was powerless, and he had this awful feeling. It was as if the two of them were being carried along in a flooded river, the occasional overhanging branch to hold onto, but never for long.

'The thing is, Jean…' her voice faltering, 'the hegemony that the country is now living under… it could go on forever. I mean, look at the ancient Roman Empire. People from its occupied lands made attempts to overthrow it, but they were never successful. It was hundreds of years before the empire collapsed, and by that time, everything had changed anyway.

'What I'm saying is that the situation's different from the Great War; perhaps it will go on and on; the Allies may never come; and maybe the Germans aren't monsters, and we should just try and get on with them. Civilisation is like any relationship – it never stays still, and if it isn't developing and moving forwards, then that means it's going backwards.'

Jean felt a horrible tug of doubt. Maybe she was right – she usually was – and he'd just finally convinced himself that he was committed to the cause…

***

Jean dismounted from his bicycle and left it leaning against the sunlit wall of the Bar Tabac. In the gloom of its interior sat Raymond with an espresso coffee and cognac in front of him. Small, dark, and Celtic-looking, with shapely little eyebrows, Raymond smiled almost mischievously at Jean as he wove his way through the tables to meet him.

'They've done their final checks on you, and they want you in,' Raymond whispered in his ear. Henri looked up from behind the bar and switched the café wireless on. Jean wasn't sure about Henri, but maybe that was to give them more privacy.

'Joseph working for the Nazis was an advantage – no one will ever suspect!'

'He thinks I've been forging food coupons. He reckons Helene's at it as well.'

'Even better!' hissed Raymond. 'Not a problem at all. Information in the Resistance is scant. It's handed down the line; everybody uses codes – numbers. You could be working alongside somebody for years and not guess. Another thing,' continued Raymond, 'is that, as a member of the family of an OT worker, you've got a special pass. To the Resistance, that's a golden card!'

'Tomorrow night is your first job; you'll be told nothing.' He laughed. 'Just like your brother working for the OT! Ride your bicycle to the place you're told, then you'll be given your next instruction. I'm sorry it's all cloak and dagger, Jean, but that's how this war will be won.'

Jean felt inside the pocket of his yellow bomber jacket and his fingers touched something. It was the Jerusalem Cross. When Joseph had returned it to him, he'd felt ashamed. Now it felt like his guardian angel.

CHAPTER 19

IN FLAGRANTE DELICTO

Joseph had thought long and hard about the visit from his sister; in fact, he'd brooded about it for months, and now it was spring again. Of course, it was the least he could do to go and confront Luft – better late than never, eh?

Several things were worrying him. He'd heard rumours. He knew that Helene was working as a clerk at the Hotel de Ville. For pity's sake, how were they going to keep the farm together if she was moonlighting! How had she got the job? Decisions like those weren't made locally anymore. It was all done at department level; people had to be referred. There were also rumours circulating about Helene and Luft, distasteful ones.

He was apprehensive of talking to Luft. He, a lowly OT volunteer – or was he a conscript? He wasn't sure now – asking a favour of an SS captain? In spite of the number of times that Joseph boasted about being "a humble man", he resented the fact that he, Joseph Fournier, a Picard farmer, was going to have to try and beg from Captain – supposedly son of Baron – Luft, evidently holder of a university degree.

Still, Joseph couldn't help liking him, and strange as it

seemed, if Luft were a woman, Joseph would like to *have* him. In fact, why limit the fantasy to that? Given that Joseph was nearly thirty-two years old and had never slept with a woman, what *was* all the fuss about anyway? In a wild thought, he had to admit to himself that this mission wasn't about support for his sister. It was fuelled by his fascination for the captain. Christ, he was on dangerous ground!

As he set out, he was in a high state of excitement, gripped with the fear of various possibilities. There was the anxiety of rejection, the worry of calling on a Nazi SS officer in his lodgings – unheard of. He was playing a lethal game. Nevertheless, he just had to see this mission through. Whatever the outcome, at least he would be out of his misery.

***

Joseph was impressed to find that Captain Luft had acquired such pleasant lodgings. The *hauptmann* had a small apartment on the third floor of a khaki-hued stone house on one of the "pretty" streets just outside the ramparts of the Old Town.

Joseph was even more in awe of the bell arrangement at the front door. Each tiny clear glass capsule contained the name of the occupant and was lit from behind, but only if its resident was in the building. If they were not at home, then the contraption was switched off to save the visitor pressing, standing, and waiting.

It was in its unlit state that Joseph found Captain Luft's little indicator sign. He hesitated; it was not too late to go back. The sign said the man was out, but Joseph had an uncanny feeling that he might be there.

As he was about to turn and leave, a smart, dark-suited and bowler-hatted man emerged from the building and offered him the opened door. Joseph didn't move. As the door was about to snap shut, his hand almost involuntarily shot out and stopped it. He crossed the threshold and stood on the worn terrazzo of the lobby floor.

He stood rigid, feeling a bit like the petrified bronze statue of the nineteenth-century local engineer he had driven past on the waterfront that morning. Now he was here, he would have to go up. If Luft was in, the worst that could happen would be that he would tell him to go. He resolved to go up and knock on the man's door.

It felt too much trouble to use the lift, so he grasped the brass handrail. It felt so cold it hurt his fingers. As he toiled upwards, the stairs seemed to become narrower, the air more difficult to breathe, and he felt a pain behind his eyes. For some fantastic reason, he kept thinking of Le Vieux Vicente. He was suddenly gripped with an idea that all his feelings and actions had happened to him before, and he had the distinct impression that he was walking through waist-high bracken, his bare legs being pricked by gorse.

Joseph had fallen into one of his fearful "cracks". Here, he was no more than a few summers old again, but in an ancient world, and he had come here alone to the tomb. His parents had told him to never go near the place. Adults didn't need to be warned. Fear alone usually did the trick.

The ancient Joseph had explored every piece of land around the village, knew how to climb up to the burial mound, had been close enough to see the low curve of its roof, so overgrown that it looked like some giant had pushed and twisted the earth.

Every time he came to the place, he was visited by the thought that if he ventured just a bit further, he might be able to look inside. Something terrible could happen to him, he might die, but even the thought of that gave him a feeling of excitement, almost to the point of sickness.

Unable to repress his feelings, he resolved to go and look. Then the thing would be over and done with, and even if the worst happened, at least his torment would be over.

He had chosen a cold, clear day for his climb up to the mound. No one had seen him leave, and he felt very agile as his feet trod lightly over the rock-hard *earthblood*. The white, powder-coated fingers of bracken hissed as his knees brushed against them.

In spite of the cold, his hair was wet with perspiration, and he thought he might spew. It was still not too late to run, yet he could smell something familiar – not just the crisp fronds of bracken his feet were crushing; it was something else he couldn't place.

He reached the dark opening in the side of the burial mound, retching with excitement. What *was* that smell?

Then he saw him. A tall man; it was almost a relief. If this was one of the walking dead, then at least he looked normal, though he seemed odd – sort of old and young at the same time, if that were possible.

Then something happened. The man did something to the young boy Joseph which he was unable to describe, or ever wanted to think about again, and as he ran howling from the tomb, he thought he heard the thing – for he was now sure that this was not a living being – wailing in despair.

He fell many times before he crossed the threshold of the only refuge he could think of: the house of the apothecary. As she comforted him, he confided to her that the man's eyes had turned white. The apothecary hung a small wood disc incised with a cross around his neck.

Joseph wrenched himself away from the "crack". His hair was soaking wet, and as he reached the top landing, he retched, but nothing came up. His climb surely was a waste of time. Yet he felt fear that Luft was there and fear that he was not.

He hovered miserably by the green-painted door, put out his hand to knock, but inexplicably, he tried the door handle instead. It opened.

The room in which he found himself was full of sunlight, and he could detect a scent, familiar, like crushed bracken, yet strangely unidentifiable. A half-open door appeared to lead into an adjoining room which was shrouded in darkness. He was aware that he had entered a private world; he shouldn't even have left the pavement below, but he *must* see what was in that room.

He moved forwards and positioned himself so that his eyes could adjust to the gloom. Two human figures were on a bed, both naked. Though the face of the man was covered, Joseph could see from the white braid on the cap – playfully placed over the supine face – that it was Captain Luft. The other figure, squatting astride him, Joseph recognised as his own sister.

Helene seemed to be in a daze, leaning forwards slightly, and it was then that Joseph caught sight of something hanging round her neck. It was a small wooden disc incised with a cross. He looked back to the male figure. Just visible under the peak of the braided cap were Luft's eyes, open but white – the pupils had vanished.

CHAPTER 20

PROMOTION

Joseph quietly closed the door of Luft's apartment building and stepped back into the street. He felt remarkably calm after the scene he had just witnessed, and considering that he had behaved in such an unusual manner, he felt quite light-headed. No harm had been done; no one had seen him. He felt a sudden light tap on his head and became aware that a seagull had crapped on him. He exclaimed out loud, 'Hmm, I'm going to have good luck all year now!'

He glanced down at the junction of wall and pavement and caught sight of two stag beetles, their exoskeletons shining in two-tone green. At first, he thought it was two males jousting, but as he looked closer, he could see that the larger male was being gripped by the smaller female and appeared to be receiving quite a sharp nip.

He was almost back at his Citroen when, without warning, he felt a violent stomach cramp and stood, his khaki-clad back arched and his hands clamped down on the fronts of his thighs as he vomited into the gutter. An ancient woman clad entirely in black, appeared from nowhere and offered him a piece of fresh cloth.

That last *thing* that he had seen, it couldn't have been… those overemotional, overimaginative siblings of his had rambled on so long about the *deildergheist* myth that now even *he* was imagining it!

It was worry which was causing all this; not receiving proper instructions from his superiors, that was the root of the anxiety and his lack of sleep.

When he did sleep, he was experiencing a disturbing repetitive nightmare that he had suffered as a child. He was lying in his cot overwhelmed with a fear. He could hear someone mounting the stairs; it was someone or something familiar to him, but he couldn't see a face. It was a force, hostile, malevolent, threatening, coming nearer, almost upon him before he realised that it was his mother.

Joseph couldn't understand how Luft and Helene had got together, and so quickly. Joseph had been dithering over this visit for six months, but even so, how in that time? He remembered the captain smiling at her the day he came to the farm almost a year ago now, but then Luft smiled at everybody, particularly his enemies. Surely Helene hated him for what had happened to Zbigniew?

As he swung his Citroen away from Luft's apartment and made an energetic left turn into the Rue St-Louis, he caught sight of the old woman in black again; this time she was crossing the road. *Watch me scuttle*, he thought as he gunned the engine and shot close behind her.

'Help that old lady somebody, will you!' he bellowed out of the window at a bemused group of local old men. 'What could they be looking so surprised at?'

***

It was September again and Joseph stood on the construction

site, staring puzzled at the watch word engraved onto the belt buckle of the general staff officer: *God is with us.* Captain Luft approached and introduced him to the general. Behind General Mezger, Joseph could see two higher-ranking generals, two bodyguards and, walking between them, Reichsminister Albrecht Speer who had come to inspect the progress on the Atlantic Wall. Joseph followed as Speer was given a superficial tour before being driven away in a waiting Mercedes.

The outcome for Joseph was a new position. Promotion to Area Organiser in charge of logistics and construction supplies to the large batteries in the area. All works now had to be completed by next summer. An invasion attempt by the allies was expected – so he was told – but no one knew exactly when or where, so the assumption had to be in the Pointe des Galets area, one of the shortest channel crossing points.

Joseph was issued with a different kind of uniform: another khaki tunic but this time with a swastika armband and the words *Org Todt*. He was also – rather ominously he thought – presented with a whip, in the style of a "cat-o'-nine-tails".

That can stay at home – I'm no sadist, he thought, *not like some of those camp guards.* But when he thought about it, he knew very well that not all camp guards were sadists either. It wasn't as if those jobs were being offered by underworld criminals, he reasoned. It was the Government, respectable jobs for respectable people, and many of the poor blighters can't even read or write. Who could blame a man or woman for wanting to better themselves in life?

As for his own career advancement, he was beginning to feel as if he'd been trapped. He was starved of information, and all the technical work was being done by a team of "others". He wasn't learning anything. Loftier-sounding promotion simply meant bigger "bollockings" when things beyond his control went wrong. He began to feel little more than a slave with wages. Dressed in his OT uniform, he felt rather like one of those sandwich board men, paid a pittance to surrender their humanity and ordered to amble up and down a street, nothing more than a sign on legs.

Standing on the bluff, his back to the sea, Joseph watched the progress of men working batching cement mixers as they prepared to pour concrete. The rumbling of the mixers became fused with another sound: a drone coming from a cloudless sky. A tiny dart appeared, travelling west, a streak of flame coming from its tail.

Joseph became aware of a man standing a few metres away, similarly dressed but much shorter, head like a boulder, and with practically no neck. *The man looks neanderthal*, he thought. It was a race untouched by the modern world and very likely the product of inbreeding. He was an "agitator", someone employed to provide encouragement to the workers. Swinging from *his* belt also was a cat-o'-nine-tails.

'That one's just been launched from the site fifteen kilometres north.' Yes, yes, Joseph knew exactly where the V1 rocket site was. Its launching pad had been built right on top of the magic pool. He'd felt bad about that, but that was life; it was war.

'They usually come directly over here from a nearer one, but it was bombed last night,' said the man with no neck.

Christ! Joseph hadn't been listening properly. That's the one he'd thought Boulder Head had just been talking about. So, it was the magic pool which had been bombed last night.

Boulder Head's eyes appeared eager. 'It's a Fieseler Fi 103,' said the head. Joseph felt a glimmer of comfort from hearing the letters and numbers, but it meant little to him.

'Just tell me what happened, will you?' Joseph should have known all this. Why hadn't he heard before? The fact was that he'd been spending too much time worrying about his brother and sister and chasing after SS captains. He could see another bollocking coming up for this.

'The raid has put the site out of action for at least one month. It probably wouldn't have done, but the RAF was helped from below.'

'Partisans?' asked Joseph, voice wavering.

'Saboteurs. They broke into the site and lit fires along the launching pad, so now we have to find more men and materials to rebuild it.'

✳✳✳

14 September 1942

How I wish I could tell Jean what I am really doing. One of the tragedies of all this – the war I mean – is all the lies and deceit. But it's all for the good.

I think that Jean has joined the Resistance. The coupon-forging thing was just a cover. He may be a dreamer, but he's not interested in the little picture. Jean wants to make a difference in people's lives. I'm worried for him. Raymond must have organised it. He's cleverer than Jean; not educated-type-clever like Jean, just knowing, like his mother.

After Robert was born, Maman got Raymond's mother to skivvy for us. You could tell she didn't like working for us because she would always leave one thing undone. Before she left, she would always say, 'I've left that cupboard; I'll do it next time,' or 'I've left the silver; I'll do it next time.' There was a kind of unspoken truculence, like she was always trying to bargain her way through life. Whenever you saw her in the village, she would always say, 'Hello, young Helene. Off out, are you?' or when Dad was coming out of the pharmacy, she would say to him, 'Just been to buy your medicine, have you, M Fournier?'

Dad would come back and say, 'That woman is a master at stating the bleeding obvious!'

Robert's got a girlfriend called Christine. He says she wants to apply for the Sorbonne as well. He says she's not a communist – not that Robert is, but we know that Jean is. The Nazis will have something on that somewhere, so with communism in the family, it's going to be best to wait and apply later.

Amazingly, the Sorbonne is still open, and Robert says it's got "normality", but then he says there's more to that than meets the eye, so he's happy in his room at Maubeuge and doing the management job now he's finished the course. He says it's a great time to learn about logistics and management because all French farm production is being redirected one way – 'Guess where?' he says. 'To Germany!'

Maman has lost weight and developed a stoop.

There's nothing I can say to Jean about what we're doing and nothing he can say to me.

I still don't know Captain Luft's first name. I bet it's Hans.

CHAPTER 21

THE STALKING

It was after midnight when Jean left the Bar Tabac and started to cycle in the direction of Pointe des Galets. He was on edge. It felt like somebody had been watching him. Last night's mission had gone well. This time they'd trusted him with all his instructions at once, so he must press on.

There was no moon, just a mass of deep, muddy-looking cloud and intense warmth, unseasonable for September. No other lights anywhere, and the hooded dynamo-driven lamp on his bicycle made a pale funnel under which the metalled road seemed to rush.

He spotted the path – some five hundred metres from the cliff edge – and stopped peddling. The dynamo stopped. Silence.

He wheeled the bike off the road and propped it up in the ditch. From there, he began to walk quickly towards the bluff. He still had a feeling that someone was watching him. He stopped and listened; nothing, but he felt no happier.

The field he was walking through had already been ploughed after yet another early harvest. The ploughing hadn't been done by him, nor his elder brother, and not by the Poles of course. The Nazis must have brought in their own farmers, and why so early?

His feet thumped and bumped on the uneven ground, and his body lurched from side to side. Then he began to get into a rhythm, less lurching, more confident...

Yes, he was like Bronze Age man setting off for a long journey equipped with hide bags – each about the size of a pair of clasped hands – looped onto his belt. Bread in one, small apples in the next, seed pod and blackfire, fire-making tools, even a bronze needle should his footwear need repairing for the return journey. Across his shoulders his bow, for defence against wild animals rather than for hunting. The fire-making tools were for emergency – the secret of a successful journey was speed. There was little opportunity to kill and cook; he would eat on the move...

Jean reached the cliff edge and turned to walk south. To avoid detection by the sentries, he had made his starting point well to the north of Pointe des Galets. His objective was to carry out a recce on the state of progress of three installations on the battery: the observation turret, the artillery casemate, and the auto mortar bunker. He knew exactly where the mortar bunker was because he had been told that it was being built right on top of the old burial mound, his place of spiritual refuge.

The first construction he came upon was the observation post, which from his view seemed to be less than half complete. Most of the concrete which had been poured seemed to be below ground level and perilously close to the cliff edge.

He took care not to venture near – not so much because of the danger of plummeting down the ninety metres but in case any distant guard picked out his silhouette against the silver light on the sea.

The tide was high, and the roar of breaking waves intensified his feelings of vulnerability. His senses couldn't compete with the din rising from below.

He marched on, though this time leaning forwards slightly and taking care to walk only on areas where the white chalk had not been exposed.

On the inboard side this time, he encountered what appeared to be a timber stockade. He began to follow the curved wall of wooden shuttering, but before he had taken more than a few steps, he tripped over a pair of railway sleepers left in the path, perhaps by a careless worker.

He righted himself and continued his journey – hugging the stockade wall, smelling the newness of the wood, and his hands feeling its roughness – until, standing on higher ground, he could see inside the stockade.

As he suspected, the timber wall was enclosing a circular patch of ground the size and shape of a small industrial gasometer. Its floor seemed to be a metallic weave of steel rods. Was it his imagination or was that a figure on the other side of the stockade? He was becoming so nervous he could no longer trust his senses.

He moved on to his third and last objective. It was raining now, though there was still a pale luminescence over the sea and a white disc of a moon had appeared.

There it was! Jean had almost failed to recognise that mound of earth which had been his place of solace for so long, which had sat there silently for four millennia and had now acquired such an unwanted, brutal neighbour. The bunker looked like some fiendish giant sugarloaf. The sand and mica in the wet concrete were sparkling in the dim nocturnal glow. He thought of the fairy tale, *What the Moon Saw*. '… *The dear old moon…*' he said aloud to himself. '… *I kissed my hand to her over and over again… oh what joy filled my heart! I saw a well-known face... of my best friend from home...'*

Before he could investigate further, he noticed a light behind him. Almost immediately, it disappeared, and he could just make out the shape of the prefabricated cabin: his brother's site office. He knew Joseph slept there sometimes. God! There would be guards around, but for Joseph to spend a night practically on top of the tumulus said a lot about the power of Nazi ideology over human neurosis!

As he moved into the shadow of the mortar bunker, his heart thumped as he saw Joseph coming straight towards him. There was no doubt, new peaked cap, OT khaki. Where had he come from? He was twenty or so metres away. He quickened his pace; he had to get clear and away from here. A confrontation with his brother was unthinkable.

Jean was sheltering against the north face of the bunker; Joseph was approaching from the north end of the path where it narrowed to three metres between the tumulus and the cliff edge. There were two options for escape. He could carry on fleeing south, make his way across the stream, and walk round the southern end of the farm. But that would mean crossing the open wheat field where Joseph would be sure to see him. Even if he reached the farm in safety, he would have to walk north again along the road to retrieve his bicycle.

No, his best chance for escape was to walk right round the bunker and the tumulus into the Field of Mars, then back the way he had come. It was risky. If Joseph decided not to follow him and came along the narrow neck of path at the tumulus's northern end, then Jean could be trapped. The two of them might bump straight into one another.

***

Joseph was driving his Citroen south towards Pointe des Galets. It was well after midnight, following a late inspection of two batteries, plus remedial works that had become necessary following the bombing of the rocket site.

He was feeling deadbeat. What's more, he was being troubled by a new voice: somebody called Carmen, fiancée of a badly gored bullfighter by the name of Francisco. Carmen had called off the marriage when she discovered the exact spot on his body where the bull had gored him. Pneumonia had claimed her shortly after her discovery and, tearfully, she insisted that she must reassure Francisco that – in the afterlife – there *was* only one kind of love.

Two kilometres north of the turn-off to the farm, he caught something in the tiny hooded beam of his headlamp. Slowing almost to a stop, he could see Jean's bicycle wedged upright in a ditch and glistening with the rain which had just begun to fall.

What the hell was going on? If Jean was on the construction site, then he was trespassing, and he must stop him before he was arrested.

Minutes later, he was pulling up outside his site hut. He must find out what Jean was up to. He made his way directly to the artillery casemate and began to make his way around its timber wall. Some careless workers had left two railway sleepers obstructing the path, and he made a note to make sure they were moved the next morning.

Suddenly, he heard a thump. He moved into the shadow of the curved timber shuttered wall and was appalled to see his brother picking himself up from the ground only a few metres away.

Hoping that the noise of the rain and sea would mask the scuffling noises he was making, Joseph made his way around the remainder of the curved wall, past the railway sleepers and back into the shadows. It was unlikely that Jean would walk round the installation twice, so Joseph felt safe.

Sure enough, seconds later, he saw his brother complete the circuit of the casemate and stumble out onto the chalk path. He watched, puzzled, as Jean changed his course, seeming to prefer to struggle on the slippery mud rather than take to the freshly exposed surface of the chalk.

Oh God! He had left the light on in the site hut. It was unlikely that it would be seen by Allied aircraft, but if one of the guards saw it and then found Jean, Joseph would be well and truly in the shit. What was he doing here anyway? He was supposed to be safe at home forging his food coupons. This was *real* danger. He must confront and warn him.

Joseph followed the most direct route to the site cabin, extinguished the light, and made towards the mortar bunker; Jean must have reached there by now.

Then he saw him standing in front of the bunker, staring right at him, the cheeky bloody monkey. But Jean looked different. When Joseph had seen him a few minutes ago, he could have sworn that he was wearing his navy guernsey under that rancid-coloured leather jacket. Now he seemed to have adopted a disguise, dressed in a long dirty vest, a muddy-coloured shawl thing, with a metal brooch which was catching the moonlight. What's more, whoever had supplied him with that lot had also unwisely lent him a long blond wig.

Joseph strode directly towards the figure which seemed to glide sideways and seawards. Got you! He felt a grim twinge of uneasiness as the figure raised its right arm. Its hand appeared to be missing.

Whatever or whoever it was, Joseph was now less than three metres away as it rounded the south-east corner of the bunker out of his sight. He raced to the spot, very nearly losing his footing and sliding down the steep escarpment. He was just in time to see the long-haired figure gliding along the south wall of the mortar bunker and disappearing again at its south-west corner. Joseph stumbled forwards, this time passing across the six-metre gap between tumulus berm and cliff edge, past the fortified bunker entrance and onto the seawards wall of the mound.

There was no sign of his fugitive. He shuffled forwards a few paces until he came to the first unblocked entrance to the tumulus and felt himself gazing into its blackness.

'Oh, Jesus no! He can't have gone in there.' Joseph felt a wave of nausea… the thought of his brother inside *that* thing. Fear, terror of the cot, the mother who was going to do Lord knows what to him. He heard himself croak beseechingly, 'Jean! Where are you?'

He tried to get a grip on himself, but it was no good – a "crack" had opened up, and he was staring in horror at himself doing something, holding something in his hand; it was a dagger, a bronze dagger, and he was trying to hide it. Worst of all, he was inside the tumulus. He could feel himself reaching up, finding a gap between two of the clammy stones. There he placed the dagger. Not in any attempt to conceal evidence, it seemed, but suspecting that his life and deeds might be seen by all as ignominious, this might at least assure him of some respect by the deities.

He was crawling, wriggling through the black tunnels within the burial mound, felt the hot skin of his body being ripped and torn against the cold stones. Then he was out in the open.

It felt like his body was trying to breathe air that wasn't there. He couldn't stop himself; he was fleeing, still trapped in the "crack". He could have taken the longer but more gradual slope back to the village, but in his panic, he took the quickest way possible, blundering across the whitestone half circle, straight over the edge, and down the steepest of the bracken-covered slopes. His limbs drove him faster and faster down the hill, first one foot stamping into the undergrowth, then the other. He was out of control, not just his body but his mind.

How could a calm, logical being suddenly degenerate into a stampeding animal? He reached the stream, didn't look for stones on which to cross, just ploughed straight through, his feet raising two arcs of sparkling water. He looked over his shoulder, no person, no thing, but he did not stop until he arrived breathless and choking at the Shadow Gate.

The "crack" closed, and Joseph found he was still rooted to the spot by the tumulus. He hadn't run away, but he had the impression that he had been making a lot of noise; he didn't want that "squarehead" guard coming across, and what the hell was the Shadow Gate?

For a moment, he considered driving round to where he had seen Jean's bike, and waiting for him, but the urgency of the moment had passed. If Jean was on his way back by now, then at least he was out of immediate danger. Joseph would have to wait.

***

Jean had taken a risk, but it was a calculated one. By the time he reached the seawards wall of the tumulus, he knew he wouldn't make it back to its north end before Joseph came around the corner. There were three entrances in the wall, all newly opened. He ducked down and crouched inside the first one. Joseph would never follow him, not in a million years.

By the time he left the refuge of the tumulus, Joseph was nowhere to be seen, and as Jean slithered back along the clifftop path, he felt a sudden disappointment. Joseph had seen him, and he had seen Joseph. Perhaps a meeting might have been a good thing after all. Jean didn't want him to know he'd joined the Resistance, but by now he might have guessed, and he somehow doubted that his brother would report him. Far more likely Joseph would use his manipulative personality to try and persuade him to give it up.

As he walked the last two hundred metres to where his bicycle lay, Jean's feet slipped sideways on the wet earth. The Zeppelin-shaped mist formations had disappeared; the nocturnal landscape was receding; and day was approaching. As his right-hand sought comfort in the inside pocket of his bomber jacket, he had an awful thought. *Where the hell is my Jerusalem Cross?*

CHAPTER 22

TRUTH DAWNS

'We're *all* playing a risky game,' warned Helene as she and Jean sat together. This time they were not at the usual scrub-top table at Chateau de Galets but in the Bar Tabac. She was looking across the table at him and seemed proud at what they'd just told one another.

'I didn't *really* think that you were forging food coupons,' she whispered.

'Joseph gave me a similar story about you,' replied Jean. 'I'd no idea what you were really up to. I'd thought you and that *Boche* captain were having an affair!'

'Look, the only reason I've told you all this is…'

As he leant forwards, he could feel his elbows – hurting as he pressed them down against the tabletop – his palms supporting each side of his head. From the "V" shape between his hands he whispered, 'You know where the magic pool was and that the *Boche* went and filled it in? Well, there's a rocket launching site there now…' Helene nodded.

'There was an RAF raid two nights ago; I was there. I think I've got away with it, probably because I'm the new boy on the team, and the *Boche* has got less information on me.' He took another breath and closed his eyes. 'Raymond and two other blokes have been arrested... I wanted you to know.' He leant backwards in his chair.

'I'm sorry,' she said. 'They won't talk, just try and relax.'

Jean didn't feel so confident.

'There's another thing I've got to tell you, just in case they come for me too.' Jean could feel himself fighting to take control of his breathing.

'We know that the Germans have flying bombs... we've all seen them, and we know that they've got stand-up rockets.' He tried to clear his throat. 'We saw something else. I hardly dare tell you what because I know it sounds like something out of a boy's adventure paper, but all four of us saw it, and we weren't mistaken. A kind of spaceship[5] – huge – God knows how they're going to launch the thing or where to.'

'First the Moon, then Mars.' Jean looked straight into Helene's amber eyes, and he could tell she wasn't joking. 'I believe you. If it's possible to go into outer space, they'll do it; they've got the best scientists in the world.' Then she changed the subject. 'The Nazis will stop at nothing – it's not just the Jews, the gypsies, and the disabled they want rid of. Next, they'll start on the Poles; the blond ones will be all right, but the ones they can't Aryanise – God help them. I know you've always said that this war was about social class, well, I'm sorry, but it's not. It's about race. You've got the right coloured hair anyway, my love.' He smiled mirthlessly.

The coffee machine coughed, and soon Henri was setting down two fresh cups in front of them. Jean knew he had to test out an idea on Helene.

'You know what I've been thinking? Those concrete bunkers that they're building up at Pointe des Galets, in a way they look like Le Vieux Vicente: long, low, dark, and underground. Well, I've seen them, and the Nazis may have ranted on about their "thousand-year reich", but the amount of concrete they've pumped into them, they'll last for at least that. They could even be here four thousand years from now, just like Le Vieux Vicente. Whether the Allies win the war or not, those buggers will last into eternity, temples without religion[6] they are... well, to their infernal ideology, that is!'

Jean took several deep breaths.

'You know your idea about ley lines? Well, they could easily have placed that mortar bunker on the south-west corner of the tumulus. I don't know a damn thing about military matters, but I know enough to see that the position at Le Vieux Vicente is impregnable to infantry and tanks. If the Allies don't arrive with bunker-busting tanks, then the crew can sit there merrily tossing mortars down into the meadow below and nobody will be able to get near. The only weak spot of that bunker is on the inner side of the tumulus facing the sea, and you'd need a piddling small tank to get between it and the edge.'

Henri was staring across at them. Jean tried to lower his voice.

'What I'm saying, Amber, is that they could have sited that bunker closer to the edge. By closing the gap, they would have achieved a hundred per cent impregnability, but they've shifted the site so...' he paused again to check where Henri was looking, '...if *your* ley line does exist, they've sacrificed an impregnable position in order for the ley line to pass through the structure... and the magic pool; they've put that rocket site on another ley line. I know I drove Joe mad since the Nazis came to power, banging on about how they were addicted to the occult, the supernatural, the mysterious...'

Then, as if she had suddenly decided to draw a line under their discussion, Helene moved on.

'Joe's in a really dangerous position.'

'You've just said we all are!'

'Yes, but he's the most vulnerable of all of us. He's spent most of his life trying to outsmart people; now he's being manipulated by the Nazis. He's just their type, the ideal personality who'll be impelled to fall in with their system, mistakenly thinking that it will meet his own ends.'

Jean looked closely at his sister. 'I saw him, you know; what I mean is, he saw *me* on the bluff by the tumulus last night.' Jean grinned. 'He looked genuinely terrified – showed some real emotion this time – I think he thought that I was the *deildergheist*! I don't think he'll give me away; he's crazy but he won't dare tell the Germans that his brother is in the Resistance, but he won't confront me either because he's a coward – he always has been.'

Jean cupped his hands round his nose and mouth and stared out of the window; then he suddenly removed his hands.

'You know he tried to kill me once – three years ago.'

'He's always been jealous of you, poppet.'

So that's all Helene was going to say on the matter. She didn't seem to want any details. It felt better to have told her, but Jean still needed to talk.

'I'm glad Robert got away from the family. It's given him the chance to see the oddities of life at Chateau des Galets and Le Vieux Vicente, rather than trying to convince himself it's the norm like Joseph has done. You've got to get away from a place in order to grow into something else. But it's important not to leave it too late, otherwise you may well get away, but you'll still have a stunted view of life.

'Joseph always argued that Paris was full of sharks and that it was the rat race, but he's made his own rat race right here by seeing charlatans around every corner. He's made a career for himself where doors won't open, and *dog eats dog*.

Doors *will* open for Robert. He'll get to the Sorbonne one day, I'm sure – he told me that it's his ambition to teach there; he'll do it.' Jean smiled.

'Maybe I'm wrong; maybe we can't change the world after all. All we can do is to change ourselves. It's as if each small shift everybody makes individually starts off a tiny metamorphosis in society; then it gets bigger and bigger, so then it's society that starts forcing each person to change, and that's the bit we don't like, so we try and change it back. It's a fear of evolution.'

This time, Helene looked out of the café window, took a sharp breath, and looked back at Jean.

'You know, people say that everything's the fault of the war. They say it's responsible for shaping us, but it's not really like that; it's our personalities which are driving us. The war hasn't turned Joseph into a difficult character; he's been like that since he was a boy.'

'I know, but you can't say that Le Vieux Vicente hasn't influenced our lives; it's had a real grip on the three of us – though Joseph's always denied it. It's been like a drug that the three of us have been taking without admitting it to ourselves. A bit like Emile's uncle who drank secretly, remember? He insisted to everyone that he had it under control but in the end, he drank himself to death.

'Joseph has always called me the dreamer, but it's him who's been living in a fantasy world. You and I have finally escaped its influence by joining the fight for our country, while Joseph is still well and truly under the thumb of Le Vieux Vicente... and what about you and Luft?' he asked abruptly.

'Now you know what I'm really up to, you see not everything is as it seems, my pet. Captain Luft is a man who is beyond healing, but I really believe that Joseph can be healed – one day.'

'You know, we've never talked like this – we could have done, easily – we should have been much closer sooner.'

'I'm to blame – too much hero worship of Joe and not enough seeing *your* good points. Mum stereotyped you as a dreamer – had me down as flighty, comical, and queer – and it sticks; no matter how much you try to change your thinking, you can't. You have to branch out, do something of your own volition, then you can really start thinking for yourself. We've done it at last.'

Jean put his hand on Helene's. 'When you see that life is not infinite, you start thinking about what might come after, what else there might be.'

'Don't think that's it, my love, if we really believed that that's all there is to life, we would be like children never managing to grow up; of course there's something more. Life on earth is just a fraction of eternal life.'

Jean smiled. 'I can just hear Joseph saying, "So, you want another life, do you? Well, you'd bloody well better try to start living this one now then!".'

'Four thousand years from now, what *will* there be left, after everything else has gone?' asked Helene. She quickly answered her own question, 'Just love.'

Helene kissed Jean on the cheek and moved towards the door.

'That's right, leave me to pay, won't you!' He grinned.

***

Ever since he had seen Jean at the Pointe des Galets, Joseph had meant to confront him, if only to warn him. His little brother had to understand that he couldn't just go wandering about the cliffs in the middle of a curfew.

At 0400 hours, on the second morning after that incident,

Joseph had a shock. Awoken by the noise of an army jeep in the farmyard, he hurried down from his bleak bunk in the gatehouse and watched as three soft-capped soldiers got out and went into the farmhouse. Seconds later they emerged, pushing Jean in front of them – clad in trousers and singlet – then into the jeep. As the vehicle pulled away and vanished into the dark, the full September moon revealed that Helene, like himself, had quickly put on a mackintosh over nightclothes.

Standing staring at one another, she spoke. Her voice sounded odd – as if it didn't really belong to her – like an automaton.

'The Allies will come; your Nazi friends will be beaten, and you, my big brother, will regret everything.' The last phrase – though spoken with her back turned as she made her way towards the farmhouse door – was sufficiently audible for Joseph to feel a pang of doubt about the true meaning of that strange tableau which he had witnessed at Captain Luft's lodgings. Should he warn Luft?

CHAPTER 23

PERSUASION

Joseph returned to his miserable gatehouse office. The more he thought about the situation, the queasier he became. Jean at liberty was dangerous enough with his floppy, unformed ideas about life, but Jean incarcerated and under twenty-four-hour scrutiny by the Gestapo would be like a loose cannon. One careless comment and the whole of Joseph's little empire could come crashing down.

He could see an obvious flaw in his first notion of going along with the intention of convincing Luft of Jean's innocence. Jean clearly *wasn't* innocent – the photographs had been found by his mother, and no doubt the Nazis had discovered something similar. It would be typical of Jean's slapdashery. Coupon-forging was a misdemeanour; it wasn't as if his brother had been involved in sabotage or belonged to a Resistance group – such organisations didn't take on dreamers.

Maman was always saying "anything can happen in war", but this wasn't war any longer; it was hegemony with clear rules, and those in charge were reasonable men.

Joseph's thoughts on the restoration of order didn't last long. Like the discovery of a rat's nest under a barn, there was something else which sprung into his mind and needed his immediate attention. Why had Jean been on the clifftop two nights ago?

Jean wasn't just batty; he was barmy. His fantasies had finally broken loose, got the better of him, and he had been overcome with curiosity to see his beloved tumulus once again close up; he'd also been coaxed into nasty little Raymond's forging enterprise. Jean wasn't to blame – his weak-mindedness had let him down – it had all been a mistake; he would be no use to the Nazis; they could send him home; Constance and Helene could keep a close eye on him – a kind of house arrest – and he would be out of harm's way. What he needed was nursing and love, and it would teach Helene a lesson; she would have to do what she was told by Luft.

***

Joseph had been rather taken aback at the ease with which he had secured a private interview with his brother. *Private*, of course, he took with a large pinch of salt. Whatever room he met in with Jean would be bugged; the event would possibly be tape-recorded, perhaps even filmed with a hidden camera. Luft sounded eager for the two of them to meet. He said nothing to Joseph about the charges, and Joseph did not ask.

Joseph's plan seemed to be working nicely, but his mind was still far from being calm. In the cave at the front of his head, he was being stalked by another voice, that of a Baron Sachaverell Ponsonby – English probably – who seemed beside himself with remorse. It appeared that his wife Emilia had eloped with a stable boy. Ponsonby had shot himself in a fever of jealousy and self-loathing. Posthumously, he realised that his performance as a husband had been so wretched that he felt compelled to tell Emilia that and to wish her well.

The meeting was to take place at the old police station, currently used by the Gestapo. Joseph parked his Citroen in the narrow street and walked to the building.

Six storeys high, the edifice had an air of the theatrical. Not an old structure, but the rusticated stone blocks around the front entrance looked as if they had been produced by a scenic artist preparing sets for an Italian opera. Joseph stared queerly at the chubby stone cherubs.

Many of the buildings lower down in the street, towards the port, had been damaged in the now frequent air raids by the RAF, but this address was on the edge of the bombing zone and, so far, unscathed.

Luft was apparently not in the building, and Joseph was met by a French policeman – wearing a white cloth armband stencilled in black *by order of the Wehrmacht* – who rattily demanded his signature and pushed him along a paint-smelling corridor.

Joseph walked, with the man following – prodding him every few seconds – and as he blundered clumsily on the terrazzo, he could hear the rhythmic sound of a bunch of keys swaying behind him.

He was shoved through door after door. *Suck, hiss; clonk, clink clonk.* It was like being inside a giant pair of bellows, and each space they passed through, the air seemed to contain less oxygen than the last, as if it were gradually being pumped out of the building.

'Stop!' ordered Joseph's unlikely fellow collaborator, the voice screechy like a magpie. 'Push!' yelled the magpie. 'Go on, *push!*' as if it had turned into an angry midwife. Joseph pushed on a shiny panel in the wall and found himself standing at the top of a dimly lit stairwell. The heat was stifling, and there was a heavy stench of linseed oil.

'Go on!' screamed the magpie-midwife. There was only one way to go, that was down, and Joseph could feel the panic rising in him as he became aware of a low rumbling, rising from far below. He could feel a "crack" opening.

In his prehistoric phantasm, he appeared to have fallen into a suffocating warren of small, dark holes, full of deafening noise.

A series of wild flashes drew the Bronze Age Joseph's eye. The caverns in which he found himself seemed to be full of the movement of many men, all engaged in different activities. To Joseph, it was rather like being in the middle of a summer thunderstorm, only instead of sky fire, there were blood-coloured lights surging up from the earth; in place of the sweet smell of warm sky water on hyssop leaves there was an unearthly stink, one of fear, battle, and death. He fought with an almost irresistible urge to retreat and shuddered as he pictured the wretched, pale slave boys and girls who were marched every day to the tin and copper mines, condemned to crawl through tunnels. Worst of all, they couldn't light torches down there, so everything was black and had to be done by touch.

The "crack" closed, and at the foot of the stair, Joseph could see a door. It looked like the entrance to a monumental safe, and the magpie-midwife was already at work strutting, pecking, and nodding while it tried every key and combination.

'Just fucking stand there, won't you!' it screeched, but there was little else Joseph could do. The accent was a southern French one. 'Come on, you bastard, help!' came the voice, and something claw-like grabbed at Joseph's arm. Joseph could feel the steel door swing outwards. The linseed oil odour was fragrant in comparison with the grotesque emanation from the space within.

As Joseph stepped across the threshold, he felt as if he was entering a pottery kiln after a recent firing. Every surface seemed to be abrasive and full of heat. The space bore no relationship to his concept of a room. It was impossible to know which planes were vertical and which were horizontal. There were pockmarked pipes, fat metal tubes, and riveted ribs running everywhere. There was no window, apparently no ventilation, no sign of a toilet – not even a bucket.

'Five minutes!' came the screech, as the door haltingly closed behind him. Joseph even doubted whether *he* might live that long – was Jean still alive?

The chamber was lit by a dim lamp mounted on a bulwark. Banged close up against a concrete rampart was a metal frame, onto which had been shoved several railway sleepers, and plonked on top of that a pad of... something, a few millimetres in thickness. Upon this hostile pallet lay a long blond-headed human, face downwards. Joseph could see it was Jean because the large stockinged feet protruded over the edge of the hellish bunk. Several seconds ticked by, but the shape did not alter its form.

'Well, another fine mess you've got us into!' chimed Joseph in his imitation of Oliver Hardy. The figure remained motionless. Joseph felt a tug of panic in his bowel.

'Have you any water?' Surely that croaking couldn't be Jean? Joseph waited for the head to turn towards him, but it didn't.

'No.'

'God! Well, *I* didn't know they'd put you in the bloody boiler room!' The only water in *this* space was inside their bodies and those sodding pipes. Jean wasn't going to last more than a few hours locked up in here.

'Look, we haven't got much time. You need to tell them what you've been doing.'

'I'm not telling them anything.'

'Don't be so bloody stupid; they know all about it anyway. They just need to hear you say it was all a mistake.'

'You don't understand.' The face remained hidden.

'Tell them! All about the coupons – and Raymond – and they'll let you out. I'll see to that. I've got some influence – so has Amber, we can get you out, look after you.'

'You don't understand; you never have.'

'All right then, if you're going to be so bloody honourable then don't tell them about Raymond; just tell them about the coupons.'

The body in front of him remained inert. Joseph's stomach turned over as he remembered Helene's last words to him: '… and you, my brother, will regret everything.' He hadn't told her he was coming here, but she might find out from Luft. He had to win this.

'Look, Jean, Mum and Amber are blaming me for what's happened to you. For their sake and mine, just confess, and they'll let you go.'

'They've charged me.'

'Yes, with coupon-forging.'

'No, with sabotage.'

'You know you really do need looking after.' Joseph was laughing now.

'I'm serious; sabotage and being a Resistance member.'

For crying out loud, what was he talking about? He had clearly dehydrated to the point of delirium.

There was a minute change in the atmospheric pressure within the chamber as the heavy door began to open outwards. Joseph leaned forwards so that his mouth was almost touching Jean's left ear.

'All right, hang on, don't tell them anything, and I'll have you out of here by tomorrow,' he heard himself whisper. Jean's face still remained obscured.

'You don't understand. You never have, and you never will.'

***

Joseph was standing alone in the cruck barn. It seemed to be the best place to meet – away from the farmhouse and Constance. His mother would know about Jean's arrest, but she wouldn't be aware that Joseph had just been to visit him.

As he waited for his sister, he found he was standing exactly on the spot where Luft had stood a year and a half ago, and as he sensed that small lozenge of sunlight warming the top of his head, he felt anger. This wasn't a new emotion of course. It was just that he'd never shown it, but what Jean had just told him appalled him. His vexation wasn't the thought of folk joining, or being members of, a resistance group; it was the sheer preposterousness of Jean's claim.

Joseph had still not spoken to Luft, so he had no confirmation of the charges against Jean, but they would certainly not be of the valiant nature which his brother was suggesting. It was all aimed at him of course. The figure lying on the makeshift bunk had been in such a fit of pique that it would not even turn its face to him. It was revenge for Joseph's superiority over the years, the skill he had harnessed to rein in his brother when he spoke out of turn. It was the adept way he had covered for Jean's gaucheness, kept him out of all manner of scrapes, and the humane way he had averted disaster that evening when Jean ventured too close to the edge of the cliff. Here was Joseph running around after him, while in return Jean was pretending to be the big fucking hero!

He heard a polite cough as Helene stepped softly on the lime and milk floor.

'Little Estelle and her big sister have come in to be with *Maman* while I'm here. Albert's still in custody. They're saying he was involved in the raid on the magic pool.'

'Well at least Jean's not in that position.' Joseph felt he had the edge now. Helene was looking subdued. Her defiant little speech of 0300 hours that morning seemed to have lost its edge. 'I'll have Jean out of there by the end of tomorrow morning. I've agreed to meet Luft very early.' Helene looked back at him oddly. She really had to understand that these situations weren't the same. Albert was a saboteur; Jean was taking part in a forging racket, and a poorly organised one at that. What's more, Albert didn't have a brother in the OT. He could see her swallowing with difficulty. No doubt she was seeing Luft that evening and was wondering how to play it. All this would have put paid to her own efforts in the world of document forgery for, like Joseph, she was a collaborator – worse, an SS whore. She was in it up to her neck now, but it was no good crying over spilt milk.

'How was he?'

'Oh, his usual self. Yes, they're feeding him. It's a bit hot in there though. Don't worry, little sis. We'll have him out by lunchtime tomorrow, but you and Mum are going to really have to keep an eye on him this time. I'm going to stress the instability issue, his impressionable nature – not too much of course, otherwise they'll pack him straight off to Grafeneck like they did with Eugene, but just enough to convince them that, with the right help from us, he could be a useful member of French society. An emotional age of say... fifteen?'

Again, Helene swallowed with apparent difficulty. Still, she said nothing, though her eyes looked as if they wanted to.

The cat had really lost its tongue this time. He'd thought for one moment in the shocking stillness of that early morning that she might have got herself involved with the *Forces Françaises Libres*, but no. Anyway, Jean and Helene were two of a kind, and those movements were serious organisations. They might be impressed by someone who claimed she could see in the dark, but they'd start looking sideways when they realised that she was more interested in stones than people, happier boiling up dandelion leaves and spouting on about ley lines than reading a real map.

***

17 September 1942

I've decided to come out and tell Joe what I'm doing. It's a big step, I know, but I've worked it out that he won't be able to do anything about it. It's complicated – too involved to write down at the moment – but he's become a kind of prisoner, and I don't think we've got anything to fear from him.

I'm sorry about Jean, but at least we know where he is, and although things may be uncertain for him, Joe is certainly heading straight for disaster.

Standing in the barn with Joe, I felt so sorry for him. Neither of us can do anything; it's like we've both been put in glass-sided coffins with the lids screwed down, and we're just lying there staring at one another. He'll go and see Luft feeling so righteous about Jean, and he doesn't have a clue. Also, it won't be just Luft; it'll be the Gestapo, and that's what I'm really worried about. I've been thinking maybe I should destroy all my diaries. The G is sure to raid the farm? But I'm not going to because the diaries are part of us, the family, I mean. It's like there's nine separate entities in this family: Dad – gone but here in spirit – Maman, Robert, Jean, Joseph, me... oh, Balzac, of course, the diaries... and I forgot one – how could I? – it's Le Vieux Vicente; Jean's right – it's become our gaoler.

CHAPTER 24

AN UNINTENTIONAL WITNESS

Captain Luft had taken the unusual step – so thought Joseph – of agreeing to meet him at 0600 hours.

He had been unable to sleep and had paid little heed to time over the last twenty-four hours. There was somebody called Mohammet pestering him from that cave at the front of his head. It seemed that the man had been battered to death by his lover Malek in a tiff over money concerning the running of the small bar in Rabat – for expats – which Mohammet had been bequeathed from Gerard, retired gangster on the run from the mother country. Mohammet wanted to tell Malek that he forgave him and that it hadn't been worth arguing over in the first place because on the "other side", the Moroccan dirham was irrelevant; there was only one currency there, and that was love.

Joseph's watch said that it was shortly before 0300; he could go for a walk in the Old Town; why not? As an official in OT uniform, he could do so with impunity. Also, he needed to relieve himself before his meeting with Luft. Then perhaps he would return and doze off in the jeep.

He climbed the hill and passed through one of the ancient stone gates which led towards the citadel. On most nights, it would have been difficult to see where he was going in the blackout, but in the light of the near full moon, the granite cobbles under his feet sparkled after recent rain.

When he reached the Palais de Justice, he turned north down a narrow, winding street which led out of the place. Unsurprisingly, there was not a soul about, and he felt as if he was on the stage of a huge theatre, in the silence before the prologue.

He was just about to enter the public urinal when he caught sight of a figure some fifty or so paces in front of him. He knew the movements of that uniformed figure well. It was Captain Luft. What was he doing here at this time? Luft's apartment was outside the city wall over to the west from here.

As the *hauptmann* turned east around a corner, Joseph sprinted forwards and peeped round just as the man was passing in front of the west end of the cathedral. What was he up to? Who was he going to meet? Joseph felt himself gripped with a strange kind of jealousy.

Why was he so interested in Luft? That disturbing feeling of familiarity had been nagging away at him. Several times, Joseph had been on the point of digging whatever it was out of his subconscious. It was certainly an entity which was at large within one of his "cracks" – definitely a Nordic hunter of a wild sort and of strange appearance. It was something to do with the hair upon the head of the prehistoric male which had been hacked to within a thumbnail's length. All that remained of shoulder-length locks was a fist-sized lump in the centre of his head the height of a man's hand, held vertically, with jelly perhaps taken from the stalk of boiled fireweed. Not only did it give the blond hunter extra height, but it also gave the impression that he was always alert and ready to receive information. The bizarre cranial sculpture had the appearance of being capable of trapping sound itself. There was a bronze bolt as well, through the man's chin. Forged in the metalman's workshop, and here it now was wobbling around as the ancient Luft spoke, acting as a kind of punctuation…

Joseph stayed pressed into the shadows until Luft passed out of sight, north this time. Joseph tiptoed past the dark opening of the cathedral's west door. Perhaps Luft would carry on, go through the north gate, and on to his lodgings? Halfway down the street, he saw the captain staring up at the cathedral's south door, before purposefully mounting the steps and disappearing inside.

Joseph had been so intent on his quarry that he almost failed to notice the three Mercedes Benz limousines parked outside and the two helmeted guards. There was a man and a woman sitting in the rear seat of one of the limousines. If he had been in his right mind, he would have continued past, but he was no longer the master of his own actions; he felt compelled by some force to follow. He was in uniform, so why not?

He bounded up the steps unchallenged and found himself standing on the stone flags of the lobby. He stared straight ahead. There was no light other than cold moonlight falling upon the stone figures which stood in niches around the base of the dome eighty metres above him. He could just make out the words *Ego vobiscum sum* carved into a stone frieze just below the figures.

To his left was a wooden door, and through its glass panel he could see a dim glow. Without thinking, he pushed it and began a careful descent of an uneven stone staircase.

The sea air which had been lingering in the lobby seemed unable to penetrate down here. His body felt hot and wet, yet the atmosphere was cold and clammy. It was as if he had entered somewhere distinctly unpleasant, but he must press on.

He found himself in a low chamber lit by a single gaslight which was mounted on the stair behind him. The floor sloped away steeply, and he was puzzled by what appeared to be the shadowy bulk of a large dog sleigh, minus dog but with an enormous driver, towering over the whole contraption. As his eyes became accustomed to the murk, the truth dawned that this was a scale model of the cathedral, made of wood, and that the evil-looking figure was in fact the elongated dome of the building.

Laughing at the strangeness of it, Joseph wondered why the model had not been wedged on the horizontal instead of being poised there, as if it was about to break loose and career away down the slope further into the depths of the crypt.

He continued down into a long gallery. The floor seemed level but so heavily pitted that he had to feel each step with caution. Some distance in front, he could see another dim light source, and he thought he could hear voices chanting, but that was probably the rain outside. There was a sound of dripping water.

A new feeling came upon him; it was as if someone or something was following him – no, following wasn't quite right – it was a presence, right behind him. Almost as if some sinister but unseen bird was weightlessly perching on his shoulder. There was still time to return to the entrance and leave, but that invisible claw which seemed to have drawn him here from the street was starting to press down on him.

As he struggled past the next gas lamp, he saw that the walls of the chambers had been painted with bold "zigzag" motifs and scenes from the Old Testament. Joseph had never actually been in an art gallery, but he had an instinctive feeling that these murals had been quite crudely done, possibly by amateurs, and in a hurry. Just by the gaslight, his eye traced a rather grubby Adam and Eve being expelled from the Garden of Eden.

He turned a corner into yet another chamber, at the end of which two more lamps were burning, one on each side of the space. This time he was sure he could hear the murmur of human voices and see a flickering of light on the rough, curved roof. There was a strong smell of damp and something else – familiar – but he couldn't place it.

He was a world away from the industry of the Pointe des Galets, and he felt gripped by that feeling he sometimes had of standing on the edge of a precipice and being physically drawn towards it. Part of him wanted to turn and run, yet the other, more powerful, part of his self just had to see what was round the next corner.

He was trying to walk on his toes, leaning against the ghastly smelling wall soiled with God knows what, pulling himself along, scraping, scratching, scarring.

The space around him seemed to be a repository for large fragments of wooden arches and crumbling stone sculptures. Some of them he even recognised as having come from other buildings in the town which had been damaged by the bombing. Standing here alone in the gloom, they appeared to be endowed with the macabre.

As he reached the end of the chamber and turned the corner, his whole body was abruptly illuminated by a pulsing light. What in God's name *was* it? Without thinking, he stamped his foot to try and reassure himself and winced as the sound answered him. He was gawping into a huge, circular space, its curved roof a mass of moving light, its volume full of human figures, and all about him were the sounds of human voices.

He could see a dark tunnel leading off to his right and had the strength of mind to drive his body into it, away from the light and the unknown figures. He stumbled on, over the stone floor, winding round to the left this time until, once again, he found himself able to view the extraordinary scene, this time without danger of discovery.

He edged forwards and squeezed himself into a niche in the wall. From here, he had a full view.

All the tunnels and chambers appeared to converge on the giant circular "theatre" which lay before him. Half of the floor area had been flooded with what looked like water, leaving an island in the centre and a dry ledge some three metres wide around its circumference.

The pulsating light he was witnessing was coming from fires burning around the edges of the space, reflecting in the water and producing a wild dancing effect on the roof. Each fire – Joseph counted twelve of them – came from within a stone urn which had been placed on a pedestal of similar material. The floor of the "island" had been marked out in white paint in the sign of the sun wheel, and he could see other markings which hinted at being characters from a foreign alphabet.

Grouped around the water's edge, Joseph could see some thirty figures, mostly wearing SS uniform. He spotted Luft, standing almost opposite him with other similarly ranking officers. Some of the figures were helmeted; at least two were wearing goggles, while another duo was – quite inexplicably – wearing gas masks. He could only speculate that they wished to conceal their identities at this hellish-looking ceremony, in a similar way to that which an executioner might wish to do.

He felt the disgusting air rush into his mouth, as at the centre of the group standing in front of him, he caught sight of the unmistakeable head of Heinrich Himmler, the torchlight flashing on his spectacles.[7] The head stared to the front, while the arms gripped a soft-looking white object. Joseph looked for women in the group, but none appeared to be present. Then he remembered the woman sitting in the limousine.

The voices continued; Joseph caught the phrases: "church of the blood" and "the blood of the people carrying the spirit of the race". The *reichsminister* dipped his fingers in a bowl offered by one of the goggle-wearers and made what appeared to Joseph to be a sign over the soft white bundle.

From his shoulder-wide niche in the side of the tunnel, Joseph's eye settled on another Old Testament fresco, and he found himself gazing at Judith dangling the severed head of Holofernes. A ghastly thought occurred to him. If he was caught here as a foreign national, he would be shot as a spy, but as a payrolled member of Organisation Todt, he would be seen to have committed an act of treason against the State and would be executed by guillotine, perhaps in the yard of the very building where he was intending to meet Luft within an hour!

He remembered Jean telling him that the Nazis were addicted to the occult. 'They're all at it: Himmler, Rosenburg, Hess...' Joseph had said it was all "tosh"; the Nazis were "down-to-earth practical men", doers and high achievers, rather like Joseph in fact.

He felt as if he was Aeneas, who had just fallen through into the underworld, but he must resurface; he had to survive and argue for the life of his brother... but to do that he had to save his own first.

Joseph knew that in order to get out of this, he must – within the space of the next few minutes – use every scrap of cunning and ingenuity. If he tried to leave straightaway, he might encounter latecomers or be challenged by the guards. If he left it too late, he could attract attention as he left the building. He even had a vision of his being locked in the crypt and missing the meeting with Luft.

The *reichsführer*-SS, accompanied by other high-ranking officers, one of whom was now holding "the white bundle", left the chamber; Joseph eased himself out of his niche and edged away from the main arena back down the tunnel.

When he reached the first long gallery, he had to pause in the shadows as groups of men poured past chattering and laughing. Then there was a hiatus as slightly less than half of the group – including the gas mask wearers – remained in the main "theatre".

It was now or never, and as the first group passed out of sight around the corner, Joseph sprinted forwards and hovered at the spot where they had just left. His heart was in his mouth. If the first group paused, or the loiterers set off while he was still waiting at the corner, he would be discovered. He almost cried out as he heard the group behind him approach the end of the gallery, but in the same instant, he saw the SS men in front of him turn the corner and he hurled himself after them.

He paused, gulping foetid air as he peered round the next corner. The group in front of him were still in the sloping chamber. Then, coming from behind him, he heard the unmistakable sound of air being pumped round the inside of ill-fitting footwear: *prup, prup, prup, prup*. Clearly, there was one man a short distance behind him. Joseph had to get off this gallery without delay; anything would have to do. He found it: a shallow niche in the wall. Only coming to chin height, and he had to bend his head sideways against its roof. *Prup, prup*, came the noise of the badly fitting boot. As it passed the gaslight nearest to Joseph's hiding place, he caught sight of an enormous shadow on the roof. It looked like a giant ostrich picking its way along. At the same time, Joseph spotted something directly opposite him which amplified his mounting fear.

Leaning against the wall of a much larger recess was a gilt-framed mirror, dusty but still capable of providing a reflection of the concealed Joseph. Oh Lord, why had he picked this place?

Standing right next to the mirror were two life-sized carved wooden statues of monks, presumably broken off from a longer frieze. The two surviving ecclesiastical figures were depicted standing in close procession, each with its hand resting on the shoulder of the body in front.

Out of the corner of his right eye, Joseph could now see the Ostrich, an SS captain dressed in a uniform similar to Luft. As the Ostrich paused level with the mirror, Joseph felt himself gagging. If only, he gasped with irony, he could have thrown a bucket of ash over himself; standing with his knees pressed together and feet splayed out into the corners of the niche, he too could have passed for a statue.

But the *hauptsturmführer* seemed interested only in his *own* reflection in the mirror, not in what lay beyond. Up came his right hand, raising his cap into the air and replacing it on his head. He repeated the action, this time slightly bending his left knee and smiling into the mirror as he did so.

This was embarrassing. Surely the others must come soon and put an end to the absurd display. Then the captain's eye fell upon the two carved monks. Keeping his body in front of the mirror, he aligned himself with the rearmost figure – slapstick style. The cap remained on his head, but only after being adjusted to a rather daring angle. His white-gloved right hand was now pointing forwards, horizontal, and poking just above the waistline of the statue in front, while his left hand thrust behind his back, palm upwards.

As Joseph squinted in horror, up went the captain's right knee. With his neck thrust forwards, the pose was clearly intended to emulate that of an Egyptian dancer, or rather the popular music hall interpretation of one.[8]

Crushed into his niche, Joseph began to sob silently; *Please God... if there is a God, please make him stop.* Clearly this was it. It was the end. He would be caught. The writing was there on the wall, and it was *his* head which Judith was dangling. He would without doubt be executed, and it was all going to be the fault of this clown!

There were murmurs from behind as other officers advanced along the gallery, and quickly the captain sidestepped out of the recess, adjusted his headgear and resumed his journey as if nothing had happened. The *prup, prup, prup* of the boot began once again. Joseph hardly dared breathe.

Soon, others were passing his hiding place. He watched them as they rounded the final corner into the sloping chamber which contained the scale model of the cathedral. Joseph followed, but he could hear them lingering at the top of the stairs in the main lobby. He would have to wait a little longer. Damn it! He could hear more voices coming along the gallery behind him. There was nothing else for it but to crouch behind the infernal scale model of the cathedral until they had gone.

Squatting down, Joseph was well concealed. He heard three new voices enter the chamber, and by peering over the balustrade of the roof of the model, he could just see them. All three were officers. Hell! They were stopping; they were going to have a chat!

One man had a very long neck and the general appearance of a goose. The second was short with no neck and looked like a bulldog, while the third man was simply very fat. He could hear the chatter. His German wasn't great, but he fathomed that the conversation was about stamp collecting. For crying out loud, why couldn't they talk about women like normal soldiers!

'King George V's collection will soon be the property of the Third Reich,' exclaimed the Goose gleefully, while Bulldog's uncle had once seen a British Guiana one cent magenta.

Joseph desperately needed to pee. The situation had been urgent even before he began to follow Luft. Now it was critical; he *had* to go. He looked around for an improvised pissoir. There was nothing. He couldn't do it on the floor; it would just wash down the slope straight under the feet of the three officers. Then, in a flash, it came to him. The model had been designed to stand outside in the rain, and like any respectable piece of miniature architecture, it contained its own built-in drainage system with a sump.

The only thing that remained was to raise his body into a vertical position, which he could do and still be concealed behind the elongated dome of the piece. Gingerly, he stood up, with his face pressed hard up against the wooden rods which acted as columns supporting the dome. He now had a view of the three SS philatelists.

As he finally relieved himself into the guttering of the model's roof, he felt a surge of heroism. The model was about the scale of 1.33 he reckoned, so this is what Gulliver must have felt like in Lilliput when he was putting out the fire. He smiled as he listened to the fat officer droning on about the Cape of Good Hope, while the Goose was claiming that it knew someone who had acquired a Falkland Islands half penny dated 1891. He had earned this moment of elation.

But something was wrong. The drainpipes on the model

must have been blocked. Instead of draining away into the sump, the contents of Joseph's bladder were filling the channel which ran around the edge of the model. Gravity had already taken most of the liquid over to the other side where the three men stood. To make matters worse, the Bulldog was now leaning against the far side of the construction; his hand grasping the edge of the channel was only millimetres away. Joseph was on the point of hysteria. If the level rose any further, or if the Bulldog stretched its fingers out, it would feel the water; it would still be warm. All hell would be let loose.

There was a shout from the lobby above. The Bulldog released its grip on the edge of the model; the three soldiers marched towards the stair, and Joseph moaned with relief as he heard the crunch of boots on stone steps. He made a final dash, paused, cautiously mounted the stairs, and peered through the glass vision panel of the door. Thank God no one was in the entrance lobby. He eased the door open, gulping the sea air. The night seemed still; the limousines were gone; and in his euphoria, he even managed a *Heil Hitler* as he raced down the steps past the guards.

Joseph walked quickly through the north gate, then doubled back to the street that would take him down towards the port and to his meeting place with Luft.

As he reached the highest point of the town, he saw that the western sky was lit from below with a crimson glow. Whilst he had been in the crypt, there had been an air raid. The river's edge, and the port, a distance of some three kilometres, had been livened by numerous fires. Some emitted white light, others pink. In one macabre scene, two steel cranes had collapsed onto one another. Lit from below by an eerie green light, they had the appearance of two colossal skeletal beasts locked in a fight to the death.

As he walked down the hill, the devastation of the air raid passed out of his sight. He reached his jeep, climbed in, and fell into a sleep of nervous exhaustion.

CHAPTER 25

AN EXPERIMENT GOES WRONG

Joseph was dreaming.

He had fallen into a large, partially frozen lake and was trying to climb out onto the ice. The fact that he was not in his own body wasn't helping matters. He had four legs and, worse still, hooves, which slipped on the jagged ice. Out of the corner of his eye, he could see upon his own head a pair of paddle-shaped antlers covered with frozen pond weed, while just below his eyes, he was aware of a large, broad, furry muzzle.

He could see the skeletal fingers of trees on the bank, tantalisingly close, could see Luft, standing smiling at him from among the crisp white powdered fronds of bracken. Joseph shouted at the captain to give him a hand but was dismayed to hear his own voice emerge no more than a miserable, high-pitched braying.

As Joseph made another fruitless attempt to climb clear of the icy water, the image of Luft vanished, only to be replaced with that of another blond man, the hair of whom was fashioned into a vertical sculptured mast.

The chin beneath the piercing blue eyes bore what looked like a bronze stud. Once again Joseph shouted, but this time, all he could raise was a sound like the bleating of a calf. He watched as the man's right forearm crossed behind his left shoulder. *A lasso*, thought Joseph hopefully, but no, the forearm re-emerged bearing a flint-tipped arrow notched to take the gut-stringed bow he was grasping in his left hand.

Joseph was frantic. He must, once and for all, convince Luft – or whoever it was – that he was *not* a moose. Yet again he tried to shout, and this time he awoke, conscious that he was making the kind of strange yodelling noise made by an agitated boy whose voice is beginning to break with the onset of puberty.

In the same moment, he realised that he had fallen asleep with the jeep window open, and as he wiped the saliva from his chin, his eye met that of an early worker on his way to the port.

It was 0555 hours. He had to meet Luft in five minutes.

The police station doors were open, and one helmeted sentinel stood in silence. Joseph strode into the brightly lit lobby, across the ringing terrazzo floor, and up to the steel-gated lift.

'Yes, can I help you?!' barked a green-uniformed figure wearing a shako-style hat. Before Joseph could answer, a squad of helmeted men shouldering rifles marched from one side of the entrance hall to the other. The last man of the group carried a flag, which – quite uncharacteristically, thought Joseph – was being trailed along the floor. *Well, that's bad luck for that squad for the rest of this year anyway*, he thought.

The crash of boots died away; Joseph was ushered into the lift, and escorted to the first floor. He was marched along more terrazzo until the shako-hatted policeman paused at a heavy panelled hardwood door. It was already slightly ajar when the adjutant timidly knocked, inadvertently nudging it further to reveal Captain Luft standing in the room.

In spite of what he had witnessed only a couple of hours previously, Joseph felt a feeling of relief at seeing Luft, but it was short-lived as the door swung open further to disclose a second person in the room.

Seated at the end of the table was a figure clad in a black leather three-quarter-length coat, a white shirt, and black tie. The coat was of such a severe construction that it seemed to hold rigid the bespectacled head of the man wearing it. The overall impression was that of a rather sinister tortoise in its shell.

Luft continued to stand, while the Tortoise remained seated in its "shell" and half hidden by the desk on which had been placed a steel box, which looked to Joseph like a sandwich container.

Joseph closed the door behind him. As he did so, something made him glance through the window down into the courtyard below. Everything in that dark exterior space appeared to move, made live by the pulsing coming from oil lamps mounted on three of the sand- and cement-rendered walls.

Oh Jesus, he had fallen into a "crack"! He knew it; he was inside the bloody tumulus again and struggling to enter the first chamber. It was not tall enough for a man to stand upright, and reaching up with his free hand, he snatched a fist-sized stone from a shallow ledge in the wall. He held it close to the seed pod he was carrying which contained the live embers of blackfire.

After four – almost noiseless – breaths, the twine and animal fats within the hollowed-out stone began to flicker, and he placed the tiny scintillating object back on the ledge.

He repeated the action and, within moments, there were no less than six lamps, each pulsing with a warm, gentle flame.

He could now see the floor of the chamber, where stood one large stone, flat-topped, roughly circular, and two lower ones, upon one of which his associate proceeded to squat.

The ancient Joseph removed the hunting bow from his shoulder and put it down upon the large stone in front of the other man. He patted himself as he did so, the sticky seeds which had been adhering to his clothes, floating off into the dark corners of the chamber. For the first time that day, he rested his arm with its heavy stone wristband...

Back in September 1942 and sweating copiously, Joseph noticed that the surface of the fourth unlit wall was heavily pockmarked, and he had a feeling that as he entered the room, he had caught sight of what looked like stretcher bearers carrying away injured men.

Why had he come here? He was unable to believe that it was in order to argue for the life of his brother. A questionable sibling, an imposter, a daydreamer, who lived in a world of fantasy. Yes, yes, Luft had told him – quite improbably – that the charge was sabotage, that he was a member of the Resistance. A bit of forgery on the side – possibly – but a Resistance member, no; he wasn't up to it; Jean hadn't got the moral fibre for that – he'd always been all talk and no do!

An outlandish thought came to Joseph as he recalled the time that he had held Jean out over the cliff edge. It had given him such a feeling of power. He could have just let him fall to his death, but instead he had spared him. It had been a charitable gesture – he had absolved a human being – and this very act had endowed him with further power.

It was almost as if that force was stored within him ready to be used. His brother's life belonged to him now, and he felt a surge of exhilaration; he would use that power to save Jean.

'Joseph!' Joseph was taken aback by Luft's use of his first name. 'I'm sorry you have felt it necessary to come here.'

There was a blink as the lamps in the yard below were suddenly extinguished.

Joseph felt confused. The strange dream, and his lack of decent sleep, seemed to have stolen that mental energy which he had felt moments ago. Luft, an occultist, worse still a *deildergheist* – surely it had been a trick of the light? He had got to put up a convincing argument.

The hegemon seated himself at the table. Joseph followed suit so that the two men were facing one another.

'My brother Jean has done nothing wrong; his arrest is a complete mistake.' Joseph felt better hearing his own voice, but even by the time he'd finished the sentence, he felt disappointment. His voice sounded thin, like some badly constructed wind instrument which blows, wavers, then peters out. Luft looked solemn. The Tortoise seemed as if it was about to take a bite out of something, as it snapped open the lid of the metal box.

The object inside gave Joseph a sickening thrill. It was the thing which Jean had so hated: the Jerusalem Cross. The tiny mother of pearl insets winked as Joseph shifted his position and moved closer to stare in disbelief.

He recalled that the only time his mother had ever struck him – when he was a child – he had sulked for hours, missing both lunch and supper. He had stood alone, in the paddock, his eyes fixed on the leaves of a silver birch tree which had trapped tiny droplets of moisture. Each time a sparrow landed on one of the upper branches, the drops rolled about like gobbets of mercury winking at him. It was the same kind of misery which he felt now.

'This was found at the rocket site after the bombing raid,' announced Luft like prosecuting counsel.

'No, it's a mistake – I can prove Jean was with me on the night of the raid. We were all three of us in my office at Chateau de Galets,' lied Joseph with a humourless smile. 'Jean and Helene had been clearing out one of the barns which we are going to convert into a *gîte*...'

Luft stared past Joseph out of the window while Joseph felt the panic rise in him. What a bloody stupid thing to say. Even if he had known of Jean's whereabouts that night, it had been a mistake to include Helene in his bluff since it was very likely that she had been with Luft. Wait though, he wasn't meant to know about Luft and Helene. Desperately, he searched for an idea. If he was clever, he could develop an argument which might have implications for Luft. It would be a kind of emotional blackmail – coded of course. Only Luft would recognise what he was talking about. The Tortoise wouldn't have a clue what was going on; it would be just him and Luft. Yes, it wasn't beyond the bounds of his intelligence; he could win the captain over, force him to be on his side. The trouble was he couldn't think of anything; his mind was a blank. Then it came to him.

He would use his powers – clairvoyant powers that is – oh God! He hadn't been going to even admit it to himself, but those people he could hear – messages he sometimes received – he could use *them*. After all, this situation had now turned into a matter of life and death.

Another bloody "crack". For God's sake! He must get on with it; there wouldn't be much time; he must free his mind. Not listen to the holy men who would tell him that his personal spirit guide was appointed, assigned for life. The Joseph of the ancient world had found out for himself that this was *not* true.

The spirit guide was within oneself, but to find it, it was necessary to free the mind. This he had done much of, sitting quietly cross-legged in his stone beehive experiencing strange sensations in his body: a pressure on the top of his head, an invisible hand resting on the heart side of his chest. Every day as he watched the furnace-makers in the workshop, he was reminded of his conviction that there was a *twin flame*, two sorts of his self, one within his body, the other outside.

The "crack" closed, Joseph's fear mingling with frustration. He had never possessed real power before – always it had seemed to be the preserve of others – and now that he had it, he did not know how to use it. For the first time, it occurred to him that there might be such a thing as a gift: a light which could lie within a person, unlit for many seasons, only to burn in a moment of need. *Never underestimate your gifts and abilities. Argue for your brother, save his life!*

He needed a focus: a personal object. Luft's wristwatch would do. He didn't need to hold it, just to concentrate on it. The room seemed very silent, and he was convinced that he was holding the two men in a kind of suspended animation. Then, in a sudden rush, he found himself speaking: 'Werner loves you. Your father loves you – he says not to worry.' Luft looked mildly puzzled. Joseph clearly needed to be more specific; more information was required, but it didn't seem to be coming. Oh Hell! If only Kurt would get out of the way, moaning on about his bloody butter dish. Then Joseph was speaking again: 'Your mother Greta, she was a piano teacher,' but the line had gone blank. Luft looked curiously unmoved, but out of the corner of his eye, Joseph sensed a movement from the end of the table; something maladroit was taking place.

With the clumsiness of a giant clockwork toy, the Tortoise brought both its arms down onto the table.

'Cut the fucking party trick, Fournier!' screamed the voice. Joseph turned. The Tortoise's face was white, the teeth clenched in a rictus and the hands twitching. In a flash, it came to Joseph what had happened. Oh Lord, it was something which could have happened to any beginner. Psychic mediumship didn't come in a perfect package; it was something you had to work at, to train, and to develop, something you needed guidance in. Joseph had got mixed up; the message hadn't been for Luft; it had been for the Tortoise. Oh *merde, merde, merde*! Murder, murder, murder!

Joseph leaned forwards towards Luft, raising both his arms from the table, palms upwards. There was no doubt – in Joseph's mind – that his face had the perfectly pained look of a priest, to whom Luft had just confessed a mortal sin, and that he (Joseph) was now gravely engaged in a struggle with God over whether or not the captain should receive absolution.

'I'm a humble man,' Joseph sighed in his gentlest of voices.

He watched a minute tick by on Luft's wristwatch. The *hauptmann* sat motionless, looking sideways out of the other window. Joseph leaned back in his seat, waiting for inspiration. It did not come.

It was no good; he couldn't think of anything. He felt wild, rough, and brutally agricultural, pitted against the smooth, degree-holding SS captain. In desperation, he took a deep breath, leaned forwards until his face was nearly touching Luft's and, with all the force he could muster, brought both his fists down on the table. Once calm again, he spoke.

'Jean was with me on the night of the bombing raid.' He began in a whisper and ended in a tiny sob. 'I swear to you on my daughter's life.'

Luft didn't move – kept looking out of the window. As Joseph's breathing returned to normal, the captain spoke softly, yet with a kind of puzzled amusement as he continued looking sideways.

'But you don't have a daughter, *do* you, Joseph?'

'Well, no, but if I did, I would!' he blustered, inexplicably wiping his mouth as he spoke.

'The cross, he hated the thing; someone else probably picked it up somewhere else and dropped it on the rocket site. He has one or two enemies, you know.' Joseph managed a slight smile; he seemed to be gaining a little ground, but his ramblings were cut short as the Tortoise raised its head out of the leather shell.

'We have evidence. There are other men in custody – one of them has confessed to both he and your brother being active saboteurs in the Armee du Crime. This man has also admitted to being your brother's lover.'

Joseph's bowels seemed to turn to lead, and he gagged as he struggled to swallow back a sudden upsurge of bile.

Joseph looked at Luft; he was unable to see the man's eyes now as they were obscured by his left hand, thumb on one side of the temple, forefinger on the other. His lips were pursed, just like they had been at that sunny morning at Chateau des Galets when Joseph had first met him. But this time, they were noiseless.

With a terrible creaking, the Tortoise rose from its seat behind the table; its head elevated while the neck seemed to stretch, and the mouth made a biting motion in the air. Finally, it spoke, in a high-pitched – almost sing-song – voice.

'Your brother will be kept here for further questioning. He will then be sent to a special detention camp near Hazebrouck.'

Without further formality, Joseph hurried from the room.

Joseph stood at the Pointe des Galets gazing towards the sea and the vast columns of cloud on the horizon. He knew that he had entered a forbidden world. Moreover, from the moment he witnessed the scene in the crypt, he realised that he had been drawn into something which was beyond the pale.

As he turned from the sea and looked towards the Chateau des Galets, he saw a figure walking up the new road of crushed chalk. He knew by the elegant and purposeful stride that it was his sister, but what was she doing coming here? This was a high-security area. The other OT officers and those "squarehead" guards were obviously thinking, *Who's* this *bird?*

He watched horrified as, after a brief verbal exchange at the wire gate, she was ushered through and turned her direction to where Joseph was standing alone, his body waving slightly to and fro in the marine breeze, like one of those buoys near the harbour mouth.

As Helene's face came into view, he was surprised to see how calm it looked. She even appeared to be smiling, but it was a smile he had never seen before.

'Mum's had a stroke and she's been taken into hospital.' She paused. 'She blames herself for what's happened to Jean. Look,' she said as the smile faded, and Joseph could see a look of "Joe, what's wrong with you?" appear in its place. 'Jean didn't join the Resistance just to spite you, you know.'

'Hmm, I didn't think that at all,' he heard himself try to justify. This was insulting. She was trying to protect him. He didn't want to be coddled and patronised; if she wanted to come and give him a bollocking, then why didn't she do it? That's what all these OT blokes standing there gawping expected: real screaming and shouting.

'I know you tried to save him, so try and make your peace with life; don't go on fighting it. Jean made a sacrifice, and you need to make a covenant with God, Joe.'

What the hell was she talking about? This was mad. Was she suggesting that Jean was like Jesus Christ? She was talking as if he was dead!

'Joseph, just make a place in your heart for what I have to say.' She seemed so calm it was making him fearful. He felt himself beginning to blink.

'You knew perfectly well what Jean was up to, and you know what I'm doing in the Resistance as well. In spite of your malicious little stories. I wouldn't go having an affair with a *Boche* captain unless there was a good reason behind it. But you know, Joe, you won't be able to do a damn thing to prevent it because the difference between Jean and I, and you, is that *we* are masters of our own destiny, while you have become a slave.

'For years, Joe, you treated those around you as menials, untrustworthy, but you overlooked the basic truth that at any moment, power can be reversed and turned into weakness. You could trot along to Captain Luft tomorrow and try and give me away, but you're his slave now, his menial, and in his eyes thoroughly untrustworthy.'

Her voice dropped to little more than a murmur.

'When Mum comes out of hospital, I'll be looking after her pretty much full-time at the farm, so we may not see one another for a while.'

She paused. 'Whatever happens, I wish you good luck.' What the hell could he say to that?

She turned and walked away, straight through the group of OT agitators and "squarehead" guards who had gathered to listen.

But she was right about Luft; he knew that in his career

of the last few months with the Germans, he had failed to "cut any ice" with them. Luft wouldn't take seriously any suggestion that she was some sort of Allied spy. Moreover, he would very likely think any such accusations were bad form. After all, Luft *was* the son of a baron.

PART THREE

Escape

CHAPTER 26

SERGEANT RITTER

North-West France, May 1944

Joseph was sitting in his office gazing at the concrete fortifications on the horizon at the Pointe des Galets. They were complete at last, and his job with Organisation Todt had come to an end.

A year and a half had passed since Jean's arrest, and he had faced his sister standing on the construction site and listened to her home truths. Jean was still alive, in custody, but he had been transferred to a detention camp at Shiel Dongwy. It was in the forest towards the Belgian border, a fair way from Chateau des Galets. Helene had been to see him three times. Train to Hazebrouck, then a clunky bus ride, she'd said. It was a four-hour journey, half an hour visiting time, then four hours back. Joseph was surprised that anyone was allowed to visit, but Helene had said that it wasn't at all like the concentration camps.

What was Joseph going to do now? How could he make a living?

There were forts in nearby areas still under construction, and repair work always needing to be carried out after

Allied bombing. He had considered applying to stay on as coordinator, but Captain Luft had advised him that as the other applicants were German, he would be better advised to find something else and "lie low" in case Pointe des Galets became a combat zone.

Integrating himself back into French society would be impossible. He'd never really been a member of it in the first place, he reflected wistfully.

His family despised him, what was left of them, with Jean gone – God knows what was going to happen to him – and their mother an invalid. Constance almost certainly blamed him for not looking after Jean. Collaboration was unforgivable. If the two sons had united in purpose against the Nazis, then if she had lost either or even both of them, there would have been some consolation.

Joseph went back to Luft and asked him if there was anything he could do to earn a living. The captain smiled ironically, pursed his lips.

'Well, there *is* something actually. You could be delivery boy and messenger to the Pointe des Galets battery.' He said it as if no other person could possibly want *that* job. 'They're not a well-organised bunch; the bunker commanders are all at one another's throats.'

Joseph didn't have a lot of choice – he needed a job to survive. He couldn't go back to working the farm; it had become a shambles.

'At least you can ride a motorcycle,' commented Luft. 'We'll need to get you another uniform. If they find out you were in the OT, there'll be all hell to pay; a lot of the fortifications have faults. Things don't work, and as you know, some of the installations were sabotaged by the labourers. You won't have any friends there. Better stick to your farming story; we'll fix you up with some references.'

That evening, Joseph went up to the battery. He was standing in the entrance to the auto mortar bunker watching a group of young men sitting inside around a simple collapsible metal table, enjoying supper. It was late spring, though no one would have guessed it, the light was unable to penetrate the concrete walls of the mess room in which they were gathered.

The men were wearing uniform but in an off-duty manner. Some had removed their tunics, others their ties, and in spite of the severity of the space, there was an air of celebration. Someone had gathered wild flowers and placed them in a steel cup at the centre of the table. Oxlip and clover florets glowed in the dim tungsten of the lamps mounted on the rough grey walls. There were even bottles of wine on the table.

Most of the men were young. A blond lance corporal appeared to be the youngest – perhaps seventeen years of age, Joseph reckoned. The other corporal and privates might be nineteen or so, whilst the sergeant seated at the head of the table looked older than any of them. It was his thirty-ninth birthday, so Joseph had been told. He'd been unable to understand how Alphons Ritter could be so old and yet still only a sergeant.

Many of the lads treated Ritter with an air of comic mystery, but they seemed to like him. Joseph had heard that he had studied philosophy at university, had opened his own bookshop, but the business collapsed after the "burning of the books". Other snippets of information he had acquired hinted that Ritter had returned to teach at the university but only on condition that he joined the Nazi Party – which he evidently had done – but it was no secret that he didn't believe a word of its ideology.

Ritter was big. He seemed almost as tall as Jean, his shoulders and chest massive under his tunic, his eyes the brightest and coldest blue Joseph had ever seen. He had a short stubble beard of muddy blond hue, his hair close-clipped and of a similar paleness. All the hair on his head appeared to be exactly the same length. Joseph thought that he looked like a failed Nordic god. One who had made the journey to Valhalla but been refused entry because he wasn't up to the job.

He had just finished telling a story which had been received with enthusiastic laughter. As the mirth died away, his mood seemed to change.

'Imagine what it would be like with all fourteen of us in here,' he intoned darkly, 'the farting, the smell, the constant scrapping,' his voice as if delivering a sermon of utmost gravity.

Joseph knew as well as the sergeant that with the campaign on the Eastern Front, the full contingent just wasn't available. He assumed that this was the reason why the platoon was being commanded by a sergeant rather than a captain.

Ritter screwed up his face, his stubble chin studded with pinpoints of gold in the tungsten glow. 'Do you know what Central Command calls us? Home guards, harbour technicians, and stragglers; that's why we're only half a crew!'

'No, we're a good crew, and we'll show 'em,' insisted the young, flaxen-haired corporal. The others joined him in a determined but somehow flat chorus.

'*Heil Hitler*,' motioned Ritter, sounding more like a non-conformist priest than a soldier.

Joseph had made his evening delivery of breakfast stores and stood watching. He wasn't in a hurry; he had nowhere else to go except to his Z bed at the gatehouse. He liked watching Ritter, and nobody seemed to mind him hanging around, even though he felt a bit like a skeleton at the feast.

Joseph had heard rumours that Ritter had been on the Eastern Front – General Paulus's divisions, Stalingrad – but he'd survived by being returned to Germany with a stomach ulcer before things turned really bad. His crew looked and sounded to Joseph like a group of fairies – rather fanatical ones and dressed in green khaki costumes. They'd probably all been in the Hitler Youth.

Before Captain Luft had departed, he had made Joseph party to an unusual piece of information. Ritter's wife Greta worked in the Foreign Office as a translator and was a secretary to Dr Goebbels in Berlin. Ritter had probably avoided revealing this to anyone – no doubt because he knew that folk would be incredulous of his relatively lowly rank. He seemed to be happy to keep it that way.

Joseph was fascinated by him: the sarcasm, the irony and, apparently, in spite of his popularity among the platoon, his credentials as a loner.

CHAPTER 27

BROKEN BOND

That afternoon, Joseph lay on his Z bed and contemplated how the landscape of life had completely changed for him. With Jean gone, he had nobody to spar against, no one to listen to his pontificating, or laugh at his superstitions, or his map fetish. Luft had mysteriously vanished, suddenly transferred to another unit so Joseph had been told.

There was the question of Joseph's mother. He had been putting off a visit to see her for months. Helene kept leaving plaintive little messages in small white envelopes pinned to the toilet door at the gatehouse. "*Maman* is now very frail…" and "She could die". But she wasn't even sixty! Nevertheless, he must do it; he had to go and see her. In a way, he was relieved that his mother had suffered the stroke. It meant that Helene was needed to look after her full-time and had to give up that madness with the Resistance.

It was 1800 hours by Joseph's watch. He had rushed back from his last delivery at the battery. His mother would retire to bed at eight, so Helene's note had said.

He lit the kerosene lamp, stuffed two badly cut logs through the door of the stove, and put the kettle on the top. He must shave.

He opened the battered cream-painted door which led to the two turrets and scrutinised the row of grubby armoires in front of him. As he began to walk towards the front turret, his boot moved one of the warped timber floorboards and the door of one of the armoires creaked open eerily, revealing the rows of farm ledgers, the latest bound in scarlet-coloured cloth, while the earliest of three generations of records stood upright, clad in dingy-looking yellow board.

It no longer mattered that the farm was becoming derelict; *everything* seemed to have fallen apart. This wasn't just because of the war. Look at the records – the farm had survived the Great War, Arnaud's illness and death, all sorts of difficulties. No, there was something else, and it was to do with him. He knew it.

He gazed blackly out of the window across at Le Vieux Vicente. Only its rear portion was now visible since the mortar bunker had been constructed against it. That very day, Joseph had been helping Sergeant Ritter and the platoon stretch camouflage nets across it, but its curved outline was still visible, strangely similar to the tumulus. He grabbed the door handle and walked back through his office. The kettle had not yet boiled.

He opened the door out onto the landing and walked past the timber stair to the second north-facing turret. From here, he had a better view of the other buildings of the battery: the kitchen block, the artillery casemate, and the observation turret.

In the late afternoon early summer light, they all looked like burial mounds. Of course, it was the best defensible form, but there was no denying that the whole coastline looked as if it was covered with prehistoric tumuli.

Hold on. He was beginning to think like Jean – perhaps Jean was dead, and that was why! This was crazy; Jean had always said that this wasn't just defence; it was Nazi propaganda. Not only would it keep the Allies from invading Europe, it would be a permanent symbol of the Third Reich. Not just a thousand-year reich but four thousand years – more! Even if it failed and the Allies won, these latter-day tombs would be immovable; they would last for eternity. It was the stuff of Wagnerian legends, Ludwig's Halls of Heroes, the Venus Grotto at Linderhof… the Godless temples had been made to look as if they contained the "sleeping heroes" who would rise again one day and save the Fatherland.

Christ! He was sounding mad now, but Jean had been right. Like the mighty stone structures of ancient Rome, Egypt, and China, these forts made of millions of tonnes of concrete and steel had been constructed by men brought from all over the empire against their will, to labour, often until death for no reward.

He had a horrible vision of a world a hundred years hence, populated by folk who would flock to the bunkers, in the manner of the outdoor museum he and his siblings had once talked about for Le Vieux Vicente. Yet that would be no more a crime than the thousands of visitors who travelled every year to gawp at the pyramids or the Great Wall of China.

Joseph had always hated the whole idea of art, but this was art all right – the art of oppression – a simple truth which for years he had chosen to ignore. He must shave…

He could hear the kettle boiling. He plucked it from the stove, carried it to his wash bowl, poured in some boiling water and added cold. As the steam rose, he looked at himself in the mirror.

He felt himself falling into another "crack" – of course, a mirror was a crack; he should have realised that. He could see himself as an ancient tribal chief, hated by his people and obsessed with himself and his own appearance. As a younger man, he (this chief) had frequently been observed by his subjects ordering the largest of flat, sticky, earth-fired dishes to be placed at intervals outside his house and filled with water so that he could gaze at his own reflection in every kind of light. He would examine his dark and mournful stare. A countenance made the more intense after long periods of intoxication. He would contemplate Joseph sober – but more often Joseph drunken – and with the aid of flaming torches pushed into the ground on spikes, he would peer into one of his mirror pools. He was seeing Joseph the troubled, Joseph in isolation. It was all *self* now – seen through his own narrow understanding – rather like the bedroom he had chosen as a child, so small that no other person could enter it when he was in there. Jean had accused him of that – the limitations of self, seen through self – but just how clear a vision did Joseph have of himself, for as a man without a wife – or lover – he felt vulnerable in that he had no close mate to measure his self against the world.

As the "crack" closed, he once again saw himself in the mirror. He was thirty-four, wifeless, childless, friendless, and now he was a slave to the Nazis. He was fucked.

He looked at his watch – it was 1900 hours. He knew he was playing for time. He had lived his life based on fear: fear of his neighbours, his siblings, the French, the Nazis, his father, and his mother. 'You two have so much in common; there's a real strong bond between you,' people had said about him and his mother – Aunt Icie among them. But he had begun to know that that bond was based on fear and doubt and very little else.

Ten minutes later, he was out in the yard and cautiously lifting the latch of the kitchen door. Inside, and standing almost opposite behind the scrub-top table, was Helene. He had not seen her properly since those last two occasions, the first of which when she came to his office, and the second that time on the cliff top after Jean's arrest.

Her face was soft in the lamplight. She looked relaxed, and was smiling just a little, while in front of her, seated at the table, was a person who, at first, he was unable to recognise. He even had difficulty deciding which gender this person might be.

The head had the general appearance of a giant dried seed pod, its veins standing out on neck and temple. The skin was ash grey with purplish tinges on the cheekbones. The face had a slightly shiny appearance as if the pod had been painted with some kind of dope designed to make the skin stretch over its brittle shell. The pewter-hued hair was pulled back and held by a black velvet-covered snood. Gone were the flowered dresses. The figure in front of him was clad entirely in the black garb which was worn only by elderly local women.

Staggered, Joseph tried to speak. 'Hullo, Mother,' he managed in a hoarse, low whisper.

The crone opposite him began to grunt "uh". The grunts came regularly: "uh" every few seconds; sometimes a double grunt, "uh uh"; back to a single grunt, "uh"; then a triple "uh uh uh"; and back to a single "uh". The head seemed oblivious to all around it; the eyes stared vacantly. Joseph could stand it no longer. Without even looking at Helene, he heard himself raise a miserable apology and slunk from the room.

As his hand clawed at the latch, he heard the rattle of a dry but nevertheless audible voice behind him ask, 'Who was that? Whoever it was, I don't wish to see him in this house again.'

With horror, he recalled the "crack" he had suffered at the tumulus that time when Jean's Jerusalem Cross had been unearthed. He remembered the way he had puzzled over the familiar look of the dead woman of his phantasm, being buried with jewels and berries. It had been his mother.

He was still imprisoned in the inertia of realisation when he heard the latch click once more behind him.

'I'm sorry, Joe. Mum's really gone downhill in the last year. It must have been a shock for you.' Joseph didn't know what to say. It *had* been a shock, but as his sister spoke, he received another.

'Jean wants you to go and see him.' Why? He felt defensive. How was that going to help matters? Everybody blamed Joseph for everything now.

'Look, Joe, I've got to go back inside. Mum sometimes forgets where she is, and she has to go to bed soon.' She turned; the latch clicked a fourth time, and Joseph was left standing motionless in the farmyard as the late spring evening light began to fade.

When at last he was released from his statue-like pose and he began to walk slowly up to his gatehouse office room, darkness had fallen. Why had Helene not spoken of Jean's request until now, when it had been weeks since she had last seen him? It dawned upon him that she had been waiting until he had seen their mother. That was to be the driver: shock.

***

14 May 1944

I've got a plan to help Joseph. I've worked it out with Jean. It's dangerous, but no more so than what any of us has been doing for the last three years. Jean may be in custody, but it's Joseph who's in the most danger, but if the plan works, it will help Jean as well.

Joseph's worst enemy is himself. If only he could stop

hating himself. This could help him... let's just pray he'll agree to do it...

CHAPTER 28

SONNENLICHT

Joseph wasn't used to bus journeys. He hadn't been on one for over five years. Neither had he travelled anywhere by train recently. The jeep had to go after the OT posting came to an end, and with no petrol privileges and zero income from the farm, he couldn't afford to run a vehicle now. No longer dressed in OT uniform, he was taken aback by the brusqueness of the railway and bus inspectors. His identity card had been scrutinised no less than six times throughout the journey so far, and he was tired of having to offer it up for inspection.

The bus was practically empty, just old folk and several children, perhaps grandchildren. A small boy sitting behind him was talking incessantly, urgently asking of the elderly grandmother sitting with him, 'Is that our house over there?'

'No, our house is in Estaires; we'll be there soon.'

'But it must be our house.'

'No, ours has a red roof; that one is grey.'

'I can see it now. I can see my bedroom window.'

'No, another few minutes and then you'll see it.'

The boy's mounting anxiety was mirroring Joseph's own mood of uncertainty. Just before Joseph rose for his stop, the small boy vomited noisily onto the wood deck floor of the bus.

Helene had said that the camp was men only, though other folk who alighted at the bus stop were both men and women; children, it appeared, were not allowed to visit.

'Don't be fooled,' she had said. He wasn't quite sure what that meant, and she hadn't explained further except to say that the purpose of this camp – or "reception centre", as it was called – was "information". *The centre of what?* Joseph wondered, *the forest perhaps*. An eerie image formed in his mind.

The reason Jean was still alive – as far as Helene could see – was because the Nazis simply didn't know what to do with him and weren't ready to kill him. Her view was that the camp had been built specifically for people who were in possession of information which might be "useful to the Third Reich" but which torture or "other means" had failed to uncover. Such individuals were therefore put into a holding position. Visitors were encouraged, though only for half an hour per day. Prisoners – or "residents", as they were called – were often folk who had exceptionally high IQs, were titled, had high scientific qualifications, or possessed unusual branches of knowledge. Quite what Jean had done to be held there, Joseph couldn't imagine.

Two timber-framed towers – the height of industrial jibs – with grey pyramidal tops appeared to rise up from the land on the edge of the forest. Joseph could see two further lookouts some distance inside the camp.

Stretched between each of the wood structures was a woven mesh of steel cable and twisted wire, so dense that Joseph found himself staring to see through it. The early afternoon sun was hitting every barb, and had Joseph not reminded himself of its grim purpose, he might have thought it a thing of beauty.

Two giant gates noiselessly opened to admit the ragged pathos of folk who had been walking with him the last few metres from the bus stop. There seemed to be guards everywhere. "Squareheads" standing at ground level and soft-capped soldiers up in towers. Joseph was impressed. Compared with the jumble of fence posts and few strands of barbed wire they had used to secure the Battery des Galets construction site, this was like the Bastille.

What he saw next gave him a surprise. Beyond the towers, he had expected a miserable shanty town of wood huts, abandoned rubbish, and the smell of decay. In contrast, the scene in front of him resembled the deckscape of a Cunard ocean liner. A sign reading *Sonnenlicht* in polished steel shone down upon him from the sweeping entrance canopy.

There were rectangles of crisp, white walls elegantly balanced upon rows of *pilotti*, green, well-attended lawns, and shining street lamps. Joseph had been convinced that within the barbaric cordon through which he had just passed, he would come upon an even more unpleasant medieval core. But here was modernity and style!

There were people moving two and fro in every direction. Some in uniform, most were wearing blue-and-white striped pyjamas. Most folk seemed to be ambling about; others were standing in groups chatting; some were even sunbathing. He could just see in the distance a game of football in progress.

He caught sight of what could be a film crew: two men with film cameras, one of whom was black, and several folk wielding poles with microphones attached. Joseph had never seen a black man before. He could see other black men, but they were wearing the striped "get-ups".

He must make haste. Helene had said he would only have half an hour, and he hadn't even found Jean yet. He passed through the main automatic door and squeaked his way across a white rubber floor. It was unbelievable; every surface shone with newness.

He slid onwards, following the dozen other civilian visitors through the gently echoing interior. Then back out into the open air – birdsong and the distant murmur of human voices – forwards again, under a ceiling of sparkling varnished planks, and through another invisibly operated door into a space, this time noisy and sticky. There were men everywhere, in clusters. He would never find Jean in time.

He passed into an atrium lit by enormous circular rooflights; a place so bright that the shaved heads of men shone. Joseph thought they looked like marble, of hues ranging from white Carrara to Nero Absoluto. Then he saw him. He was sitting – almost nonchalant – at one of the dozens of white tables and talking excitedly to other men pressed close to him.

Jean had already spotted him.

'Talk to Louis,' Joseph could see Jean mouthing amid the din and motioning towards a mild-looking man seated three places away.

What the hell was going on? He'd come to talk with his brother, not some stranger.

'Don't be taken in, Joe,' said the mild man, echoing Helene's words, as Joseph took the only vacant chair next to him, looking at his watch as he did so. There were twenty-five minutes left. 'What you're seeing is just "surface"; we call it Teutonic hygiene.' The man was well-spoken, and Joseph calmed a little. Louis produced a small, grubby square of paper which Joseph had just been watching as it passed from Jean along the row of men. He handed it to Joseph.

You can trust Louis; he's one of us.

What, exactly, was "one of us"? thought Joseph. Was he a farmer? Did he mean he was a homosexual? Perhaps he had been in the Resistance? As he began to write a reply, Joseph glanced across at Jean, but he wasn't looking.

'You can have tea or coffee...' said the mild-looking, smiling man, as Joseph contemplated a gaping hatch set in the shiny, white, vertical surface behind his head, '...but the kitchen staff are bastards – they're Frenchies – a mixture of "moles" and "lizards", but they've got their own slang, and if you don't ask for it right, they won't give it to you. If you want water, you've got to ask for "lix". Milk is "bull", and margarine is "slab". Bread is "bars". They're a real pain in the arse – kitchen scum! Everything here is about information,' continued Louis. 'Once you're through the Chateau d'If, as we call it, there are no security checks – you'll have noticed – no "sign-in"; that's because the *Boche* have a system. People are encouraged to mingle. The Gestapo know that friends and relatives come here to swap information, so they don't stop them doing it. The trick is not to be intercepted – as most people are – without knowing it's happened.

'To avoid that, you have to know who's who, and because men are coming and going here every day, most folk don't know. The people to really avoid are the "moles" – or *momes* as they're known – you know, "*lytel* friend" or "li'll chick"...' Joseph completed his return note for Jean and handed it to Louis.

'All right, make sure that a *mome* doesn't get hold of this then,' he said cockily. He had the distinct feeling that everything that was happening was above his head and that Jean and Louis had other ideas for him.

Just give them the information they want, names, places, you know. I'm sure they'll let you go, his note said. There were nineteen minutes left.

'...Then there're the "lizards" – those chaps with the white armbands...' Joseph remembered the "magpie" at the police station. They were French collaborators, reptiles who had changed the colour of their skin. '... Oh, and there's the g'rilla"...' Jean's return note arrived.

You know I can't do that. The hastily written script stared up at Joseph.

'... He's the commandant. Prisoners rarely get a glimpse of him. If you get more than that, then you know you're really in the shit.'

Jean was staring out through a glass wall behind the throng. He had expected the accommodation huts to be crude and rustic – cynically extreme versions of sentimentalised Tyrolean hideaways – but he found himself looking at rows of slick modular units. Pre-cast lightweight concrete panels the hue and texture of deerskin, deliciously inserted into simple galvanised steel sashes. God, it was clever; they even had windows. Inexpensive prefabricated units like these could be erected or added to in a day, built all over Europe to a single blueprint. It was a dream!

'Nobody has ever escaped from here,' enthused Louis. Christ! Joseph had been drifting off while Louis was wittering on. He looked at his watch. There were ten minutes to go. 'That's because people think in terms of probability rather than possibility. Jean and I have been here quite a while – as you know – and most folk don't want to escape; they just want to hang on here – so do their relatives once they've been to visit them.'

Joseph had turned his attention to the white expanse of tabletop; it was finished in a material unknown to him. It was smooth, monolithic; he tapped it with a coin; it seemed harder than diamond.

'That's where you come in, Joe.' Joseph forced his attention away from the tabletop and looked into the eyes of the mild man. The eyes themselves were anything but mild.

Joseph managed a smile. There were six minutes to go. 'And, Joe, don't forget, you can say "no".'

Joseph felt a sudden surge of excitement. 'Jean has a plan,' announced Louis. 'It's to change places with you, and remember, Joe, you don't have to agree to it.'

Joseph felt as if he was holding a solution of freshly squeezed lemon in his cheeks. There were tingles like small electric shocks passing through his stomach, and his breaths were coming in short, thrusting-like movements.

He would do it. There was no question about it. He would sacrifice himself for his brother, would die an honourable death in this architectural Shangri-La – he would redeem himself with his friends and family, perhaps even be remembered in the form of a small monument in the village at Chateau des Galets. But how the hell were they going to do it?

'But the security is like Devil's Islands, how on earth is Jean going to walk out of here?'

'You're thinking just like everybody else, Joe; you need to look at it sideways, but your Devil's Island comparison is a clever one because that's the key. Practically nobody ever even *contemplated* escape there. People here have basically got what they want: comfort, sociability, even a kind of freedom, all in extraordinary surroundings. Few people die here; they're well fed, exercised, receive sunray treatment – I mean, when was the last time you saw your brother looking as well as he does?'

Joseph had to admit that he had never seen Jean looking so fit. His head may have been shaved, but little bird's egg-like freckles had appeared on its surface, and he was gently tanned. His eyes were bright, his body confident.

'But the Allies will come soon – I mean, why not hang on?'

'Oh, Joe, how little you know about the Nazis. What do you think all those railway lines are for? That's what Germans do all day; they're constantly shunting people round Europe, dividing, confusing, reordering, plonking people down in places where nobody knows anyone else. You can be sure that by the time the Allies reach St Omer, the Nazis will have closed this place and have us all in cattle trucks heading for Upper Bavaria.'

'I'll do it.' Joseph looked up the table, but Jean still wasn't looking at him.

'Oh, three things, Joe: before you next come, shave your head, and for Christ's sake remember to bring a cap – make it two, in fact, so you've a spare. Lastly, don't bring a coat, even if it's raining.'

There was the dry quacking of a klaxon, and Louis was on his feet; then he seemed to vanish into the crowd. Joseph looked for Jean, but he too had gone.

CHAPTER 29

ANOTHER SECRET UNCOVERED

In spite of being deafened by the roar of the overpowered engine, and thrown this way and that by primitive suspension, Joseph was enjoying his return bus journey. He was in a strange state of elation. In a manner of speaking, he too was *in* the Resistance now, and *who* would have thought it! It would probably end in his death – if it didn't happen at Sonnenlicht then it seemed that it might well be asphyxiation on the boards of a cattle truck, but he had to die somehow. At least Jean would have a chance of reaching his unit if his contacts were still good.

In 120 seconds, Louis had explained the plan to him, in a briefing which must have rivalled the most special of special services groups. Though spoken, his commands had been delivered in the form of bullet points:

- 'On arrival, locate kitchen staff toilet door and enter without being observed; if seen, you *must* abort plan. We can't risk discovery, otherwise nobody else will be able to use the plan again.

- 'Inside are two tile-clad shitters, open to the ceiling. Choose the left one; if occupied, don't wait – you *must* abort plan. Note that there are three pissers in the lobby so others may come and go while you're in the cubicle.
- 'Cubicles have doors but no locks so beware if a second party enters lobby. They're squatters but have high-level cisterns, behind which will be concealed one pair of bluejams and slippers.
- 'Put on bluejams and hide your clothes (including underpants and vest) behind cistern. Put shoes inside the cistern. And don't you dare walk out with your hat still on. That goes behind the cistern.
- 'Leave the toilets, but only if no one is in the lobby; if they are, and they don't move in time, then we're all fucked.
- 'Re-enter dining hall and make your way straight to shower block.'

Apart from the obvious danger of being seen entering and leaving, the weak point of the plan seemed to Joseph to be the concealing of the civilian clothes. They were considerably bulkier than the jams, might be visible, and the interval of time between Joseph leaving the cubicle and Jean entering it must be kept to a minimum.

But it was no good rushing the operation either. If Jean emerged, togged-up in civvies, into the dining hall too soon, then he would have time to kill before the klaxon and there was more chance of being recognised by a "lizard" or *mome*. Louis had said this would be a dangerous period as Joseph would be agitated and more likely to make a blunder. Going for a shower would get him clear of the public area. By the time he was out of the shower, Jean would be out of the front gate.

It was 2000 hours by the time Joseph stood under the apex of the cruck barn roof at Chateau des Galets. What would he tell Helene? She would want to know all about it, how Jean was. He couldn't possibly tell her that he hadn't spoken a word to him! She obviously knew of the strange environment, and its weird systems, but did she know about Louis? He could hear the polite light cough as she entered the barn.

'Jean looked very well,' he said optimistically. When he thought about it, he should have said, "Jean *is* very well" – she might suspect they hadn't spoken. She smiled, was disconcertingly silent.

'He seems to know a lot of people.' She gave a frown. *What a bloody stupid thing to say*, he thought.

'What I mean is he obviously gets on with people.' She gave him an even odder look.

'There're a lot of people there.' Christ, this was hard work; that sounded worse than ever; of course there bloody well were – from all over Europe – *Help me, Amber*, he thought. *Ask me a question!*

'There's a centre for women as well, some distance away, but it's smaller.'

He had an idea. 'Do you think we should take it in turns to go and see him?'

She seemed to brighten at this suggestion. If he was volunteering to go, that would indicate to her that things must be improving between the two men. But did she know about the plan? She couldn't possibly – it was too insane; the risks were too high; and she could end up losing both brothers. Then he remembered that meeting with her on the construction site. After what she had told him about what she was doing, she was capable of anything. Had Joseph really agreed to this crazy operation of his own free will, or was he the last piece of *their* jigsaw?

'Yes, that's a good idea, Joe,' she replied, walking towards the door of the barn, and out she went in her own dissident female way into the gathering darkness.

***

Joseph began to have thoughts about the future. Not the *gîte* he had once planned but survival. He was beginning to worry about his own death. He dared not set foot in the village where anyone might take a potshot at him.

His dogsbody-style job for the *Festungkommandant's Heer Artillerie* kept him busy almost twenty-four hours a day. Raw materials for food arrived at the battery and were prepared in the kitchen block, so all he had to do was to get to the site and distribute the food containers. But it took time. Then he had to collect the empties. No questions were asked, though he was sure that everybody was suspicious of a *Frenchie* doing the job, but who could blame a man for wanting to survive? At least he was safe here for now.

It was if... no, *when* the Allies came that frightened him. Supposing he didn't go through with the Sonnenlicht plan, or if anything happened to Jean *before* they put it into practice? The best thing he could do was to surrender as soon as he got the chance and take the lengthy prison sentence which he would receive for his part in overseeing slave labour when they found out who he was.

He kept remembering Jean's riposte about the afterlife, and he was convinced that Jean – if he died – would try to reach him. He listened apprehensively for those disembodied voices in his head; what an awful mess he'd made with that Gestapo officer that time!

He was fearful about having to go to the auto mortar bunker in its location next to the tumulus. If Jean's ghost was going to appear to him, it was sure to be there. So many times, he'd seen things up there over the years, and that was when Jean was alive, so God knows what kind of spooks he would encounter if Jean died.

***

As Joseph made his way to the auto mortar bunker the following afternoon, he was counting his blessings that this bunker was occupied by Ritter and his platoon. The young men were aloof with Joseph, but Ritter was downright matey. Joseph spoke a little German – one of the legacies of Aunt Icie – but Ritter spoke better French.

After he'd returned the lunch empties and delivered the evening meal, he began to dawdle. The late afternoon sun was warm, and he sat down on a wooden pallet next to where he'd left his motorcycle and sidecar: Zündapp KS750 – ex-Panzer division. *Nicht rauchen* proclaimed a sign stencilled in Gothic script by the gas lock door of the bunker. Some of the men emerged for a smoke in the late afternoon sun.

While the young men divided into two groups, the blond lance corporal – perhaps seeking a few moments' solitude – entered the old burial mound. Joseph shuddered. He watched the soldier as he moved – like a crab – along the low stone gallery into one of the empty chambers and disappeared from sight.

This was the last of Joseph's deliveries, so he was in no hurry to return to his makeshift office. He would stay on his pallet and enjoy a few more moments' quiet.

After some time, the boy machine gunner emerged from the tumulus looking excited.

'Don't tell anybody, but look at this!' he exclaimed, striding towards Joseph. This was a change; the boy normally just stared at him.

In his outstretched palm lay a wedge-shaped object, grubby, but as the boy's hand waved it around, Joseph could see flashes of purple and green. He was no archaeologist, but he knew a dagger with a bone handle when he saw one.

Without warning, a wave of nausea came over Joseph as he recalled the nocturnal scene on the bluff two years ago when he and Jean had stalked one another.

As he swallowed, he felt the bitter taste of bracken in his throat, and his hand touched his forehead, pouring with sweat but stone cold, in spite of the warmth of the late afternoon.

'Where did you find that?' he heard his voice ask cracklingly, knowing damn well what the answer was going to be.

The gunner spoke in a rather strange way. German, it appeared, was *not* his mother tongue – and he was breathless with excitement, which added to his peculiar theatrical performance.

'I was just going to light a cigarette when I thought I saw a flash of green near the roof of the hole where I was sitting,' the young soldier animated. His elation made his explanation seem even more comically elaborate. Joseph felt curious but queasy.

There was something vaguely familiar about this young man, the pale hair, the thyroid eyes, the blond eyelashes, and pinkish skin – almost porcine – but Joseph couldn't place him.

'To look closely at where the source of light seemed to be was difficult because of the low height of the ceiling…' the young soldier persisted histrionically. '… So, I found myself adopting the gymnastic pose of a discus thrower.' He demonstrated crazily with his arms. Joseph was feeling hot one moment and cold the next.

'With my upswinging left hand operating the lighter, and my downswinging right hand gripping a chunk of that honey-coloured stone, I managed to achieve perfect balance and prevent myself from toppling over,' he continued zanily. Joseph felt very sick; it was coming in waves.

'This time I saw it, a metallic seam wedged between two giant flat stones.' Joseph had begun to shiver. 'With the lighter locked in my left fist, and my shoulder tight up against the stones, I brought my right hand up, without being able to see. This time, I ran my fingers along until they met an object of a different texture.' The boy gave a shrill, nervous laugh, grinned. Joseph badly wanted to share the amusement, but the only laugh he was contemplating now was a liquid one.

'Rocking it backwards and forwards, I felt it begin to loosen. Finally, it was released into thin air, emitting a bewitching musical note.'

The contents of Joseph's stomach forced themselves into his mouth, and his body jerked forwards, emitting its own discordant and distinctly unmusical note as his hastily ingested meal of tinned meat, eggs, bread, and red wine was noisily disgorged onto the crushed chalk. The boy seemed to have neither seen nor heard him.

'At first, I thought I was staring at a Masonic trowel. Its shape was rather like the silver-plated object my uncle once showed me…'

'Just stick it in your pocket and keep quiet,' gagged Joseph as he wiped his mouth, mounted the Zündapp and kicked down on it.

'Was it something I said?' queried the boy, hardly looking at Joseph.

The motorcycle roared beneath him, and Joseph watched the young corporal walking back to the bunker mess room as he neatly dropped the dagger into the left breast pocket of his shirt and buttoned his tunic over it.

CHAPTER 30

THE BATTERY

'Wake up, you bastards, and stop playing with your sausages! You've got drill parade in five minutes; then we've got a bloody film crew coming to take pictures of us running up and down steps with klaxons blaring.'

Sergeant Ritter's words made Joseph smile. The first event was true enough, but the second was a typical Ritter ploy to keep his platoon constantly ready for a scramble.

Unspecified "dignitaries" were always on the point of arriving – "ready to inspect" the lads – and the sergeant insisted several times a day to each member:

'Don't forget that I made you what you are today.'

The last point was one of irony. Ritter was the last person who had been responsible for shaping their young minds over the years. Though perhaps, wondered Joseph, he felt sadness, and even collective self-blame, for the way that these young men had been indoctrinated.

Ritter had decided to accompany Joseph on his rations run. Ritter liked to play a game. Though there were only five years between their ages, Ritter would adopt the role of an "old hand", a kind of father figure.

The story given to the battery *personalreferent* by General Mezger's staff had been that Joseph was Joseph Barbusse, a farmhand who had worked on one of the larger farms inland which had been "commissioned" by the Germans and that he was simply "renting a room" at the nearby Pointe des Galets farm. Though Joseph had been delivering rations for some weeks now, Ritter would always treat him as if it was his first day.

'Settling in all right?' Ritter would ask him daily with tedious regularity. 'By the way, you're not related to the novelist Henri Barbusse, are you? A communist, you know, but he got out, defected to Moscow.'

Another of Ritter's cringing standard lines was: 'Are you courting yet?' A question which particularly depressed Joseph, for even if he had wished to strike up a relationship with a *local lass*, he had no time which was his own. There was also the distinct probability – given his display of loyalties – that if any such person existed, she would ask the Resistance to deal with him, or even quietly poison him herself.

The sun of the early morning had by now been obliterated by a fog of disorientating density. Ritter seemed to be put off by these sudden mists; he obviously wasn't used to them.

'This is a real eye-opener,' barked Ritter, losing no opportunity for irony. 'Every single one of those battery crews is at one another's throats. It's supposed to be defence in depth, a system of mutual support, but the only thing that's mutual about it is a feeling of loathing. This will be a rare opportunity to see your fellow man in his habitat; don't be surprised if he shoots the messenger.'

The two men picked up stores from the kitchen block and piled them into the sidecar. There was practically no room for the sergeant, and as Joseph kicked down on the Zündapp, Ritter crouched, leaning forwards, his feet planted just inside the well of the sidecar. Joseph thought he looked like a large pilgrim in the act of prostrating himself in penance.

As the two men rode in the half light of the swirling fog, the sun seemed to be somewhere… working its way back through the murk, and lighting a small patch of ground way ahead, giving Joseph the impression that this spot had some special significance. He thought about Jean – what *was* going on in Sonnenlicht, and could Joseph make any difference? But the hopeful glow died away and merged back into vapour, tumbling alongside them like loose fragments of tattered gauze, while the motorcycle lurched like a rocking horse bewitched.

They stopped abruptly, within three metres of what seemed like endless concrete wall. Joseph knew exactly where he was. It was where he and Jean had stalked one another in the dark, the night after the raid on the rocket site.

'You're on your own now,' muttered Ritter darkly as Joseph grabbed the first of the ration boxes.

In the gloom, Joseph followed the curve of the concrete wall, running his hand against its surface. He could see little, but he could feel its abrasiveness, its wetness. He also became aware that he was about to enter another "crack".

His ancient self was plodding along, feeling the air growing colder, seeing the light fade, and there was little doubt that his fears were about to be realised – he was walking into a wall of sea smoke. He had been travelling with somebody, but he had lost them; they had become separated in the fog. It was eerily silent; not even a roar from the sea, and there was an icy chill of moisture on his face. He seemed to have a wound to his hand. The sun's strength! It was really hurting now. He dragged himself forwards, stopped, and waited. He would turn around – yes, that's what he'd do – and follow his own marks on the wet earth.

The Bronze Age Joseph walked back the way he thought he had come, searching for tracks – he found them, but there was an area of hard packed earth and grass, and the footprints disappeared. He knelt down, examined the individual blades of grass, but each was dripping with fresh moisture, and it was impossible to tell whether or not a human foot had been there. The urge to call out was almost irresistible, but resist he must. Daemons haunted these clifftop areas, and there were stories of giants walking out of the sea. He began to panic and called out in a loud whisper, but the air felt heavy with moisture and no sound was able to leave his body. He blundered on. Perhaps somewhere, way above this dead cloud, was the sun. It would clear soon. Suddenly, his body gave an almighty jolt. A few paces in front of him stood something terrible: the dark mass of a gigantic human form.

There was no point in trying to run; he just stood there shivering. As he overcame his fear, he could see that the lowest part of the "thing" was motionless, while the taller form was moving, pulsating. At last, it came to him that the solid object was a standing stone; the sun *had* been trying to penetrate the sea smoke, and in so doing, it was making bright the fog itself around the stone; it was an odd thing to see. Somewhere, way above the sea smoke barrier, was a pale, rising sun, and if he walked away from it, he should reach the cliff edge. The sun's beam had strengthened and was throwing a long shadow – not upon the ground but upon the sea smoke itself. The shadow moved in waves like the sea, pulsing, it seemed to be guiding him.

As Joseph prised himself back out of the "crack", he became aware of a sparkle upon the surface in front of him. The emerging sun was catching the microscopic facets of the mica fragments within the sand of the concrete, and now –

even in the dankness – he could feel the air – with its strange electric taste of ozone – blowing against his face. Then he saw the figure of a bare-headed soldier, apparently suspended in mid-air.

The fog blew to one side to reveal that the man was sitting astride the barrel of a colossal gun.

'Rations delivery!' Joseph shouted up to the man on the gun, in good German, he thought. Silence. Then – closer – he noticed three further pairs of eyes looking at him, sullenly. Soldiers two and three were sitting on camp chairs playing cards. Soldier four, seated on an ammunition box, looked up from what appeared to be a letter he was writing. No one seemed interested enough to respond.

As the mist lifted for a moment, Joseph caught sight of the end of the gun barrel thrusting out from the man's groin like a giant steel penis; the heroic member aimed out into the mist of the English Channel.

An *unteroffizier* emerged from the gas lock door in the side of the casemate, pushing aside the camouflage netting, and Joseph shoved the ration box into the soldier's hand without thanks.

Feeling his way back along the wall towards the Zündapp, he saw the tiny glow coming from a cigarette which Ritter had placed between his lips. He could hear the thump of gunfire.

'Are those from the guns at Cap Gris-Nez?' Joseph found himself whispering as he neared the cigarette. He was pretending to sound as if he hadn't a clue.

'Yes and no,' replied Ritter cryptically. 'There's a time delay. The ones you just heard are firing from Dover. Ours go "whup"; the Dover ones go "boom". It's a bloody strange conversation they have...' Joseph stamped down on the motorcycle.

After the surliness of the artillery crew, the men of the observation bunker seemed almost cordial. This time, Ritter held the rations box, walking in front, as the two of them entered the building between two high walls of concrete.

'Rations delivery,' roared Ritter. A head clad in an M40 steel helmet popped out of the interior gloom.

'Come and observe,' invited the head. The two men entered the concrete cylinder and stood in the middle of the floor. One metre above their feet was a giant horizontal slit which followed in an arc, to almost half the circumference of the building. Joseph recalled – with some satisfaction – the moment at which the mighty steel ring beams had been craned into position and bolted together to create this unsupported space.

The irony of the invitation to observe became immediately apparent. It was possible to see through the colossal window, but what lay beyond wasn't even recognisable as space; it was unknown dark matter. Visibility was zero.

A second helmeted man stood peering vainly through field glasses into the void. Ritter quit the bunker, but the helmeted corporal seemed keen to give Joseph a tour. Joseph didn't say a word; he knew every centimetre of this structure, and he smiled as he thought that he, *Joseph*, should be giving the corporal the conducted tour.

'I'm not doing any good standing here,' lisped the corporal, 'and you look like a nice enough chap – oh, that's Lance Corporal Menzel, by the way.' He nodded, the steel helmet inclined towards a bare-headed figure in a green tunic. 'Fancies himself as an artist.'

The soldier was squatting over an upturned wooden box, a small bottle of Indian ink in his left hand, a sable brush in his right.

He was translating from brush onto concrete, the third

of a trio of figures: Mickey Mouse, Snow White, and Goofy.[9] It was strange to see the much-loved cartoon characters – too recent for Joseph's childhood but very much part of his brother Robert's – taking shape on the wall of this artificial world of men, at the hand of one so young.

'Your sergeant has a reputation as an intellectual,' whispered the corporal. 'He only swears because he thinks that's what sergeants are supposed to do.' Joseph smiled.

'Oh, and while we're at it, we may as well have a look at the toilet facilities,' announced the grinning *rottenfuhrer*, kicking open a pulverised wooden door which led into a coffin-like enclosure.

At the rush of cold air coming up from the floor, Joseph recalled what to expect next, and as he moved closer to its clammy source, he peered directly through the perfect twenty-centimetre circular hole and out into the mist.

No more than two metres directly below, he could just make out a nest of kittiwakes in a crevice in the cliff face.

'They normally crap on us, so now we get an opportunity to get our own back,' smiled the corporal. Joseph surprised himself by laughing, not at the man's predictable joke but at the irony that had it been a clear day, they both would have been able to see past the kittiwake's nest and right down onto the rocks below where lay the remains of Joseph's tractor, the result of the ploughing mishap years previously. *That idiot farmhand drove my tractor over the edge and now the Germans are crapping on it!* thought Joseph.

'Come to the upper deck,' urged the corporal.

The two pairs of boots clicked up the concrete steps and into a room of shape and size similar to the observation chamber they had recently left. Another helmeted figure stood gazing through field glasses.

'Have a look,' the soldier said to Joseph, handing him the

field glasses. This time, unlike the soup-like vista of the level below, Joseph found himself staring out at the whiteness of the sunlit English chalk cliffs, now visible above a field of rolling cloud.

CHAPTER 31

THE FIRST ESCAPE

It was a dull, overcast sort of day on which Joseph made the journey, first on the train to Hazebrouck, then the jerky bus to Shiel Dongwy, and the last few score metres on foot to Sonnenlicht.

At Louis's instruction, he neither wore, nor carried, a coat. He had donned his smartish tweed jacket, while upon his newly shaved head sat a tobacco-hued tweed cap. A similar cap nestled, furled in one of his side pockets. In his inside pockets were his tickets and ID – what the hell was Jean going to do with those? Still, that was his business.

His mood see-sawed between elation and gloom; he would miss Ritter – that was an odd relationship, not a friendship exactly, but the man was interesting. Anyway, Joseph didn't want friends. He was still uncertain as to whether or not he had chosen the destination towards which he was heading. In his mind, he would have liked to have imagined that he was journeying towards the light – the real Sonnenlicht, but all he could see was a nebulous dark mass. While the route he appeared to be following seemed like a spiral, as if he and those dingy clouds of gas were being drawn – slowly at first, then faster – by some unseen extreme form of gravity, into the black hole at its centre.

He passed through the armoured outer barrier of Sonnenlicht, with its bogus Gothic lettering, its adumbration of stories by the Brothers Grimm, and its sham hint of heroism. He experienced a frisson, as if he was teetering upon the edge between the universe which man understands and those places of extremes, which will be forever unknowable.

Once through the automatic doors and standing within the slick, shining white of the Sonnenlicht reception area, he caught sight of a lounge of "lizards" busily engaged in cleaning one of the white porcelain hand basins so incongruously mounted on the wall. The white armbands of the "lizards" flicked two and fro as they wiped and polished.

At the basin on the wall opposite stood a member of the pathos of visitors, running his hands under water. Perhaps indulging with hope in some ritual of purification to be carried out upon the threshold between that which was real and that which seemed unreal.

Joseph crossed the rubber floor, past the long, low ramp rising away to his right which led to the "g'rilla's" office. There were twenty-eight minutes to go before the departure klaxon would sound. He noticed that his breathing had become shallow and that his mouth was dry.

He entered the dining hall. Even under a dull sky, its surfaces – both inanimate and those of the humans who thronged it – shone beguilingly. He made his way slowly through the mass of folk and towards the rear of the hall, looking for Jean or Louis. He could see Louis, but no Jean. There was no time for contact anyway; he had been told not to on this occasion.

He stood in front of the elongated hatch at which men, civvies and bluejams, were queuing. He knew to walk to his right, to pass between two glossy pale walls, where he found himself in a long, low, curving corridor, brightly lit with fluorescent tubes. The floor was sticky, and there were people passing: "lizards", civvies, even the odd "squarehead". Jesus, how was Jean going to get in here? How was he going to get out? Someone was bound to notice the seven-centimetre height difference between the two of them. A ghastly thought occurred to him. Supposing escapes were actually encouraged so that the escapee would inadvertently draw the Gestapo to their contacts?

The corridor turned to the left and he saw it – just as Louis had said – *Kitchen Staff Only*. There was nobody – what luck! He lightly gripped the door handle, made from some pale-looking metal; it felt reassuringly cool as he pressed down on it with the side of his palm.

He was in! Hell! The left-hand cubicle was occupied. It was what he'd been dreading. They couldn't abort the plan now – surely? He crouched down to look under the door. Yes, there were boots; there would be. Kitchen staff wore bluejams and white elasticated headgear, but instead of the putty-hued slippers worn by the other prisoners, they were issued with black boots. He dodged into the right-hand cubicle and closed the door behind him. Twenty-three minutes to go.

He hardly dared breathe. Standing there with his palm against the door, he began to panic – supposing they had left bluejams behind *this* cistern? He checked; no. Were these toilets siphonic – or was the word symphonic? Joseph wasn't sure. The action of several litres of water being released down the flushing pipe was usually sufficient to clear this type of toilet, but without the additional suction coming from the vacuum created by an "S" trap, it was necessary to provide a lidded galvanised steel bin to take the less soiled pieces of toilet paper and prevent them blocking the drain. With the care and precision of a dealer handling a piece of Meissen porcelain, Joseph removed the lid of the container, but there were no items concealed there. He could only afford to stay in this position for another two minutes. Then he would have to abort. Why was there barbed wire stretched along the top of the cubicle walls? Who would want to climb up there, and why? But these toilets were for kitchen staff, and God knows what strange practices they indulged in. 'Kitchen scum,' Louis had said.

After half a minute, he heard a noise which made him want to hallelujah – it was the sound of shiny interleaf toilet paper being drawn from its porcelain holder. Eighteen minutes to go. He listened with a kind of ecstasy to the retching of the chain being pulled, followed by the rattle of the contents of the cistern dropping down the vertical pipe.

As he heard the outer door being closed, Joseph sprang out of the tiled cubicle and hurled himself into its neighbour. Yes, the bluejams were there, and a pair of the putty-hued slippers. Suddenly, the outer door opened. Oh Jesus, Jesus! Why? He heard the door of the next cubicle bang shut, and the almost imperceptible sound of light trousers – yes, they would have to be bluejams – being dropped. How was he going to get undressed without making a noise? Even removing his jacket in this confined space could arouse suspicion. It was no good waiting until the unknown person had gone; there wasn't time. He pulled the chain on the cistern, and under cover of the hiss of ballcock and valve, he removed his jacket, took out the bluejams and slippers. Off came his shoes and socks, ramming the socks inside the free jacket pocket. He clumsily stuffed the jacket and his hat in the fifty-millimetre gap behind the gurgling container, then his shirt, trousers, underpants, and vest. It was a messy job; only a blind person could fail to miss the concealed clothing if they opened the door and looked in. These toilets were too clean; you needed grime to conceal things. The ball cock was rising now, its valve still hissing, and Joseph felt a still small urge to rejoice.

He also felt a sudden overwhelming need to urinate. There were twelve and a half minutes to go. How long would it take him to piss? Six seconds? Could he – no they – afford it? He recalled the severe eyes set within the mild face of Louis. 'Every second counts,' he had said. 'Always think of the possible rather than the probable. Maximise your chances of success; minimise your chances of failure. Every action we take has cause and effect.'

To pee or not to pee? Joseph howled inwardly at the human absurdity of it, as he imagined an awful scenario of Jean failing to get out of the dining hall before that terrible klaxon sounded, leaving the two of them incarcerated together, bluejammed and slippered, waiting to die together in Sonnenlicht, never having spoken to one another again because the plan had failed, failed because Joseph used six precious seconds in which to have a wiz.

In the end, it took him four and a half seconds. On went the bluejams and slippers. Finally, he removed his wristwatch, dropped it into the breast pocket of the folded jacket, and cautiously opened the cubicle door, praying that he would not be caught. There were only twelve minutes to go; Jean would have to race like mad to get here, get dressed, and get out.

Joseph's heart suddenly thumped. As he tiptoed past his neighbour's door, it opened. A man was standing there, shaved head, tall, dressed in blue pyjamas.

'For Christ's sake, get a bloody move on, will you?' hissed Jean.

Joseph stared at him, said nothing but lunged for the external lobby door, peeped out sheepishly, and stepped once again onto the sticky floor of the corridor.

Out in the dining hall, Joseph was in a daze. He must not make eye contact with anyone; just follow the left-hand side of the hall – as Louis had instructed him – until he came to a wide opening. People were milling everywhere, and he had to move this way and that to get through the crowds.

The corridor into which he stepped was less populated than the hall, and he was able to scrape along the – this time – slightly abrasive floor, through a broad opening in another shiny wall, past a "squarehead" guard, and into a five-metre cube lit from above by light canons. Two of the four walls of the cube had small hooks, one row above the other, from which dangled several pairs of grubby-looking bluejams.

He was standing in what was (according to Louis) effectively the *core* of Sonnenlicht: the shower system – Teutonic hygiene, as he had called it. It was through this system that Louis – or Jean – would have obtained the second pair of bluejams.

The cube – designed for the removal and discarding of jams and slippers – had a twin space which lay some distance away. Between the two pavilions was a wide, white-tiled corridor – four-fifths of which was open and occupied by communal showers. The remaining space was divided into toilet cubicles – six squatters on either side – open to the corridor; there were no doors, and all spaces were lit from above with generously proportioned light canons.

"Residents" would disrobe in the first cube then proceed – via the toilets (*zeds*) – into the shower areas. From here, they would enter the second five-metre pavilion where attending "lizards" would issue them with white towels and, when dry, they would be given fresh jams and slippers before they made their exit, past the second "squarehead" and back out into the main glossy corridor.

Guards were changed every hour, but not both at the same time, nor did the incoming guards arrive before the outgoing one departed, so an agile "resident" – if they timed it right, and once rerobed – would be able to nip back round to the starting point and remove pairs of bluejams and slippers in the sixty seconds before the incoming guard arrived and before the soiled garments were removed by a "lizard" for laundering.

Joseph no longer had his watch. Nor was it likely that any other residents possessed a timepiece. The multiple diurnal brayings of the klaxon would provide a basic time structure, from which residents might know when to rise, at what time to eat, and when to vacate the building so that the rubber floors could be scoured by the "lizards" and allowed to dry. But these were just temporal baselines. How could any man calculate with accuracy? Perhaps most didn't care and were happy to exist, to drift in the spaces between one amplified bronchitic wheezing and another. As Joseph gazed upon the whiter than white of the surfaces which surrounded him, it came to him. The answer lay in the word *sonnenlicht*. Every white surface was different, and each possessed their own luminal value. Shadow lengths were changing every second. One didn't even have to have *sonnen* all the time, even on a day like today. The tone and shade of every surface was critical. As the seasons changed, so would the shadow lengths. The whole building was a timepiece if one was only able to see it like that.

Even at night, the vast, black, roofless expanses of glass would transform into a scienceless observatory from which – through crystal skies above the forest – man could reacquaint himself with his primeval origins.

Away from the tumulus at last, Joseph had thought that he had escaped the "cracks", but as he gazed at the umbral fingers cast upon the wall by the rooflight glazing bars, he felt himself once again falling into an earth upon which his like had walked millennia ago. He was guided by the luminous patches which seemed to emanate from the land surface outside a village and by a number of the larger light specs in the sky. Bronze Age Joseph had studied these light specs. He had interpreted patterns by transposing their forms onto pieces of flat stone and marking the surface using powdery whitestone. He drew straight lines, joining up the brightest specs, and found that the shapes he produced resembled familiar things: a fish, a fish with two heads, a human figure, wild creatures. He had been doing this since he was a boy, and in his workshop was a collection of such stones. He had even begun to use these patterns as ideas for bronze body decoration. He followed one of the light specs in the still-dark sky. This spec was well known to him for it was scratched in whitestone on one of that collection which had lain on his workshop floor for many summers now, and it was easy to find in the early sky for it was the most prominent in a curving configuration of eight…

Once showered and rerobed, Joseph decided to venture outside. He could see through the glass walls. It was drizzling, and hundreds of men were noiselessly sliding over the concrete paving; some had ventured onto the greenness of the lawns. He made his way back through the dining hall. *How long has it been since the departure klaxon*, he wondered, *forty minutes?* It must be about 1510. How long would it be before he could measure time by shadows? How many months before he was able to follow the stars?

The shower environment had been curiously odourless. Here in the vastness of the hall, he was reminded of the ever so slight smell of coffee, disinfectant, and male bodies, which the humming air conditioning had failed to remove. The floor was stickier than ever; the klaxon would perhaps belch out its order for all to leave the building soon. As he stepped out onto the concrete paving, he noticed its dampness; the drizzle had become slight rain. No matter, when the floors were dry and he went back in, he would go through the shower routine again; it would be a good time adjustment. It must be fifty minutes gone now.

What about Jean? He hadn't seen him take that processional walk through the various automatic doors and along the honey-hued pathway leading to the two medieval siege towers. He'd been told not to watch. It would have been too nerve-wracking anyway. If Jean hadn't got through, Joseph would have heard about it by now, surely? *Is Jean on foot?* he wondered. *Has he got the nerve and know-how to use the bus? Where will he sleep tonight? Maybe he hasn't got far to go to get to his unit and he has simply disappeared into the forest.*

What about Joseph's accommodation? Louis had told him which block Jean had been in. Nobody would be surprised to see a newcomer. Roll calls were casual, hurried through by "lizards" on a block-by-block basis, and it would only be an incomplete list which aroused suspicion, not a different voice.

His eye caught that of another man, tall and with something of the hunted about him. His cheeks were non-existent, just scoops of skin, tiny caves without entrances. Catching his eye wasn't quite the right word because there was something about those eyes, as if they were no longer the primary organ of the senses. Contact like this was bound to happen sooner or later.

The head moved close and planted itself in front of Joseph as he tried to avert his eyes, but it was too late – Joseph had become the centre of its attention.

'I haven't seen you before,' said the man.

'Oh, I've been here a few days,' lied Joseph, trying to make his voice sound convincing.

In the pause which followed, Joseph's mind was racing. Had such an encounter taken place in the street, he would have had an escape route: to run for a bus, a person to meet, a task urgently requiring attention. For the first time, it occurred to him that there was no escape; he was a prisoner in many ways, bound to this man and forced to endure whatever outcome there might be of such a meeting.

He desperately groped around for something to say. It had to be a comment which would have no consequences, would lead nowhere, nor would require the making of decisions, the expression of like or dislike, for this man was almost certainly a *mome*. Sport! That would be a good subject.

The man's face was millimetres from his own, and before Joseph could speak, the mouth moved again.

'Do you like the great Grimaldi?'

The name meant nothing to Joseph. This was almost certainly code – perhaps the stranger was a partisan and was waiting for Joseph's coded response. With barely a pause, the voice continued, 'I'm rather partial to the harlequinade – even thought of becoming a Joey meself at one time.' What on earth was a "Joey"? Joseph felt his panic begin to rise.

'I'll tell you a little story,' the man continued, as if all would be explained, that centimes would drop; they would be friends for life. Joseph felt more uncomfortable than ever. 'It goes like this: two men both sit down on the same park bench. The first man looks glum. The second man says to him, "You look a bit downhearted, old fellow," and – while pointing at a poster pinned to a nearby tree – then, "You should cheer yourself up a bit – why don't you go and see the great Grimaldi?" Then the first man looks more miserable than ever and says, "But I *am* the great Grimaldi!".'

Joseph became aware of a gentle digging against his chest and looked down to see the man's elbow nuzzling his breastbone. 'Get it? *I* am the great Grimaldi, heh heh heh.' All Joseph could think to say was that he must go and relieve himself, which he indeed must.

As he passed through the wide gap in the shiny white wall leading to the *zeds*, he turned and once more caught sight of "Grimaldi" standing amid the throng, his head close to that of another man, and Joseph could just hear him saying yet again, 'I am the great Grimaldi, heh heh heh.'

***

When the moment came, it was a complete shock to Joseph – a coincidence which was almost beyond reason. He was on his third trip through the shower system. Freshly jammed and slippered, he slithered into the corridor, unexpectedly catching the eye of the "squarehead" guard. As he shuffled towards the dining hall, he recalled the eyes; they were the eyes of the young lance corporal who he had encountered at the observation bunker. It was the youth who'd been armed only with a sable brush and a bottle of Chinese ink. It was the boy who had been squatting on a pallet, meticulously reproducing the figures of Mickey Mouse, Snow White, and Goofy onto the dehydrating concrete of the bunker wall. Oh, sweet Jesus! Was this fresh-faced lover of Walt Disney to be his nemesis?

He must keep calm. What would Louis suggest if Joseph could see him to ask? But Louis seemed to be keeping out of Joseph's way.

Assume non-recognition; after all, it was three weeks ago since they met.

Shaved heads all look the same, whereas a full head of copper hair...

Eye contact was only a split second – when they'd met in the bunker, he'd only turned away from his concrete "canvas" for half a second.

Even if he'd recognised Joseph, he wouldn't remember who, where, or when.

Forget the possible, and consider only the probable.

But it's the eyes, isn't? It's always the eyes. They are all different, like snowflakes or fingerprints. 'Ooooh, he's got his dad's eyes, you know.' No, he fucking well hasn't, because they're all fucking well different!

He made his way over to the glowing hatch in the dining hall to queue for supper. How long could it be now? The klaxon would retch out its supper call at 1830 hours; that must be close now, so it had been four hours. How far could an escaping man get in that time? Had chance been maximised sufficiently?

He was going through the motions of rehearsing "lix", "bull", and "slab" when he felt his wrists grasped, both of them. Mezger – no, Menzel, that was it, Christ, if Joseph could remember his *name*, then of course a capable, observant artist would remember Joseph's eyes. Only, for some reason, he was no longer Lance Corporal Menzel but Private Menzel; perhaps he had travelled a Walt Disney figure too far, been demoted, and sent instead to be on shower duty at Sonnenlicht.

Joseph could feel himself being manhandled up the ramp. The rubber floor was soft as soft here: *pha pha, pha,* about-turn; *pha pha, pha, pha pha…*

Once inside the "g'rilla's" office, the *gefreiter* and his "twin" vanished, and Joseph found himself standing in a spacious, glass-walled room.

The view to his left was identical to the view to the right of him but "mirrored"; green lawns, deerskin-hued concrete panels, and in the dull distance of the remains of the day, a fine, silken, metallic mesh with perhaps a hint of moisture.

In front of him was a panorama, a roofscape of curved white walls, an expanse of pale asphalt punctuated with the upstands of scores of rooflights.

The only solid wall in the room was the one through whose door Joseph had just been marched. In the train of his eye, he could feel – rather than see – a wallscape composed of box files resting on elongated slabs of some near-black exotic wood supported on shiny metal brackets. The desk in front of him – for he assumed it was a desk – was a monumental tablet of hardwood, stripey, garish, and devoid of any material obstruction save a black, shiny button recessed into its top, the size of a one-franc piece. Where was the real work done – all that meticulous planning?

The human figure – presumably seated – behind this sepulchral piece seemed to Joseph to be an intrusion upon a kind of perfect aesthetic order. The body, green-uniformed but capless – to call it bare-headed would be to award it humanity it did not deserve – had the appearance of a giant potato.

'Delighted to meet you, M. Fournier,' came a sound, tumbling out of a hole in the face. What was it about these Nazis? There was the icy formality of Luft, Ritter, sarcasm with a twinkle, but there was something indefinably brutish about *Oberwachtmeister* Kartoffel. In spite of the fragility of his predicament, Joseph was possessed by a nervous urge to laugh out loud.

'How do you like our facilities?' And without waiting for a reply, 'I gather you are a man of many parts, M. Fournier – a farmer!' The voice sounded surprised. 'We have a little something in common; I was a dairy farmer, you know, milk production. They call it "bull" in here, and so much "bull", as the Americans say.' Joseph – still standing in front of the closed door – could feel his breaths coming in pants; his mouth was dry.

'I hear that you are a capable builder; what do you think of my office?' Again, there was no waiting for a reply. 'And now you're a food distributor to the Wehrmacht, though I gather that at one time you were providing a bespoke butchers service to your fellow countrymen, and at *such* reasonable prices.'

Oh Lord, so they knew about *that*!

'You know… your brother will soon be recaptured. And then… and not till then,' he added – black eyes gazing upon Joseph with the persistency of those "eyes" in potatoes which are often so difficult to remove when you're peeling them, 'I'm afraid that it will be the end for him – "curtains", as the Americans say!'

Joseph must be calm; he had to be brave, but he felt compelled to ask, 'What will happen to me?'

'Oh, M. Fournier!' The voice had the tone of "You should be ashamed of yourself for even asking". 'You know, M. Fournier, you and I are not important in this world. We are small – how is it you say – "cogs"; small cogs. Without us, the machine will continue to run, and without you, M. Fournier, the sun will continue to set.'

That was it then. They were going to shoot him, quietly – or noisily – against one of those perfectly proportioned building units, make a mess of those deerskin-hued pre-cast concrete panels. It was more than he deserved. He couldn't even make a decent job of sacrificing himself for his own brother.

Joseph stood, swaying ever so slightly, and wondered what was going to happen next. Without warning, the potato head rolled to one side.

'You can go,' it said, in a perky tone, as if Joseph was being told that he had just won a much-coveted prize.

Even as he was being escorted back down the ramp, he still believed that they would not let him go. He had just assisted a "criminal" in an escape, not to mention *his* crimes and misdemeanours. This was a trick to prevent him from panicking, struggling and shouting. Menzel was probably luring him to a gallows, cunningly concealed, elegantly proportioned of course, and no doubt beautifully crafted from the finest Chilean teak, standing there ready to launch him into eternity.

Then the logic dawned upon him, logic with its particular Naziness. When he returned to Chateau de Galets with his story, all would assume that he had once again become a collaborator. *I mean,* they *wouldn't let him go just like that, not unless he had brokered a bargain for his life.* All Joseph's attempts at his own redemption had fallen pitifully flat – through no fault of his own, he would be ostracised once again.

'I've no clothes,' he said uselessly to Menzel. As if in reply, a white door at the bottom of the ramp noiselessly opened and a brown paper bag – rather like a potato sack – was thrust at him by a khaki-clad disembodied arm. Joseph looked in the bag. There appeared to be clothes: a charcoal-grey suit, white shirt, socks, underwear, tie, shoes, and, mystifyingly… a bowler hat. 'Where do I change?' asked Joseph. Menzel shrugged his shoulders. And so, standing in the long, white gallery of the outer entrance lobby at Sonnenlicht, with "squareheads", "lizards", prisoners – and no doubt the odd *mome* among them going indifferently about their rituals, Joseph shamefully removed for the last time his bluejams and slippers and clumsily staggered into the large, white underpants, the vest, and the baggy trousers.

He pulled on the freshly laundered white shirt and struggled to fix the detachable round collar with its little gold stud, cufflinks as well...

It was a beautiful suit – the jacket reveres hand-stitched – though the shoes were at least two sizes too big. They would probably have fitted Jean.

As he stood, dressed, bowler hat in hand, the white door opened once again, and the khaki arm appeared, this time holding a rolled umbrella. Joseph took it meekly and wondered what was in store for him now.

'You go!' whispered the *gefreiter*.

Joseph clumped his way past the automatic glass doors, shambled under the long, curved canopy, and waddled down the wide, concrete paved path between the green of the lawns. It was beginning to rain. He reached the first two timber towers; the steel mesh gate between them opened silently and apparently without the assistance of human hands.

As he passed between the second and final pair of towers, he looked upwards, holding his hand against the top of the bowler as he tilted back his head. He could see several soft-capped, green-uniformed soldiers. One of them, wearing a pair of round spectacles, peered down at him.

'Hey! Charlie Chaplain.'

Other guards crossed the wooden platform and looked down at him.

'Charlie Chaplain forever!'

He emerged into the road, where more voices were chorusing. The men on the second tower were leaning over the wooden rail and shouting. The rain was coming down smartly.

He tried to walk quicker – away from the towers – but the oversized shoes made it difficult. The rain was pouring now, making little *pa* noises on the dome of the bowler hat.

'*Pa*, Charlie, *pa pa*, Charlie, *pa*, Chaplain, *pa, pa*. Charlie.'

A man on a bicycle came pedalling along on the other side of the road.

'Why don't you put your umbrella up?'

Joseph walked on towards Shiel Dongwy. He had no money, no ID. He felt his free hand exploring the beautiful wool jacket whose interior he was now inhabiting. First the side pockets, empty. Then the left-hand inside pocket, also empty. In the right-hand inside pocket was a small buff folded card, an identity card – not unlike his own, the one which Jean now possessed. He opened it. The name was typed and signed by its previous owner: *Schlomo Pearlman.*

Joseph walked on, through Shiel Dongwy. It was pointless continuing to Hazebrouck; he had no money for the train. He turned west, heading cross country towards Desvres, hoping for side roads. The rain was less, but the sky no lighter. His eyes began to feel prickly. There was water on his face from the sky, but it seemed to be coming from his eyes as well and, without warning, he heard a long, low moaning sound. It appeared to be coming from his own body. It was born in his belly, raised through his lungs, and launched into the world through the red opening which was his mouth. The moan became a howl, then a bellow, then a roar.

It was he, Joseph Fournier who was making all this noise. It didn't matter – nobody could hear him – so he carried on howling. He howled for the brother he hated and bellowed for the brother he loved, for it seemed that these two elements – love and hate – had so mixed that they had become a single stable compound. He roared out of the fear of his father, bawled for – what he had thought was – the love of his mother, that which had also turned out to be fear. He hollered at his hatred of foreigners and clamoured against his own life, so full of uncertainness, ambiguities, and unfairness. As he walked, his lungs fought for more air, new air, untainted with hatred. He could feel his blood pumping, and as his body moved through the dark landscape, it was as if he had entered a giant cardiac valve, forcing out from its minimum diastole and pulling into its peak systole. These were the first tears he had cried since he was a baby, but they were real, and it was a start.

After a while, he began to recover from this unexpected outburst. This is what it must be like to be human, normal, to fit in with other humans. Though he knew he could never quite be "normal" because he had this thing inside him: the special gift of clairvoyancy, the power of psychic mediumship. He felt new. Whatever happened to Jean – or to him for that matter – he would endeavour to make use of this gift, wherever, or whoever, it had come from.

He trudged on. The whole experience had left his body feeling numb but not sufficiently to anesthetise his feet which were hurting like hell, so he tried taking the shoes off, tying them round his neck, and walking in stocking feet, but after half a kilometre it was even more painful, so back on went the shoes and slower became his pace.

After he had gone some distance further, he had a shocking thought. Supposing the Nazis had publicised his release, posted notices in village squares. He wouldn't exactly be difficult to identify. Partisans and Resistance groups would be sure to see it and lie in wait for him. They would be bound to make him dig his own grave before they shot him.

His heels and instep must be red and raw. He had an idea. Why not remove the vest and underpants he was wearing and wrap them round his feet? The shoes would fit better then. He found a spot to change. There were three poplar trees growing by the side of the road and he dodged behind the middle one. It was dusk; the rain had gone; it was unseasonably warm for late May, and the air was still but for the occasional far-off bark of a dog.

What joy to remove those shoes! The socks were damp and dirty now. He shed the lovely wool suit, stepped out of the cotton underpants, pulled the vest over his head. Then he dressed, taking more care with his wardrobe than he had done at Sonnenlicht an hour or so ago. He even felt a touch of pride as he adjusted the cufflinks and reinserted the collar stud with a positive flourish.

Then he sat down on a nearby log and got to work with the conversion of the vest and pants into a pair of chunky socks. The vest adapted like a dream and was bulky enough to knot round his leg after it had encased his foot. But the underpants seemed cumbersome until he got the hang of drawing the elastic tight and then knotting it, rather like a garter belt. He slipped the shoes back on and fastened the laces. They were a perfect fit now – he would be able to walk forever like this. The blisters which had started to form would be cushioned. He picked up the bowler hat and placed it carefully back on his head, smiling as he did so. He was ready for anything now.

As he turned to go, a soft noise broke the silence. At first, he thought it was some animal roaming about in the field, until he recognised the unmistakeable sound of a light female cough, followed by a giggle. It was almost dark now, but less than four metres away, he could make out two human figures. One was male, perhaps nineteen or so years of age and dressed in blue denim overalls like a farmhand. The female was no more than sixteen and wearing a putty-coloured blouse, dirty beige dress, shoes and grubby white socks. They were sprawled on a bank of meadow grass, and the dirty beige dress was drawn up at the front to reveal an even shadier pair of culottes, into the top of which was inserted the young man's right hand. His left hand was resting inside the putty-coloured blouse. Both faces were watching him.

How in God's name had he not seen them before? The girl giggled again and slowly – and rather tenderly – the youth removed his right hand and held it in the air, raising his thumb as he did so.

'Mush!' he barked, grinning as if he was giving encouragement to a team of huskies. The girl giggled again.

Joseph managed to raise his own hand in response. It reached just above waist level – fingers slightly parted – before it sank back to its former position against his worsted-clad thigh. It was the kind of movement – he imagined – made by a very elderly pontiff close to the point of expiry.

As the sun rose, he passed a farmer loading boxes of vegetables into a cart and was aware that he was being watched, this time by three tiny girls, while three older female children helped the farmer. The man asked if Joseph would like to come in and join them and his wife for breakfast, but he refused, accepting only water. For now, he would fast.

The second night he spent cowering under bocage, wondering about Jean. How far had he managed to get in that four hours before Menzel had seized him? Things weren't necessarily that bad for Jean, anything was possible, he could be halfway to Spain or England by now!

It was about midday when he arrived at Chateau des Galets. He limped straight to the auto mortar bunker, fearful that he would have lost his job.

'Frigging hell!' exclaimed Ritter, who promptly offered his condolences, assuming that Joseph had been called away to a funeral. Joseph explained that he had been to visit his brother in Sonnenlicht.

'Sonnenlicht eh! All right for some,' chortled the sergeant. Joseph enquired plaintively about his job.

'The lads here and I thought that you'd eloped with a young lady… oh we got another Kraut to fill in temporarily, so you're all right. Nobody wants *your* job, mate!'

***

It was 2000 hours, and Joseph stood uneasily under the apex of the cruck barn. He had managed to eat something, wash, change, and had even done the early evening delivery at the battery. On his head was one of his spare tweed caps – a faded straw colour – which, though protecting the crown of his head, would still reveal at close scrutiny that his head had recently been shaved. He heard the light, polite cough and watched as Helene glided into the barn.

He couldn't decide whether or not she looked surprised to see him. If yes, then not very. Slowly, and rather clumsily – for he was deadbeat and more than a little confused – he told his story: Louis, "bull", "bars", "lizards", *momes*; Major Potato, Walt Disney, Charlie Chaplain. Still, she seemed unshocked, though perhaps there was a slight air of apprehension about her. When he had said all, and the air around him seemed to fill with silence, he heard a familiar noise. It was faint at first, but gradually it became louder, until he recognised it as the sound of a motorcycle. A similar – if not the same – motorcycle which he had seen and heard two years previously, consisting of a khaki-clad and steel-helmeted dispatch rider and his khaki-painted motorcycle, arriving with the request from Luft that he should meet with him and Traugaut in the barn and thereby launching his career with Organisation Todt.

Joseph strode out of the barn, anxious that the dispatch rider should not knock at the farmhouse door and alarm their mother. Helene followed. Joseph took the telegram from the soldier, opened it, and read:

SONNENLICHT. JEAN FOURNIER
RECAPTURED AT 1200 HOURS YESTERDAY.
DISPATCHED TO CAMP IN GERMANY.

Dispatched – a commodity – just like a telegram or an order of stationery for Joseph's office. As the rider vanished, Jean handed the telegram to Helene without looking at her.

'I knew about the plan,' she said as she finished reading it.

So, she did, did she! So, he had been right about him being the last piece of their jigsaw. The two of them had assumed that Joseph "the collaborator" would be feeling cornered, humiliated, and would be desperate for redemption. Of course, he would agree to the plan. They had manipulated him. For all their principles in life, for all their holier-than-thou motives, they were no better than he. After Jean's first arrest, he – Joseph – had had no choice: a collaborator, a short life as a double agent, and now a collaborator once again, and a target for Resistance groups and Partisans. He had to be! He wouldn't be standing here alive in front of her if he hadn't done a deal with the Nazis. Fucking principles! His mother had been right: 'It's war, Joe, anything can happen.'

'You did your best, Joe,' she said quietly as she walked back towards the farmhouse.

CHAPTER 32

ATTACK

Yes, he'd done his best. Joseph awoke, wanted to look at his watch, realised he no longer had one. Somehow, he knew it was about 0430 hours. He lay, exhausted. He was in his Z bed at the upper room of the gatehouse at Chateau de Galets, getting no more than half an hour's sleep each night, and he had to be on duty at 0500 that morning. He was no stranger to early rising, but the real reason for his weariness was that he was frightened to go to sleep.

He recalled that conversation long ago in the days when he and his siblings sat round the scrub-top table talking. The subject had been ghosts, and *do we believe in them?* Normally when a topic like this had been introduced, he would have taken off elsewhere, but this time, something had made him stay.

Helene had said that ghosts weren't "wispy things, dripping with ectoplasm", nor did they appear like real people. 'Ghosts are clever,' she said. 'If they *are* going to haunt you, they won't try to do the impossible; they'll simply enter your subconscious when you're asleep, so in that way, ghosts *do* exist; in fact, nobody can say that they don't.'

Perhaps things might be better if they could be sure about Jean, whether or not he was dead. At least then – as Helene would no doubt suggest – they could "give him back", but how could they if they weren't even sure?

He gazed – submissively now – into one of his "cracks". He was in a skinboat on the sea, his arms moving in a perfect circular motion, but his thoughts were muddled. As he drove the wooden paddle through the water, he thought about his brother. It was as if something was levering away at his head and wouldn't leave him alone. Could things have been different?

As the phantom Joseph quickened the rhythm of his arms, he braced himself ready to be drawn up a mountain of solid water and through "the rock gate". His skinboat was well positioned now – centre of the two pillars – but he couldn't get away from those thoughts of his brother; he just kept coming upon another, and another, like strata of metal ore in a rock face. Sun and Moon! If he had turned a moment sooner than he did…

The "crack" closed.

At first it was as if he and his two siblings had been swept along in a river. What Joseph had done was wrong, but he had little choice, and Jean had – possibly – paid the ultimate price for his struggle against evil. Was Jean's death a punishment for Joseph's acts? There was no point in punishment for punishment's sake. Good can be reconstructed out of evil, but to put right what you have done wrong, you have to go back and start to make decisions at a point where choice becomes possible, and from the time Joseph had entered Sonnenlicht, the choice was there for the taking…

The awful "crack" opened again, and Joseph found himself peering in, witness to a gruesome prehistoric ritual.

A circular pit had been dug into the chalk: about six hands deep and of sufficient diameter to accommodate a human body in the foetal position. Joseph could feel his ancient self forced to look at the gruesome scene; first the victim's right hand was severed using the very implement that his skill had produced, the hardened bronze edge cutting easily through the skin and bone. Then the conspirator was strangled with a length of twine. Joseph could see the bulging eyes of the executioner. The brows meeting, nostrils dilating, his fists clenched as he throttled the life out of his victim. Finally, the head was struck off with a bronze axe and placed, together with the body, in the pit inbetween the calf and thigh, while the severed hand was positioned behind the shoulder.

Many times, Joseph's ancient self had woken to the screech of starlings coming from the gorse bushes just outside the Shadow Gate, which signalled the coming sunrise, but he knew that even before the first sign of sun, the chalk pit would have been levelled, and the party of men who had completed this grim task would have passed through the gate and gone about the business of the day.

The "crack" closed. Joseph knew that his vision had been of the mysterious skeleton found by Arnaud when he dug the foundations for the gates… at least he hoped it was that. He rose from the bed and *he also* began to go about the business of the day.

It was a brilliant early morning at Pointe des Galets. The pale wall of the auto mortar bunker provided a luminous scenic canvas, in front of which a troupe of actors might perform, but today it was the perfect backdrop for Sergeant Ritter's parade, with Joseph as its audience.

Ritter seemed to be in a curiously jocund mood.

'Answer me this,' challenged the sergeant of the platoon. 'There were five men going to church and it started to rain.

The four who ran got wet, but the one who stood still stayed dry – who were they?'

No one spoke. 'Come on, it's bloody obvious: a body in a coffin and its bearers!'

As the sergeant delivered the answer, a motorcycle and sidecar bounced up and swayed to a stop within a metre of where Joseph's Zündapp stood. It appeared that Joseph, and the corporal who had just arrived, had doubled up. Ritter's platoon was about to receive a second delivery of rations.

The corporal who had been riding in the sidecar climbed out carrying the box containing the provisions. Unaware of his error, he tried to hand it to Ritter, but the sergeant blocked his way.

'You cannot pass; you shall not pass,' yodelled Ritter, standing with his feet wide apart and arms folded, like a giant goblin in a fairy tale.

'You must first answer this riddle; if you are wrong, then it will cost you a forfeit.'

The corporal looked bewildered as the sergeant's voice raised an octave and half sang, half spoke.

'There were four brothers in this world that were born together. The first runs and never wearies. The second eats and is never full. The third drinks and is always thirsty. The fourth sings a song that is never any good. Who are they?'

Occasionally, Ritter met his match and encountered an adversary who had heard it before or, through powers of superhuman perception, guessed the answer.

'Lucky for you!' he would sometimes be forced to exclaim, but not today; the corporal didn't even seem to grasp what was going on.

'Last chance,' bellowed Ritter. 'Well, the answer is earth, air, fire, and water, so hard luck, my friend – your forfeit is ten press-ups. We Germans have a reputation for acts of cruelty, so we must *not* disappoint,' he shouted, as the hapless corporal prised himself up and down on the still-dewy turf, to the hoots of laughter from the platoon.

If the irony of Ritter's mood escaped the soldiers, the gravity of the next event did not, and as the laughter died away, Joseph heard the roar of a second motorbike engine. The rider did not even bother to dismount but merely raised his goggles and called to Ritter.

'The enemy has landed in Normandy and has secured a beach head. An order has been issued to capture the channel ports, so make sharp.'

'A bloody disaster,' exploded the sergeant. 'All our artillery pointing out to sea, and we're going to be attacked from inland. I told the buggers not to build casemates round the guns; now you can't move 'em.'

The machine gunner corporal continued to look bright-eyed, but the rest of the platoon looked nervous.

'Don't worry,' grimaced the sergeant, 'you'll have seventeen thousand cubic metres of concrete and forty tons of steel between you and the enemy when they come.'

Joseph could imagine that, as an academic, and student of the history of siege warfare, Ritter would be well aware that only a small percentage of sieges are unsuccessful. Once an enemy appears – rather like blackmailers – they rarely lose interest and go away; if their supply lines hold, then it's just a matter of time. The defender can either surrender or die.

***

The summer wore on, and Joseph discovered that the Allies were pushing directly inland. That would give those at the Pointe des Galets battery a reprieve, of sorts anyway. Signs of autumn even began to appear.

He continued to make his visits to the auto mortar bunker, and often he and Ritter would share an hour of one another's company, making the round of the other installations on the battery.

He had got to know Ritter better – in this short time – than he had done Captain Luft throughout the whole time they'd worked together. Luft had been aloof, literal, and – fortunately for Joseph – untouchable. It felt to him that Ritter was the first person in his life to really treat him as a human being. Perhaps they were just two *oddballs* together?

'We're not supposed to know,' a messenger muttered to Sergeant Ritter, 'but the Canadians have taken Le Havre and Dieppe.' Joseph could overhear from where he was standing a few paces away. God! The end might not be far away now. He must somehow try and make sure that he was in the farm rather than *here* when the invading force arrived.

At first, Ritter said nothing as he opened what looked like a letter from his wife. Eventually, he spoke.

'Well, our friend Dr Goebbels has evidently been made "Reich Plenipotentiary for Total War" – whatever that means,' he read aloud.

'Have you any children?' the boy machine gunner demanded without warning. Joseph thought he meant him and was just about to answer – he still thought the young man looked familiar. Ritter shook his head without a change of expression.

'I'm very keen to have children…' suggested the youth.

'Hold your horses, you randy devil, you're only seventeen!' smiled the sergeant.

'… But I don't think love is important; I don't think it even exists – not between people anyway – only for the Fatherland,' persisted the boy.

'Oh, you don't, do you,' snapped the sergeant. 'Well, I'll tell you; you have to find it first, and it isn't bloody obvious; it's inert; it doesn't grow on its own; it has to be brought alive, nurtured, cherished…'

Was Joseph hearing correctly? Were these really two soldiers talking about love?

'Yes, but I think it's a social duty to pass on one's genes. We must survive and reproduce, to obtain the fittest future generations, and in order to survive, we must compete…'

The skin over Ritter's clenched teeth puckered into an angry knot.

'If that implies mistreating the weak and those less able, then where do you think that leaves us? That's not civilisation; it's the opposite – it's savagery,' Ritter was shouting. The boy still went on.

'Wars are not bad, you know, they are an opportunity for a nation and individual to make many achievements in a short space of time…'

Joseph heard the sergeant exhale loudly.

'I'm not against fighting as such, I just see it as a last resort in the struggle to promote humanity, but the way we're going about it, we're using it as a first resort to inflict more of man's inhumanity.'

Ritter had had his business destroyed by the burning of the books, and now here he was, his life possibly going to be brought to a sudden end by trying to defend the indefensible – why was the boy persisting like this?

'Homo sapiens…' Ritter's voice resumed its usual calm but ironic tone, '…now our leaders are telling us to make way for a new species, the Homo superior[10]. It's true, Homo sapiens may well have outlived its use, but the name was never quite correct in the first place: *sapere* – to know – no man can really *know*, but any one of us can be a seeker of the truth, and sometimes we may find it's been right under our noses all the time. Anyway,' he added, fully returned to his ironic self, 'I rather prefer the term Homo *spiritualis*.' He looked almost pleased as he turned to meet the mystified faces of his platoon.

Joseph also wasn't any the wiser than they, but he had to admit to himself that he liked the idea of seeking the truth. He also had a distinct feeling that he had come nearer to the truth – whatever that was – than he had ever been before.

Ritter was a master; he was like some kind of priest. Instead of giving orders, he had used logic and reason; he had responded to the boy's almost mutinous outburst and brought calm to the situation.

Joseph, Sergeant Ritter, and the lance corporal stood together with other members of the platoon, listening to the bunker radio. Joseph could hear the voice of Dr Goebbels ranting away – 'Resist with utmost fanaticism!'

***

Throughout the 24th and 25th of September, Joseph could hear the sound of almost constant gunfire. On the 25th, he arrived with additional stores, and at about 1000 hours, he completed his second round of the battery and started to head back to the farm. Damn! He'd forgotten to drop off the extra powdered milk ration at the mortar bunker. He dismounted the Zündapp, kicked the stand out from under it, and began to walk over to where Ritter and two platoon members were standing.

He got no further than two paces from his machine when the air was filled with the violent braying of a klaxon.

'That's it,' shouted Ritter, 'leave your bloody motorbike

and get in the bunker with us; you can't travel back now – the enemy has been sighted.'

The prospect of being incarcerated in that *thing* was the worst that Joseph could think of. He felt himself avoiding the sergeant's eyes, heard himself make a noise in his throat like hysterical laughter. Rather like the tons of steel mesh which had been packed into the bunker's construction, he felt the vagueness of all his fears welding into the impenetrable knot of a phobia.

'You won't get me in there in a million years,' his voice wavered as he started to run. If he ran straight down the steep slope – he knew where the minefield was, for Christ's sake – he could be back in the farm in five minutes. He could feel Ritter's right shoulder pressing against him. Something snapped, something cold and shiny, and Joseph looked down to see that he was manacled wrist to wrist with the sergeant.

'For Christ's sake, let me go,' he screamed as two corporals appeared and dragged him backwards into the chamber. The door hissed closed behind him.

Inside the bunker and now separated from the sergeant, Joseph stood helplessly watching the blond *oberstabsgefreiter* at his post by the MG42 machine gun. This was puzzling; he felt an unexpected sensation of safety, like some sweet warm liquid was being poured over his body. After all, *he* had driven a tractor round the tumulus; not only that, he had skilfully guided a team of ploughing horses round it. He knew the exact clearances.

Approaching from the north, it was impregnable to an invader, whilst from the southern end it would take a tank driver with nerves of steel to risk squeezing between the end of the bunker and the cliff edge. Anyway, no German tank could get through there, and he doubted if the Canadians had a machine small enough to do it. Perhaps they would be safe after all?

It was not easy to hear any sound from outside, but when the steel embrasure was open, it was just possible for Joseph to hear birdsong over the hum of the air conditioning. The boy also seemed to be able to pick out the sound, the intonation of a song thrush. It must be perched on top of the bunker.[11]

As Joseph strained to listen to the purity of the repetitive fluting notes, he recalled a moment, nine years previously, when he had listened to a very similar song. It was the time when he knelt in front of a water trough, as the shadow of Aunt Icie fell across him.

Seeing clearly can be perilous. There is a point in the process of realisation when the mind – having groped around in the close confinement of uncertainty – suddenly plummets through into an abyss of discovery. The experience can be one of horror, and like the thunderbolt hitting the tumulus that night years ago, it struck Joseph that the boy soldier in front of him grasping the machine gun was Otho, Icie's missing son.

The two men's eyes met. If the lance corporal had recognised him before now, then he had been skilful in concealing it, but any pretence there may have been was over.

While keeping his left hand on the machine gun, the boy's right hand slowly drew from its holster a Walther P38 pistol.

'Joseph Fournier, you little shit of a Frenchie farmer, I'm going to kill you *now*.'

Joseph was terrified. Without warning, here he was, imprisoned in the very concrete bunker whose construction he had sacrificed himself to help build, and now he was facing what would seem to be certain death at the hand of the boy – no, that little pig-like child with blond eyelashes – that he had punished all those years ago.

There would be no recriminations on behalf of Joseph. The lance corporal would simply have been seen to shoot the messenger who had panicked in combat and tried to open the gas lock door from inside.

All Joseph's anodyne thoughts that he might be safe seemed to suddenly explode. His only consoling notion was that a bullet through the head was going to be preferable to being incinerated by Canadians who could be just about to arrive outside.

The two men had become the condemned and the executioner, and as the one sat, and the other stood, they could still both hear through the embrasure the lilting of the thrush, nature oblivious to the human drama taking place below its claws.

Ch ch prr prr, ch ch prr prr, prr prr prui. Ch ch prr prr, ch ch prr prr, prr prr prui... As both men listened, the birdsong was overlaid with a strange new resonance. It sounded to Joseph like an army of bicycles being ridden over a rough cobbled road surface.

Joseph hadn't a clue what to do. He hovered by the gas lock door, watching the lance corporal in the steel tractor seat gripping the MG42 – the pistol was now back in its holster.

He saw the boy pull the trigger on the machine and release two short bursts of fire. The noise sounded like a street pneumatic drill.

If – it occurred to Joseph – he turned his head through ninety degrees, he could get a view through the covering embrasure, and he watched, mesmerised, as he saw the rounds strike the berm, raising clouds of dust. There was no return fire.

He could hear the alternate hollow thud and twang of outgoing mortar rounds from the chamber almost directly above him. After every five rounds, there was a pause; in the silence, he could again hear the song of the thrush, miraculously undeterred, until once more, the purity of harmony was overcome with the dry rattle of a tank forcing itself over a surface of crushed chalk.

Sergeant Ritter appeared within the internal door of the entrance lobby. He was carrying three Panzerfaust 30 anti-tank shells. The men seemed oddly silent.

In order to change from machine gun mode to that of anti-tank gun, the boy gunner needed to tilt the steel embrasure plate and increase the aperture for a moment.

Through the side opening, Joseph could see the front part of the caterpillar of a Sherman Firefly, as it began to emerge at the end of the berm onto the Field of Mars. He could hear the bronchitic wheezing of its engine and stared as its turret rotated.

His eye travelled back to the lance corporal, watched him level the anti-tank weapon, but before he could fire, the boy's body was propelled backwards. At the same time, Joseph felt a violent swing in the air pressure, became aware of a series of head-splitting metallic clangs, followed by a smaller sound very close to his right ear, like someone popping a wet paper bag and snapping a stick. A large sack of what appeared to be butcher's meat – like the scrag-ends he'd sold to his fellow countrymen for outrageous profit – fell against Joseph's right hip.

Without turning, he could see that it was the headless body of Sergeant Ritter, red liquid jetting upwards to the concrete roof above Joseph's head. In front of the machine gunner, he could see the torn steel embrasure plate and a red glove which had been planted against its jagged edge. To his horror, Joseph realised that the object at which he was staring was the boy's right hand.

The incoming shell had failed to explode. Instead, it had hurtled through the embrasure, tearing the edge of the steel plate and scattering lethal fragments, ripping off the defender's right hand. Next, it had careered through the open door where Sergeant Ritter had posted himself. From where he was standing, quaking, Joseph could see Ritter's M40 helmet inverted and spinning on the other side of the mess chamber floor, the severed head still in it.

How could one unexploded shell coming inboard do so much damage? As he could no longer hear the sound of mortars firing, he had to assume that everyone else in the bunker were dead. His mind began to drift. He was unable to absorb the reality he was seeing; there was nothing he could compare it with. Reason had ceased to be the foundation of certainty. The certainty with which he had created order in his work for the OT had suddenly turned into chaos. This had to be what Hell was like. He found himself thinking of images once shown to him by Aunt Icie, scenes painted by the artist Hieronymus Bosch. The thoughts of the paintings seemed to draw him backwards, away into some unchartered void. In a desperate bid to comfort himself Joseph began to recite within his mind, first the map reference. *62/C3 1*38/50*45*. It was futile. Then, a simple arrangement of words, in a sequence which reduced each meaningless sentence down to his very core, the 'I'. *For it be the have and to that of a in of I. Be of I have it to that and for in a. It and to have of that a in I for. Have I that for it and of a. And a in that have it for I. In that I have it for a. I that it have for in. I that have it for. Have it for I. I for it. For I. I.*

I for. It for I. I for it have. For it have that I. In for have it that I. A for it have I that in. I for it have that in a and. A of and it for that I have. For I in a that of

have to and it. A in for and that to it have I of be. I
of in a of that to and have the be it for.

Sobbing, Joseph wanted one thing only. The urge to get out was uncontrollable. He began wrenching the gas lock wheel. He had to, before the troops triggered a flamethrower. He was a dancing crazy flurry of limbs, and his feet slithered as they frantically tried to find purchase on the slimy red duckboards.

As the gas lock door swung open, light fell upon the body of the juvenile gunner. It was rhythmically rocking backwards and forwards like a giant internal organ of some animal, the heart of the fresh rabbit, still pulsing after its chest has been ripped open. Surely the boy couldn't still be alive?

It righted itself into a kneeling position, and then, only with Joseph's help was it able to continue its progress, lurching towards the open door. The boy soldier pitched forwards out into the sunlight, trying to shield his eyes with the bloody stump of his right arm. Joseph followed with both of his hands raised above his head.

'Stretcher bearers over here!' he heard his voice croak, as if he were a toddler trying to utter its first words. Joseph could see three Canadian infantrymen converging on them.

CHAPTER 33

RESOLUTION

6 November 1944

Dear Joe,

It's such a relief to know that you are safe.

Be patient. None of us can know exactly what the future holds, but I have a belief that it will not be as bad as you think it may be and that good will come to us all in the end.

I wrote to Aunt Icie with the news that Otho too has survived and is recovering in the POW hospital. The piece of shrapnel from that horrid steel plate on the bunker was deflected from his heart by a prehistoric bronze dagger he was keeping in his breast pocket would you believe! A Canadian field doctor stopped him bleeding to death, but he really owes his life to you, Joe, for getting him out of that dreadful place before they stormed it.

Sad news for us all, Joe, Maman *passed away the day before yesterday. I know that you were upset last time you saw her, but it's happened for the best. She had no joy left in life, so why try to hang on?*

Robert is coming over from Cambrai to assist, and

guess what? Little Estelle from the village has agreed to come and help sort through all Mum's things. She was orphaned last year in that terrible business with the reprisal after those Germans were killed by the Resistance. We're all orphans now, Joe; sounds odd, doesn't it!

I'm going to come and see you before they move you.

I was going to leave it until I saw you, but there's something else I must say now. The authorities at the Hotel de Ville have published a list of names of those killed by the Nazis and yes... Jean's name is there... well, it doesn't actually say "killed", but the list includes people who were working for the Resistance. Many of them were sent on what people are now referring to as The Death Train[12] and it says Jean Fournier on that, so that's as sure as we can be about what actually happened.

I've decided that when the war's over, I'm going to go and work for an organisation that they are founding in Switzerland for helping children all over Europe who have lost their parents. The main thing they are asking for is language skills, and I've got those – thanks to Aunt Icie!

I'm going to close now. Rest assured, my love, I will be there.

Your little sister Helene

***

It's late afternoon on the same day Helene's letter arrives, and Joseph is standing outside the wooden hut which has been his home for over a month now. It's dark and raining.

There's a small covered area where prisoners can stand out of the rain. He looks out towards the wire fence, waiting. Tomorrow, they'll move him; that's all he knows. As for his trial, that could be months away – next year even.

He hopes that she'll come.

She was right, of course, he's been a slave for years, and prison is going to give him a kind of freedom. It's been one shock after another: the sight of Jean on the cliff that night, his sister and Luft together, the scene in the cathedral crypt, and the awful interview with the Gestapo officer. He's been in the grip of the Le Vieux Vicente; he knew it all along, but he's never been big enough to admit it, even to himself.

Now the tumulus has done its worst. Like some giant cat grown tired of playing with a captive mouse, it's had its sport with the three of them, and they are free.

For the first time in his life, Joseph offered genuine help to someone; after all, he's got nothing against Otho. He's taken a real interest in the boy, asking the guards if they know anything, but this letter is the first news he's had. He's asked about Sergeant Ritter as well. Had anybody known him, met him even? Nobody had. Joseph says that he pities those who had never had that pleasure.

There's little he can do now except wait, have faith, hope, and yes – love. A kind of prose verse that Helene used to recite comes into his head:

I said to my soul, be still, and wait without hope
For hope would be hope for the wrong thing; wait
*   without love,*
For love would be love of the wrong thing; there is yet
*   faith*
But the faith and the love and the hope are all in the
*   waiting.*[13]

He'll try and help Helene; it'll take time; yes, they'll help one another. He can't expect to live in isolation; he needs her. He isn't mad, but he knows he needs help, so that's a start, and if the offer's still open, he'll let her help him, heal him. He hopes she'll come.

Maybe he can get training to use his clairvoyant powers? He's had neither "cracks" nor voices since the event inside the bunker. He hopes he hasn't lost his powers – who would have thought it! Millions have died in this war. That means that there are millions more who are bereaved. Perhaps he can do something to help, put some of them in touch with one another; it isn't so daft. He'll need proper guidance, of course – real tuition. He can learn to cope with those strange voices from Daniel, Carmen, Baron Sacheverell, Mohammet, and even Kurt, bless him, moaning on about that butter dish. 'Yes.' He laughs aloud. 'I can even put up with you, Kurt!' But will Helene really come?

Those "cracks", he's been thinking, he's had so many of them… and then that loss of his mind in the bunker, yet since that awful event, he's been able to recollect something else. He can only recall one thing at the moment. It was when he, Helene, Jean, and Robert went to search for Helene's dog – he can't remember the dog's name…

They were all walking up the hill in the dark, towards the tumulus. Jean was over to his right, Helene beyond, and Rob was on his left. He couldn't see any of them, but he could see the lights of their lamps. Jean's lamp always seemed to be slightly ahead of his, and that made him feel angry. It must have been that which brought on the "crack", and it's only today that he's realised what he missed while he was in the "crack".

He remembers thinking, *It really doesn't matter anymore; why go racing on, what's the hurry? There's no need to beat Jean to the top.*

Each lamp they were holding was different, but the light was all one, and the glow from the moon, they all seemed to be part of the same source. Their voices all came from different points on the hillside, but they were all one, and the sound of the wind was part of the same sound. Their waterproof raincoats, his tweed cap, the bracken stems, the floating seeds; they were all one. Their four bodies, their bones, the bones of those in Le Vieux Vicente, and the stones, were all one. There was nothing to fear. It no longer mattered who arrived at the tumulus first because Joseph could see, even before any of them got there, that the dog was dead. He could see where the dog had gone as well. He had felt love for his siblings, felt love for Jean. If only he hadn't missed everything by falling into that "crack".

If Joseph can remember that event, then he'll be able to recall others. Were these "cracks" timeless? Was the action of his recollection taking place in "normal" time? They couldn't both be happening at the same time, but perhaps they were? So maybe there was something in what Aunt Icie said about "the thin places". Perhaps Helene was right about time not travelling in straight lines.

One thing is certain; his watch won't give him the answer.

***

There are about a hundred other men in his compound, collaborators like him, but never exactly the same; everybody has a different story. There's been trouble. Some, like him, have been OT workers and are guilty of serious crimes. He'll plead guilty, of course, to organising slave labour; there's no question of that – none of that "Oh, *they* made me do it!". For Christ's sake, it was his decision, and he'll stand by it, even if his choices had been limited in the matter.

He can see people arriving outside the wire, mainly women; some have come to see loved ones, while others are here merely to shout abuse. He wishes to God she'd come.

He's lived all his life by fear, and now his only fear is that she won't come. He feels like a little boy waiting for his mother to come and collect him from school.

A disturbance by the wire catches his attention. A woman tries to throw a pot of white paint over one of the prisoners. It catches on the mesh and bounces back, its contents splashing over two other women. Someone begins screaming. The Canadian guards take no notice and light cigarettes. The screaming continues as more prisoners move towards the wire to see what's happening. Joseph follows them. He can feel the rain on his face; everybody seems to be shouting.

Then, in a split-second lull, he hears a woman's voice calling something... it's Helene; he only catches one word at first.

'... Escaped...!'

His heart gives a gigantic leap.

'Escaped?' *He's* escaped? Has he really? He repeats it aloud to himself.

At last, he can see her now – she's laughing! Her face is wet with rain, perhaps tears. He franticly fights his way towards her until they can touch one another through the wire. Now she's kissing him.

'Joe, you escaped,' she says it quietly and very slowly this time, so there's no mistaking. 'You escaped from the temple.'

END

ENDNOTES

1   "The Fatal Avenue" – the phrase was coined by General de Gaulle during the interwar years when he was campaigning for more tanks.

2   "The spirit…" – meditation phrase.

3   William Blake, "Eternity".

4   The whole sentence is *Do what thou wilt shall be the whole of the Law.* It comes from *The Book of the Law*, a magical doctrine written by the occultist Aleister Crowley. Crowley claimed that the document was "received" in the form of a kind of unearthly dictation from one Aiwass. Practitioners of this philosophy he called Thelemites who, contrary to the popular understanding of the statement, were not indulging egoistical fancies but were finding and following their true spiritual paths.

5   Given the Nazi ideology of *lebensraum*, the motivation is plausible, though in terms of Nazi scientific application, it is not. Even if Jean had seen a prototype, it would have been at Peenemünde, not in the Saint-Omer area.

     German ideas about space travel appeared more in the 1920s in the form of Hermann Oberth's *Feasibility of Space Travel*, but the technology of the 1940s was concentrated on weaponry. Nevertheless, the real beneficiaries of the skills and work of Wernher von Braun (a committed Nazi) were the USA and, eventually, the Apollo space programmes of NASA. A fact very much played down at the time of the 1969 moon landings.

6   Between 1958 and 1965, the philosopher and writer Virilio documented the fortifications of the Atlantic Wall and referred to them as "… small-sized temples without religion".

7　To the best of my knowledge, there is no evidence that Reichsminister Himmler attended an occult ceremony held in the crypt of any cathedral. There is, however, inexhaustible evidence that Himmler and other major, and lesser, Nazis were "heavily into" the occult.

8　Refers to a stage dance routine entitled *Cleopatra's Nightmare* performed by Wilson, Keppel & Betty in the 1930s.

9　The three Walt Disney characters were photographically recorded by the author as found on the internal wall of an observation installation, in the Boulogne area in 1975. They almost certainly date from 1943–4 and are far too meticulous in their execution to have been done by a casual visitor. Also, most of these installations are "off limits" to the general public.

10　If one is sticking to Latin, then I suppose it should be *Homo superius*. I chose "superior" in reference to the chilling words of David Bowie's 1972 "Oh! You Pretty Things", which is generally acknowledged to refer to Aleister Crowley's concept of an "alien invasion" being aided and abetted by society's youth, viz. Homo sapiens has outlived its use.

11　I have not researched the weather conditions in the Pas de Calais area for 25 September 1944 and therefore am not able to claim that a thrush would have been able to give song. However, as the fictitious songbird seems capable of competing with mortar, machine gunfire, and the sound of an approaching Sherman tank, who knows what conditions it might be prepared to perform under?

12　The museum at the La Coupole, V-2 rocket site near St Omer contains a list of those sent on The Death Train. I visited the museum in 2009, at which point Jean Fournier was established as a working name in this novel. I was therefore astonished to find this name on the list of those sent on the train and made the decision to carry on with it. Any similarity between the fictitious Jean and the person on the list is coincidental.

13　"East Coker" by T. S. Eliot from *Four Quartets*.

ACKNOWLEDGEMENTS

To Kylie Fitzpatrick for early mentoring on behalf of Cornerstones Literary Consultancy. To Alice Jolly and Edward Docx tutoring on behalf of the Arvon Foundation. To Judith Mead Cann and Angela Burt for early close reading and to Matador Books for painstaking publication and an excellent cover design.